ESSENCE

THE ELEMENTALS TRILOGY BOOK TWO

DEBBIE KUMP

This is a work of fiction. Names, characters, places, and incidents are products of the author's imagination or are used fictitiously and are not to be construed as real. Any resemblance to actual events, locations, organizations, or persons, living or dead, is entirely coincidental.

World Castle Publishing, LLC
Pensacola, Florida
Copyright © Debbie Kump 2017
Paperback ISBN: 9781629897110
eBook ISBN: 9781629897127
First Edition World Castle Publishing, LLC, June 12, 2017
http://www.worldcastlepublishing.com

Cover: Karen Fuller
Editor: Lisa Petrocelli

DEDICATION

For Dad who loves a great journey.

PROLOGUE

I had failed.

Those words weighed heavy on my soul. I helplessly watched San Francisco burn, ravaged by the Earth Elemental Gaia's massive quake. Flames engulfed entire blocks, causing great billows of black smoke to rise high above the city. The air felt gritty, hot, and thick, making it impossible to breathe without choking on soot that rained from the sky.

Structures slanted at awkward angles until they tumbled and squashed the residents' cars tightly lining the steep streets. Rows of townhomes collapsed like playing cards stacked upon one another. Giant fissures opened in the earth, cleaving the black asphalt of the street in half. Nearby, freeways buckled as large spans of elevated roads crashed to the earth. The trusses buckled and broke, sending a few unfortunate motorists airborne. Car alarms blared unheeded, unintentionally set off by the violent shaking of the ground. Trolley cars crowded with commuters tumbled on their sides. Sounds of shattering glass and cracking masonry mixed with the panicked screams of residents when fires ignited entire neighborhoods.

Seismologists would later pinpoint the epicenter to the nearby geologically unstable San Andreas Fault, but I knew the truth behind the destruction and loss of life.

Gaia created this quake.

Still, I couldn't stop blaming myself for the utter destruction that surrounded me. As an Elemental, I possessed the power to generate fire, but not to halt its course. Hydros—the Elemental master of the watery realm—was the only one capable of achieving that feat by dousing the uncontrollable blaze with a sudden outburst from the sky.

And she couldn't do a thing to help...because *I* had destroyed her.

Guilt heaped on my mind as thousands, perhaps millions, flocked to the streets. I darted away from the chaos to the top of the nearest hill for a better view. The widespread destruction affected everything in sight, sparing nothing and no one.

"You may feel powerless right now," said a voice, "but I can assist you."

I turned, startled by the noise and its familiarity that echoed in my ear. A few yards away stood the lava woman from my dream. I spun around to face her, instantly recognizing her long trusses of silky hair—as black as a moonless night—that spilled down her back and fell in waves to her bare feet. I thought back to my dream in the hospital, remembering the molten lava that hardened beneath her toes. I could never forget her powerful dark eyes, filled with intelligence...and her sudden flare of anger, generating a tempestuous eruption of lava with a swift flick of her hand.

"Who are you? And what do you want from me?" I asked, hoping for a verbal response this time.

She stood silently, stoically amidst the destruction—a reminder of the persistent threat. And in that moment, I understood the truth behind her sudden appearance. I must stop the remaining Elementals, but couldn't complete the difficult task alone. She gave a small wave of her hand, beckoning me to accept her assistance. Suddenly, I understood her full meaning: she could train me to complete this formidable task. I only had to follow her.

I glanced back over my shoulder, ashamed to leave this city in ruins.

When I didn't move from my spot, the lava woman challenged, "You may have stopped them once, but what about the next time?"

"Please. Help me to save these people now. Everything that's happened is all my fault!" I folded my hands together, begging her to halt the destruction and spare these innocent people. If she truly held the power to move the earth, couldn't she also silence Gaia's shaking?

She gave me a small, sympathetic smile before she turned on her heels and disappeared behind the rubble of a fallen building. I ran after her, desperate for her aid. But I found only a wispy trail of vapor that danced on the breeze. And after a minute, the trail vanished from sight.

I suspected she held the secrets I sought but chose to conceal them from me…at least for now. I dropped to my knees, burying my head in my hands with despair, knowing that I could have prevented the city's destruction and tragedy.

If only I had left this place in time.

Chapter One

I flew up in bed, my heart pounding in a cold panic that drenched my hospital gown. Instead of the scenes of chaos that flooded my mind, the sterile white surroundings of the hospital room enfolded me. A simple pair of lithograph prints of generic foliage decorated the off-white textured wallpaper, and a small flat-screen TV hummed with the city's latest news.

Outside my door, the nursing staff complained about the havoc of the tempestuous storm that hit the city only two days before. I strained my ears for more details. With no view of the outside, I couldn't guarantee the threat had truly passed.

My injuries from battling The Three had healed with astonishing speed. Better yet, the danger had diminished with Hydros gone. The Elementals didn't present as great a threat toward humanity. And for that, I allowed myself a sigh of relief.

But another thought clouded my mind. If the threat was gone, why would the lava woman call me back to finish my work? What more must I do? Everyone should be safe—*I* should be safe—at least for the moment.

I removed my blankets and pulled up the hospital gown to survey my wound. A thin crescent of shiny skin remained, barely perceptible across my belly. I vaguely remembered the nurses say they couldn't understand how I'd recovered so quickly. But the details of their conversations eluded me, blurred into a fuzzy memory from the effects of the prescribed painkillers that allowed my body to rest and heal. Remnants of nasty olive green and purple bruises surrounded the scar, but I surprisingly felt little pain. Almost like magic or a miracle had intervened, allowing me to survive and finish my task. I placed my gown over the wound and covered my body in the hospital's warm blankets, trying to forget the echo of the lava woman's words that sent a chill up my spine.

On the television, a newscaster reported, "Emergency efforts are underway as search and rescue teams have uncovered twenty-six survivors trapped under the collapsed freeway spans of the Bay Bridge to date. California Governor Burnham recently announced the city has been granted federal aid damage relief, though he estimates the bridge will take several months to repair. Commuters should expect considerable delays as higher volumes of traffic congest other routes into San Francisco."

I folded my hands, praying those individuals were not seriously hurt. A new wave of guilt consumed my soul when the news report shifted from the full screen aerial view of the bridge to the homes crumpled in Gaia's sudden quake. Had these images instigated my most recent nightmare? Or was it the TV station's repeated airing of black and white archived photos from the legendary 1906 quake?

I wasn't sure, but one thing I knew. I alone could have prevented the damage.

I cursed my injured arm, trapped inside a cast for too many weeks. And my impressionable heart that craved normalcy. Why did I have to grow so attached to Sully, Micah, and the Trudeau family? It would've been much easier if I'd lived alone.

A short rap on my door distracted me from my thoughts. "Come in," I automatically replied in a rough and scratchy voice, realizing I'd barely spoken since my battle against the Earth, Water, and Air Elementals.

"Why are you listening to that junk?" Sully blurted. He barged into the room, crossing its length in a few long strides to turn off the TV. Despite his harsh tone, I smiled, pleased to see Shayne Sullivan, who preferred everyone (including his teachers) call him by his nickname "Sully" instead.

His pale blue eyes surveyed me with disapproval. Short hair poked out the sides of his baseball cap, reminding me of the color of coffee with cream brought to my bedside with breakfast. "No one blames you," he reassured me. His hand subconsciously grazed the back of his head, remembering the pain from his concussion when the bridge trusses collapsed upon his sister's car.

How I wished his words were true. I closed my eyes, sniffling softly while scenes of destruction replayed in my head. Horrible memories rang in my ears: the crunching metal of the weakened Bay Bridge before its collapse, the screech of tires swerving to avoid collisions, Cam's cries when the car frame crushed his small body, and Sully's staggered steps down the street in search of help.

"Scientists said they already determined the location of the epicenter of the quake," Sully continued, "and blamed the weather for the storm surge along the coast."

My glossy eyes met his, a frown deepening across my lips.

"Hey, it's not your fault. You tried to warn us, we just…didn't listen." Sully cautiously sat on the side of my bed and placed a gentle hand upon my shoulder. By the expression on his face, I suspected he'd forgiven me, for most of what had happened at least. Still, I couldn't help but feel guilty for letting him and Cam get hurt.

Noticing my despair, Sully quickly added, "I mean really, Jordan. You have to admit, your stories seemed kind of far-fetched."

He was right. They did sound unbelievable. Concerned

with his safety, I tried to blow him off after that long kiss we'd shared, even though he insisted he could take care of himself. He had never believed an ominous threat existed or that I was that different from everyone else.

Until it was too late.

A fat teardrop rolled down my cheek. I squeezed my eyes shut, trying to forget the horrors. Still, my body heaved, shaking with uncontrollable sobs.

"It's okay. Really," Sully said, leaning in and wrapping me in his warm embrace. His short hair tickled the side of my cheek, but his arms felt strong and secure. In that moment, I wanted them to protect me from all I'd endured and all that was still to come. The smell of his cologne filled my nose. I breathed in deeply, letting him hold me for a long time to quiet my tears.

I slipped my arms around his back in return, comforted in his embrace. All of a sudden, I wanted to tell him how much I had worried about him. How I was confused and scared, and how uncertainty had clouded my emotions. Because now that it was just us, I quickly forgot all the reasons I had forced myself to avoid him in the first place. Had I actually liked Micah more than him? Or was it an easy excuse to prevent myself from getting too close to Sully and risk losing him?

Maybe I'd made a huge mistake. Deep inside my heart, I knew I'd never stopped liking Sully. It was safer to keep those thoughts locked inside, in case the other Elementals returned once more. I couldn't chance placing him in danger again.

With a heavy sigh, I unwound my arms from his back. Sniffling once to rid the flood of emotions from my mind, I said softly, "So Cam's really okay?"

Sully slowly released me before replying, "Yeah. He really is."

"But how? Yesterday, I thought Cam was in dire condition. Are you saying he actually doesn't need a transplant anymore?"

Sully's mouth widened into a broad smile. "Nope. He's all good. No transplant, nothing. I guess it's kinda like a miracle. The doctors are keeping him to run a few more tests, but Micah said it's strange. He'd been bumped up the list of recipients, then all of a sudden, the doctors couldn't find anything wrong with him."

My brow crinkled. "Is that normal?"

"No. Not at all. Cam claims he had some angels visit him in his sleep and they healed him," Sully explained.

"Angels?" I repeated. All my previous thoughts and concerns vanished in an instant. I focused solely on that single word — *angels*. Under different circumstances, it sounded innocent, pure, and heavenly. But used in this context, it dredged up fear within the recesses of my soul. Could that explain my remarkable healing, too? I hid my trembling hands beneath the hospital blankets. I swallowed hard, my stomach knotting with dread, before daring to speak, "How is that possible?"

Sully shrugged. "He's six. Six-year-olds say funny things sometimes."

It was possible Cam witnessed real angels from Heaven. But more likely, it was something — or some*one* — else.

"I want to see Cam," I announced impulsively.

Sully shook his head. "Y'know, I'm not so sure you're supposed to leave here yet. I don't think the nurses would want you to…"

"I want to tell him I'm sorry," I interrupted, "for what happened on the bridge."

I did want to apologize to Cam and Micah and Celia. But I also realized that if Cam had fully healed and the doctors released him, I would never know the truth unless I visited him *right now.*

Sully's face clouded. "Um, I'm not exactly sure that's a good idea."

I knew that look. He hid something from me. "Seriously,

13

Sully. It's my fault he ended up here in the first place. The least I can do is apologize."

"If you say so," Sully mumbled, his eyes unable to meet mine. He stuffed his hands deep into his jeans pockets. "But don't say I didn't warn you."

"Warn me about what?" I wondered aloud.

Sully didn't answer, but hesitantly offered me a hand to sit up in bed. Instead of a bolt of pain piercing my abdomen when I climbed out one side and slipped on a robe, the action caused me no discomfort and I suspected I knew why.

Outside my room, the hallway felt chilled with the air conditioning running at full blast. I wrapped my hospital robe tighter around me, partially from the cold and partially from fear that Cam's story would confirm my suspicions and leave me in more danger than I imagined.

A few doors down, we reached Cam's room. Inside, a woman's high-pitched voice sounded agitated. Suddenly I began to think that I should have listened to Sully and stayed in my room. When he moved to knock on the door, I grabbed his hand in restraint. He shot me a puzzled look.

"Wait a minute," I whispered and pressed my ear to the door. Inside the room, Celia's voice sounded strained so she wouldn't wake Cam from his slumber.

In hindsight, I should've walked away. But in that instant, a desperate urge to hear the truth grabbed me. I had to know what Celia thought of me, now that my actions had revealed my true identity to her.

Sobs contorted her broken voice as she spoke. "I thought I did the right thing, Micah. You understand, don't you? I couldn't imagine leaving her alone on the streets, not after what happened." She paused to heave a deep sigh. "How was I to know that something like her even existed?"

Shock registered on my face. Her words stung my heart like

salt rubbed into an open wound. Instantly forgetting my concerns about Cam's angels, I bit my lip, unable to stop the tears from pooling in my eyes.

I'd never be able to regain her trust, not after what had happened. My head dropped into my hands while her unforgettable comment echoed in my mind, tearing my heart in two, those three words defining my entire existence: *something like her.* And to be honest, I couldn't say which realization hurt more — the fact that she'd never forgive me…or that I'd never be normal. Ever.

CHAPTER TWO

"It was definitely a big mistake, and I know you warned me against it," Celia continued, unaware I listened through the door.

"Yep. I did," Micah agreed.

His words stunned me. I'd thought we were friends—and more. Now, I knew exactly how he felt. I remembered how he objected to Celia's offer to have me live in their basement after he'd accidentally broken my arm. I remembered the grief he'd endured—grounded from the car for a month and losing his cell phone privileges for a low score on his French test. It probably didn't help that I beat him on the test.

Then again, I did stand up for him when he'd thrown that impromptu party in Celia's absence. Had he forgotten about that? Or about how he'd felt, right before he kissed me?

I guessed so since Micah refused to utter a single word in my defense.

"But I didn't listen," Celia added with a deep sigh. "I'm sorry, I never meant for any of this to happen. Will you forgive me?"

A long pause passed before Micah replied, "Of course, Mom."

Why doesn't he stand up for me? I slumped to the floor in shock. And here I'd planned to apologize when I came to check on Cam. How could I go in there when I knew she despised me for creating this mess?

Sully offered me a hand. I glanced at his outstretched palm,

16

but shook my head, unable to speak. Celia kindly took me into her home, and look how I repaid her hospitality...putting her sons in mortal peril. Some appreciative guest I turned out to be.

"C'mon, Jordan. You know Celia," Sully whispered and knelt by my side. "She may get mad quickly, but she forgives even faster."

I squeezed my eyes shut. The truth behind Cam's miraculous healing no longer concerned me. I couldn't face Micah's family again, not now that I knew how they really felt.

"You can go back to your room or you can get this over with, right?" Sully reminded me.

I looked up at him, biting my lip nervously. Tears glazed my eyes. Her words echoed in my mind. *Something like her.*

"Go on," Sully prodded, turning the door handle for me. "No time like the present." He flashed me an encouraging smile.

"Yeah. Might as well." I muttered, knowing Celia's protective motherly nature accounted for her anger. I hadn't wanted them to get hurt. She had to understand that, didn't she?

"I'll be here if you need me," Sully said and pushed the door ajar.

"Thanks." I tried to mask the hurt in my wounded voice. When I stepped through the doorway, the room felt noticeably colder, even with my hospital robe wrapped tightly around me. It seemed the cold originated from within, radiating from my core the second I spotted Micah.

Before, I'd felt drawn to Micah's hazel eyes, engaged and sympathetic at times, disinterested at others. I often wished he'd look at me in the same way he did at Tessa. I'd found his short dark brown hair particularly cute, how it spiked up a bit in the front and trailed into sideburns.

Funny how quickly my perception changed. Now, I couldn't stand to look at him, knowing our friendship was a farce. He had claimed he cared about me when he saved me from The Three, had even kissed me sweetly when I lay on the hospital bed. But his reaction to Celia told me all I needed to know. Everything he'd said and done had been a lie.

Even Celia didn't seem herself. Her normally styled hair appeared scraggly and unkempt. With one side flat and matted, I imagined she'd spent the night sitting upright in the chair next to Cam's bed. But from the look of her red, puffy eyes, I doubted she'd actually slept more than a few minutes in a row since she received Micah's call. She draped a protective arm over Cam's shoulder. Her eyes gauged me with suspicion and trepidation.

Her face changed, perhaps from regret for her previous kindness. If only she hadn't opened her house to me, if only she hadn't been called into work and missed Cam's game, if only she hadn't seen me for who I really was, then her son wouldn't be in this situation.

"Don't worry, I'm leaving," I said coolly. "I only came to say good-bye."

"Where will you go?" she asked. I noticed Micah's curious eyes met mine for a flash of a second. "Will you finish school?"

I didn't see why she cared. I wasn't a normal teen, regardless of how hard I tried. Shouldn't my education be anything but traditional?

I shrugged. "What does it matter as long as I'm far from you, right?"

My comment came out harsher than I intended. But the shock of her hurtful tone still lingered in my ear. Micah didn't say a thing, unwilling to choose a side.

Fine, Micah. Whatever. The thank-you-for-everything kiss we shared meant the world to me...and nothing to him. I blinked back another round of stinging tears and turned to leave.

I almost reached the door when I heard Cam's soft, groggy voice. "Is that Jordan?" he asked, hopeful.

Well, at least one person seemed glad to see me.

18

I wiped my eyes, and slowly spun to face him, forcing a smile despite Celia's hurtful words. I needed to appear brave for the little boy who reminded me so much of my little sister, Sarah. I desperately wanted to sweep him into a hug, grateful he survived Gaia's wrath when my own Sarah had not, but I hesitated in taking a step toward Celia's reproachful face. "How are you feeling, buddy?" I managed, straining to keep the sadness at bay.

"I'm all better now," he replied. "Thanks to them."

"Them? Them who?" I prompted, pretending I'd never heard a word about his angel story. I forced my anger and hurt aside. If I could get him to elaborate, he should be able to confirm or deny my suspicions. I hoped for the latter.

"The angels," Cam replied in his sweet, soft voice. "They came into my room and made me all better."

"You know Cam," Celia said through tight lips. "He's got a pretty active imagination." She patted the top of his head.

"How'd they do that?" I asked, my voice shaky with anticipation.

"It was pretty cool," Cam said. His face relaxed. "The old woman put her hands under my back, right where it hurt the most. Her hands got really warm for a long time. And then the pain was gone."

"All gone?" I asked.

"Yep," he said, flashing me his toothless grin, "Like magic."

I felt the blood drain from my face. "And these angels…" I began, my hands starting to tremble. "Do you remember what they looked like?"

"Sure," Cam replied. "One had a soft, round face, kind of like the moon."

I didn't recognize his description, but still had one to go. I took a deep breath. "And the other?"

"She had really long, black hair."

"Long?" My throat grew dry. I dared to ask, "How long?"

19

Celia eyed me skeptically. I could tell my questions made her uneasy. I seemed to know too much for someone who hadn't heard his story.

Cam didn't appear to notice his mother's concern. He shrugged. "I think it reached all the way to the ground. And it was hot."

"Hot?" I swallowed hard. Not exactly your typical adjective used to describe someone's hair.

"Yeah," Cam said, nodding his head. "It was kind of melting."

"You know kids—sometimes they say the most ridiculous things," Celia said with a nervous laugh. "I mean, really, since when are angels on fire?"

"Melting?" I repeated. My eyes didn't leave Cam's face. "Like lava from a volcano?"

"Yes!" he exclaimed. "Exactly!"

"Oh God," I mumbled.

Celia gasped. "Don't tell me *you* know what he's talking about." She wrapped her arms around Cam's body, shielding him from me.

I felt the blood drain from my face. I backed toward the door, afraid to admit I *did* know exactly what he was talking about.

"It's her," I breathed. I glanced at Sully, my face filled with fear. "She healed Cam, knowing that would make me indebted to her, that I'd have to seek her out. It was her way to guarantee I'd find her to complete my training."

"What are you talking about?" Celia asked, panicked. "Who is she?"

"Cam's fine now," Sully told me, reassuringly. "You don't have anything to worry about."

"No," I shook my head, resolute. "I have to go. I'm supposed to find her."

Micah shifted uncomfortably in his chair, but remained awkwardly mute. Celia opened her mouth to speak, but shut it again, afraid to delay my departure.

Only Cam bothered to wave. "Bye, Jordan, I'll miss you," he chirped from behind the shelter of his mother's arms.

I wished Celia realized I'd never intentionally harm someone as sweet and innocent as Cam, especially when he reminded me so much of Sarah...before I lost her forever. I braved a smile, wishing I could hug him good-bye. But I wouldn't have that chance, reminding me I never got to say good-bye to Sarah, either.

"See you," I managed, my voice choking on each word. I turned on my heels and closed the door behind me with a note of finality.

CHAPTER THREE

I only made it four steps down the hall before I heard Micah's voice. "Jordan, wait."

I stopped, feeling conflicted with surprise and disappointment. I glanced at Sully to gauge his reaction.

"I'll just go hang out in your room," he offered.

"You don't have to stay," I told Sully. "I doubt Celia wants you around me, either."

"I'm a big boy," he said. "I can take care of myself. Besides, she's not my mom."

I wanted to smile, but I guarded my emotions, unsure of what Micah planned to say after he offered me no defense against his mom's harsh words. I watched Sully make it down the hall and into my room before I turned toward Micah, my face contorted into a bitter glare.

"Thanks for sticking up for me," I hissed, unable to hide the resentment in my tone. Without waiting for him to respond, I continued, "I don't understand. I thought you…you know…"

"I thought you were going to die," Micah interrupted. "I felt bad for you, just like anyone else would. It wasn't fair that you had to sacrifice yourself so we could get away."

I nodded, realizing that statement was probably as close to a compliment as I'd receive from him.

"But things changed. Both you and Cam healed in ways the

22

doctors can't explain."

"And now you have to live with the reality that I'm still here," I finished for him.

"I didn't mean it like that," Micah protested.

"Of course you didn't," I said with biting sarcasm. "Besides, you wouldn't choose me over Tessa."

He flinched at the severity of my tone. "Jordan, Tessa and I have been together for almost six months. What did you think I was gonna do? Dump her after just one kiss? Look, I'm sorry if I led you on. Things weren't supposed to turn out like this." Micah sighed in frustration. "Can't you see how difficult this is for me? I have to keep everyone happy…my mom, Cam, Tessa, Sully… and *you*."

My eyebrows pinched together. "So what are you saying?"

He glanced toward the door to my hospital room. "It's easier for everyone if I let you go."

I blinked, understanding Micah's intent. "Sully still likes me?" I wondered aloud.

Micah nodded and jammed his hands deep inside his pockets.

My fury toward Micah dissipated in an instant. I stood there in awkward silence, staring at him, searching for the right words to express my final good-bye. I settled for a mere, "Thanks."

He gave me a small nod and a wish of, "Good luck," before returning to Cam's room.

Heaving a deep breath, I straightened my shoulders and walked the rest of the way down the hall, more eager to see Sully than I had imagined.

I opened the door to my room and smiled at him.

"Celia's just a little shocked and upset right now," Sully assured me. "But she'll get over it." He walked up to me and slipped his reassuring arms around me. "I'm still here for you."

I thought of the time I'd wrapped my arms tightly around his waist, zipping over the hills on his motorcycle. I recalled how he'd fearlessly scampered to the edge of the rocky cliffs to peer at the churning ocean far below. And I thought of him rushing up the side of an icy wave on his skimboard, only to be launched off once he'd reached the summit of the breaking crest.

"That's because you've always been attracted to danger."

Sully broke away from the embrace, giving me a look of feigned perplexity. "Is it that obvious?" he asked with a wink.

"A little," I admitted.

"You know me too well," Sully said, flashing me a crooked smile.

God, I love that smile. My heart took an unexpected leap inside my chest, thinking about Micah's words in the hall. A part of me wished things had never changed between us and the threat of the Elementals had never loomed on the horizon. If I could go back to that night when he'd invited me to his house, would I still break away from his kiss?

"Well," Sully said, digging the keys from his pocket. "I should probably get going."

"Already?" I didn't bother to hide my disappointment.

He paused for a moment and let his keys drop back inside his jeans. "I guess I don't have to...if you don't want me to," he offered.

I breathed a soft, but honest response. "I don't."

For a long moment, he looked at me, speechless. He stood in front of me, his fingers lightly brushing the side of my cheek while a conflicted look formed in his eyes.

I swallowed hard, my eyes locked with his, waiting to see what he'd do next. With Hydros gone and the storm diminishing, maybe my life would prove less dangerous. Maybe I could have the normal teenage existence I'd always wanted. Maybe.

I clung to that hope and to the idea of being with him.

His fingers left my cheek and slipped behind my neck. He leaned toward me, his face pausing mere inches above mine. My mouth parted expectantly.

Only the briefest space of air remained between our lips when the door popped open and Bethany Donovan flew into my room. Her short blond curls bobbed with each rapid step. Startled, Sully leapt backward.

"Oh my God, Jordan! I'm *so* glad you're okay!" she gushed and threw her arms around me in a quick hug. She pulled away just as quickly, nervously running her fingers through her curls in case our small embrace had messed up her hairstyle.

"How did you find me?" I asked cautiously. After all, I was under the impression Bethany only wanted to befriend me to get closer to Micah.

She plunked down on the empty chair in my room before disclosing her secret. "Micah texted me and said you were here. It's amazing you're even alive after what happened!"

First off, since when did Micah start talking to Bethany? And second, exactly how much did he tell her? That the Bay Bridge had crushed Sully's car or how I had made a fire tornado? Did she know I'm an Elemental? Then again, did she even know what an Elemental was?

"He did?" I shot Sully a worried look.

He shrugged his shoulders to say I had nothing to worry about. Even if Micah deliberately chose to ignore me, he wouldn't go around and blab about my fire powers to everyone at school, especially not to Bethany who couldn't keep a secret if her life depended on it. I took a deep breath, knowing Sully was probably right. Besides, chances were nobody would believe the truth if they heard it.

"Of course! He said you outran a tsunami and escaped the bridge collapse from the earthquake," Bethany continued without pausing for a breath. "And he pulled his little brother out of the car and picked you up just in time to save you from a tornado coming down the street. Can you believe it? A tornado in Oakland! Oh my God…that makes him like your hero, doesn't it?"

"Yeah. Something like that," Sully muttered. Clearly irritated, he dragged another chair across the room next to Bethany and slouched into its seat.

I snorted. Leave it to Micah to exaggerate the story in his favor. But at least he was nice enough to omit a bunch of the details I'd rather she never know.

Bethany's eyes anxiously flitted across the room. She smoothed out her jacket in a fidgety manner and wound a lock of hair around her index finger, twisting it repeatedly. "Is he here now?" she said in a low voice.

"Nah," Sully answered for me. "And don't expect him to be swinging by anytime soon."

Bethany's face turned into a disappointed frown. She smoothed her hands down the length of her short skirt and glanced at Sully, noticing him for the first time. "Weren't you with Micah when the bridge collapsed?"

His eyes met mine for a fraction of a second before he answered. "Unfortunately. It was my car that got totaled."

A part of me wanted to correct him, reminding him it was his sister's car that Gaia destroyed.

Bethany reached over and laid a hand upon his knee. "Ohmigod. I had no idea. Are you okay?"

Sully sighed a little heavier than necessary when he replied, "Yeah. The docs tell me I got a concussion, but I'm okay. It's really Cam and Jordan that I'm worried about."

"You are too sweet," she said, batting her eyelashes twice at him. Within seconds, Sully's face and neck turned a bright shade of pink.

"Oh, brother," I muttered under my breath, somewhat surprised when jealousy boiled within my veins. All of a sudden, it no longer mattered that I had originally broken things off with

Sully. Who did she think she was to start hitting on him right in front of me?

Before Sully had a chance to reply, I sat on the edge of Sully's chair and slipped my hand in his, squeezing it possessively. "Yes, he is too sweet," I told her. Sully shot me a quizzical look.

Bethany's gaze shifted toward our entwined hands, a small frown forming across her face. "Oh, my bad," she apologized and stood to leave. "Well, if you see Micah, tell him I say 'hi.' I guess I'll see you later, Jordan." She gave me a small wave.

In that instant, I wanted Sully back so badly so Bethany couldn't have him. But I reminded myself of why that would never happen. Regardless of my feelings, I couldn't take the chance. Not after what had happened.

"Sounds great. Thanks for stopping by," I fibbed, upset by the reality of my situation. Even though I didn't want to release him, I forced my fingers from Sully's hand.

"Bye, Sully," Bethany said, batting her eyelashes in a disappointed way. "See you at school, I guess."

"Yep. See ya, Bethany," Sully replied, his tone a bit too cheerful for my liking. As he watched her leave, his face rapidly changed, another thought suddenly popping into his mind. Freed from my grip, he leapt off his seat, blurting, "Or if you want, I can walk you down to Cam's room to see if Micah's still here."

Bethany turned, her face brightening from his offer. "Would you?" she declared in a helpless way. I rolled my eyes, watching them leave without another glance in my direction before Sully quickly closed the door behind him. *Let him go*, I told myself, driving thoughts of our interrupted kiss from my mind. He didn't need my permission. His lips had never touched mine. We had no commitment, especially when I had ended things before.

I crawled into my bed and rolled over on one side, pulling the blankets up to my chin. When I closed my eyes tightly, a fat teardrop slid down my cheek, dampening my pillow. It wasn't for losing Sully, but for my desperate plea to live a life of normalcy. I must discover the reason the fire angel called me back to finish my work in this world if I ever wished to have that chance to be like everyone else.

The only place I knew to look for her was in my dreams. I squeezed my eyes tight, forcing the hurt from my mind. I willed myself to rest, anxious to meet her once more. Eventually the exhaustion of my confusing emotions overcame me and I entered a fitful sleep.

Thoughts flew through my head of lava bombs plunging from the sky and the cracking sound of bridge tresses gave way under the unnatural strain of Gaia's tremors. *It's not worth the risk*, I repeated to myself. If I didn't let myself fall for anyone again, the other Elementals would have no leverage over me. They'd have no one left to hurt in order to gain control. *It's a solid, foolproof plan.*

"Or you can protect yourself and those you love," said the voice of Cam's fire angel.

She's here. Inherent curiosity piqued my interest, compelled to learn more now that my strategy had worked. Still, I feared her explosive rage. With hesitation, I sat up in bed. My eyes scanned the room, searching for the woman with the long silky hair that ended in molten lava.

"Protect yourself and those you love," the fire angel repeated.

A flash of white fire infiltrated my mind, blinding in its intensity. This must be her way of telling me to seek her out immediately, before other dangers befell the ones I loved.

That's it! Her meaning registered in my brain. I'd hurt so many people I loved because I couldn't defend them from The Three. Now she offered an alternative…a way to increase my powers until I eliminated the threat forever.

A relieved grin spread across my face. She presented the perfect reason to train and learn how to protect the people I cared about most. Now all I had to do was find her and begin. I closed my eyes, confident and secure for the first time in a very long while.

Suddenly, the door burst open with a deafening bang. A fierce gust of wind rushed into the room, blowing off my covers. It knocked the framed prints from the wall and shattered the television monitor. I curled into a fetal position, shielding my face and body from the shards of broken glass. From my spot on the bed, I peeked with hesitation and uncertainty at the door as two figures strode into my room.

Gaia and Skye.

"You're alive?" I gasped, though deep down I knew it would take more than a fire tornado to destroy The Three all at once. "But how did you find me?" I shouted over the wind.

They uttered no response, surveying me through steely eyes. Raising their hands toward my cowering form, they paused for a moment, preparing to synchronize their powers and finish me.

"Search deep inside," the fire angel's voice suggested. "Fuel your powers from your core."

My core? What did that have to do with my powers? I wondered. I attempted to heed her advice, assuming her training began at that precise moment. I strained to concentrate my anger and fear deep within, an energy cell feeding my entire body. My heart and soul committed fully to the cause. I closed my eyes and allowed the raging burn to build inside my chest, then course outward through my arms and legs. My eyes stewed with anger and resentment as the power mounted inside me. Fearlessly, I rose from my huddled position on the bed, surprised to find the floor covered in a fiery mass of boiling lava. The lava spilled out toward the corners of the room, consuming everything except for my hospital bed, perched safely in the middle of a molten sea. Strength and conviction filled my face. My mouth wound into a proud grin. *It begins now*, I told myself, defiant. I sat taller upon my bed.

Panic clouded Gaia and Skye's countenances. They inched toward the door, desperate for escape. But before they could turn and flee, Sully entered the room to check on me. He immediately froze, stunned by the destruction before him. My grin faded. My gaze shifted toward Gaia, contemplating her next move.

She looked from me to Sully and back again, her emerald eyes flickering with evil. Her lips snaked into a sinister smile that sent a chill racing down my spine.

"Leave him alone!" I screamed. Before she could lift a hand in his direction, my entire body turned white-hot in a glowing orb. Shock filled Gaia's expression. She whipped her head from side to side, searching for an escape.

Determined to save Sully this time, I stepped from my bed and held the handrail, startled to discover everything I touched instantly melted — the handrail, the mattress, the walls. My eyes glowing with revenge, I strode toward Gaia, reaching my hand out toward her arm.

"No!" she shouted, recoiling from my touch. She backed herself into the corner. Pinned against the wall, she had nowhere to go. I took another step toward her, my hand outstretched, only inches from her skin.

But before I could touch her, I felt a strong, comforting hand upon my shoulder. "Jordan? Jordan, are you okay?" I heard Sully ask in a soothing voice.

My eyes instantly simmered. I blinked into the bright hospital room, shocked to find everything still intact. The bed, the framed prints, the television monitor — everything returned to its original state. Only my covers lay strewn in a messy pile upon the immaculate floor, kicked off in my fitful state.

"What happened?" I asked in alarm, my eyes focused on Sully's face. "Where are they?"

"Bethany, Micah, and Celia left a few minutes ago. Cam's

30

sleeping again so they figured…"

"No, not them. The *Elementals*," I said, dropping my voice to a forced whisper.

Sully let out a hearty laugh. "They're gone. Don't you remember finishing them off? And here I thought *I* was the only one who got hit hard in the head."

I managed a small smile of relief at his comment. *He's okay. I'm okay.* I surveyed the room again, still intact. Gaia and Skye hadn't come back for me, not yet, at least. It was all just a bad dream.

But the Elementals would inevitably return. Only this time, I promised myself I'd be ready — with the help of the fire angel, of course. Though one major problem remained. I had no idea how or where to find her.

CHAPTER FOUR

My racing heart gradually subsided, the calming reality of my hospital room registering in my brain, followed soon after by a grating irritation of Sully's willingness to impress Bethany Donovan. "Thought you'd still be with Bethany," I muttered.

"Bethany?" Sully replied with surprise. "Why's that?"

I rolled my eyes. Hadn't he noticed her fawning over him, right by my bedside? "Oh, I dunno," I said, heavy on the sarcasm. "Maybe because she likes you?"

"Me? You really think so?" he said. His expression changed, suddenly remembering that we'd almost kissed before she arrived.

It's better this way, I reminded myself, ignoring the ache in my heart.

"I'm sorry, Jordan," Sully explained. "I just showed her the way to Cam's room."

"Always the helpful one, aren't you?" I grumbled and rolled onto my side away from him. Scenes from my dream repeated in vivid detail — lava pooling on the floor, my white-hot molten touch, Sully's casual entrance that nearly cost him his life. No matter how hard I squeezed my eyes shut, I couldn't rid the nightmarish images from my mind.

Sully let out an exasperated sigh. "All right. What is it this time? I mean, I left you and you were fine. And then I come back a few minutes later and you're thrashing around on your bed. You can't really be that mad about Bethany, right?"

I closed my eyes, steadying my nerves. Slowly, I rolled back to face Sully and gazed into his pale blue eyes. "You're right. I'm not."

A smile brightened his face. "Okay, then. So what is it?"

Under other circumstances, I would have buried my thoughts deep inside. But I could trust Sully, even if he didn't entirely believe everything I said. And right now, I had no one else to trust. "It's Cam's angel. She keeps visiting me in my dreams."

Sully attempted to hide his snorting laughter behind his hand. When the tears of hilarity faded from his eyes, he exclaimed, "Cam's angel? Don't tell me you actually believe his story?"

"How else do you think I knew so much about her?"

He shrugged. "I just figured you're pretty good at making stuff up."

I rolled my eyes again. "She sent me a message. Not only do I owe her for saving Cam's life and for healing me, but I believe she can teach me to protect those I love." I might never have a normal life, but I could prevent the Elementals from taking anyone else from me...assuming I found her. "Only I've got a huge problem."

"Yeah?" Sully asked as one eyebrow lifted dramatically high on his forehead.

I sighed, still unsure he believed a single word. "I don't have a clue who she is, much less how to find her."

"Well, maybe I can help," Sully offered. He settled back in his chair and rotated his hat around backward the way he usually did when he wanted to focus. "What did she look like again?"

"She's beautiful. Very beautiful. And she's got a quick temper. She can make a volcano erupt. And her hair is super long and ends in lava."

"Makes volcanoes erupt? Hair like lava? Hmm...gimme a sec," Sully said whipping out his phone.

I frowned. I crossed my arms over my chest and blew the hair from my eyes, wondering why I always placed a distant second to that small, inanimate object.

He turned the screen toward me to display an illustration. "You mean like this?"

My jaw hit the floor. I stared at the picture on his tiny screen, unable to believe my eyes. "Oh. My. God," I gasped in disbelief. Her face looked as beautiful as I remembered, with high cheekbones and full lips. She wore a crown of red flowers around her head. Long black locks trailed from strong shoulders to form the sweeping slopes of a mountain. The ends of her hair glowed hot with molten lava contacting the sea. The artist even portrayed the fiery temper that flared within the woman's warm brown eyes.

"Who is she?" I dared.

"That's Pele, the Hawaiian goddess of fire," Sully explained. "Some people say you can find her by the active volcanoes on the Big Island of Hawaii."

I blinked. "How do *you* know all that?"

"I'm not a total wash in history." Sully chuckled and puffed out his chest proudly. "I actually remembered a couple of stories from when my family vacationed in Hawaii a few years back."

For a second, I recalled the puddle of spittle that collected on Sully's desk during Mr. Tabor's US History lesson and tried not to laugh. "If only Mr. Tabor knew the real you," I joked.

"If only," he agreed. His smile widened into that same cute one he'd flashed me before—the one I chastised myself for finding so alluring. I wished I had a strategy to help me focus on my task at hand that worked as well as Sully's spinning baseball cap routine. Because right now I couldn't think about anything besides finishing our interrupted kiss.

Luckily, Sully remained in focus-mode. His fingers flew over the miniscule keyboard on his phone as he spoke. "Sometimes these upstart airlines have pretty good last-minute deals…oh, wait, here's one called Skyways Air."

A shudder ran up my spine. The name alone scared me, dredging up memories of my last contact with the Air Elemental.

But Sully didn't seem to notice my reservation. "It says they fly into Hilo on the Big Island of Hawaii."

"Hee-low?" I repeated, my eyebrows crinkling on top of my head.

"Yep. And their one-way tickets start as low as $99."

I frowned. "I don't have that much money." I supposed there was no need to tell him I don't have any money at all or a place to stay, now that Celia forbade me anywhere near her boys.

"So? You can borrow it from me," he offered.

Shaking my head, I said, "Sully, I appreciate what you're trying to do here, but I can't ask you to —"

"Think of it as a gift." He shifted in his chair before continuing. "And all you have to do in return is set a date for me."

"A date?" I asked, surprised at his suggestion. Perhaps he wasn't as interested in Bethany as I'd thought. "But how is that possible? I won't be anywhere near you."

He held up his phone. "It's easy. We can see each other using the Internet. It's like a phone call with a video feed."

"But I don't have a phone," I objected. "Or a computer."

"No, but libraries do — and you can use it for free." He looked back at his phone, quickly touching the screen to flip to the calendar mode. "In a few days, I'll be starting up a new job that'll carry over into the summer. My parents said I had to start saving for college, y'know."

"You did? Doing what?"

"Construction. A lot of places need fixing up after the superstorm's tsunami hit Pacifica."

"You mean Hydros's tsunami."

"Regardless," he continued, "why don't we just plan to talk

when I'm done with work? Like a phone date."

My mind fixated on his last word, even though I'd be halfway across the sea. A broad smile filled my face. "Deal," I agreed, no longer trying to hide the rising blush in my cheeks. I'd still get to talk to Sully every day. I deliberately ignored the voice in my head that reminded me I had no guarantee I'd ever make it back to California and see him in person. But I could figure that out later, certain Pele wouldn't let me return until my job was done... if I even survived that long.

"Hey, look! They've got a ticket left for tomorrow," Sully added. "After you get released, I can take you to the airport, if you'd like."

I had to admit Sully was sweet, just as Bethany had said. "You don't need to do that."

He shrugged. "Maybe I want to say good-bye."

My heart fluttered inside my chest, wondering if I'd get a second chance at that kiss. "I'd like that," I admitted.

"But this time, *I'm* driving," he said. An infectious grin spread across his face.

I couldn't keep myself from smiling back, perhaps a little too wide for my own good.

I would've given anything for one last ride on Sully's motorcycle to the airport, letting the wind whip through my clothes as I clung tightly to his body. I longed for the sensation of zipping up and down the hills leading into the city, along the same route I'd used to escape the tsunami. But Sully didn't want to strain my injury, even though it seemed fully healed to me. So, I had to settle with sneaking glances at him across the console of the rental the insurance company had provided while they sorted out the claim on his sister Vanessa's crushed car.

Since I was under eighteen and had never flown before, airport security permitted Sully to pass through the checkpoint and accompany me as a personal escort. Once security finished scanning my backpack full of borrowed clothes from Vanessa, we continued to my departure gate. We walked side by side past one gift store after another, strategically situated to entice last-minute shoppers before they boarded the plane. Racks of postcards stood outside each store, displaying colorful images of the sights of cable cars traversing San Francisco's famously steep roads, the Golden Gate Bridge immersed in a sea of fog, towering Redwood forests, and the old island prison of Alcatraz. I stopped for a moment when my eye caught a picture of the Bay Bridge spanning the distance between the city and Oakland. Only now it lay in ruins, completely unusable. I visualized the scenes from the news report of irritated motorists stranded in mile-long traffic jams and the unfathomable number of man hours required to repair the structure…all because I couldn't get off the bridge in time. I never should have let my heart get in the way of my decisions.

"C'mon," Sully said, placing one arm over my shoulder to direct me away from the souvenir stand.

Still, the images reminded of the nightmarish threat I posed to him. Even though I had tried to warn him before, he chose to come back. I attempted to block the horrifying thoughts from my mind and rid them from my memory. I made a solemn promise that with Pele's help, I would never cause him harm again.

In the waiting area, the TV monitors highlighted one news story after another, each more depressing than the last. I squirmed uncomfortably in my seat, wishing to say good-bye to Sully, but finding it impossible to concentrate with the newscaster's horrific tales of accidents, shootings, drownings, and suicides. Our conversation resorted to small talk as travelers crowded the seating area.

"Sorry Micah couldn't be here to see you off," he finally said. I noticed his eyes had difficulty meeting mine.

I slipped my hand inside of his. "I understand. Cam needs him now, anyway." *Plus, he's got Tessa. Someone Celia approves of.* "Thanks again for all of your help," I added. "I really couldn't have done this without you."

Sully glanced at the time on his phone. "They'll be boarding soon," he noted.

I nodded, my anxiety levels rising, as we sat in awkward silence, each avoiding the other one's gaze.

The Skyways Air gate attendant took her position behind the check-in counter. She pulled her hair tightly up in a high ponytail that bobbed with every slight motion of her head. Her heavy makeup strongly accentuated her angled cheekbones. Wearing a white button-down shirt beneath a fitted navy blazer and a matching mini skirt, she raised the microphone up to her ruby lips, a signal to begin. The intercom buzzed with an alto voice, heavily encrypted in loud background static. "We will now begin pre-boarding for Skyways Flight 1107 with service to Hilo. All passengers who are traveling with children or need extra time are welcome to board."

I looked at Sully and felt suddenly very confused now that I had to leave. I liked Micah. Okay, scratch that. I *had* liked Micah, but couldn't have him. But a small part of me had never stopped liking Sully. Was it the fear of the Elementals that initially drove me away from him? Or my desire to win Micah's affection?

It seemed so long ago, I couldn't recall the minor details. All I knew now was Sully had always been there for me—picking me up on his motorcycle on the long walk home from school, taking me out for pizza after I flunked out of Driver's Ed, and waiting by my bedside when I finally revived. Shouldn't that be enough of a reason to like him?

The intercom buzzed again as the gate attendant continued her boarding procedure. "Now boarding Rows fifteen through thirty on Flight 1107 to Hilo."

I glanced at my ticket with row number twenty-eight written in bold ink. Shooting Sully an apologetic look for my lame good-bye, I slung my backpack over my shoulder and stepped into the long line of passengers. Suddenly, I second-guessed whether I should leave at all. But the words I wanted to say to him inconveniently stuck inside my throat.

"Now boarding all rows for Hilo Flight 1107," the gate attendant declared over the static of the intercom.

Sully gave me a small, sad wave and turned to leave. His shoulders slumped as he walked away, filled with disappointment. I knew I should board the plane without looking back, but sought comfort in his familiarity. A swift terror to venture into the unknown consumed my heart. I knew I couldn't risk repeating the tragedy on the Bay Bridge. It was too dangerous for me to stay, regardless of my feelings. And if I intended to destroy the remaining Elementals, I must act now. That was the reason I needed Pele's help. The reason I must leave.

I watched Sully walk away, wishing my decision wasn't so difficult. I hoped he'd look back so I could say good-bye one last time.

A deep frown settled over my face as I stepped forward in line. Half a dozen people remained ahead of me, each waiting to present their boarding passes to the flight attendant. I glanced over my shoulder again before bolting from the line.

"Sully!" I called, sprinting to catch him. He turned, his head cocked to one side in a quizzical way.

"What's wrong?" he asked, confused.

"Nothing, it's just that..." My voice trailed off, unexpectedly at a loss for words. Unable to convey all my thoughts toward him, I took a step closer, bridging the gap between us. Rooted to his spot, his eyes held mine. And that was all the confirmation I needed.

My conscience warned me to return to the line and board

the plane so I wouldn't complicate our precarious relationship, but my emotions suddenly overruled logic. Before I could stop myself, I stood on tiptoes, pressing my lips softly to his. A look of pleasant surprise quickly replaced the initial shock registered across Sully's face.

I kissed him without reservation. I knew I didn't deserve this, not for how I'd treated him in the past. Still, I couldn't break away from our kiss. Fear had a funny way of clouding my emotions and influencing my actions. Now with the element of fear minimized after Hydros's death and the superstorm receding from the Bay Area, I could relax slightly and appreciate Sully. Especially when he was here with me now…

And Micah wasn't.

"Final boarding call for Flight 1107 with service to Hilo," the gate attendant declared over the crackling intercom.

I broke away from our kiss and peeked nervously at the door of the Jetway, my boarding pass clenched in my fist. The flight attendant looked at me disapprovingly for complicating her job.

"I don't think I'm ready," I admitted to Sully.

"But I thought you said this was the only way you'd get the answers you need."

The intercom buzzed again with the gate attendant's irritated call. "Paging Skyways passenger Jordan Smith," she announced. I glanced over my shoulder. The woman pursed her lips and tapped her foot on the floor, waiting impatiently. Looking me straight in the eye, she raised the microphone to her lips once more. "Jordan Smith, please return to Gate D3 so your plane can depart on time."

"Guess it's time," Sully said with a crooked smile.

Trepidation filled my body, uncertain of what lay ahead.

Sully planted a quick peck on my cheek. "You'll do great. I know you will."

I smiled thanks as the intercom buzzed again. "Just a

reminder, this is the *final* boarding call for Flight 1107 with service to Hilo. All passengers must board at this time."

I shot the gate attendant a pleading look, desperate for one last minute before they closed the Jetway doors. She replied by tapping her index finger to the face of her golden wristwatch in an aggravated way. Maybe she needed to loosen that ponytail and relax a tiny bit.

"Hey," Sully said, brushing his fingers across my cheek to get my attention again. "I'm still here for you. Remember that, okay?" He gave my hand a final squeeze.

I braved a smile, grabbed my bags, and dashed for the door. The gate attendant set the microphone upon the counter. Her three-inch heels clicked on the protective floor mat as she met me by the gate, her ruby lips turning into a smug smile. Snatching my boarding pass from my hand, she scanned it with a jerky motion. "Welcome aboard. It's nice of you to make it," she said, her voice thick with sarcasm. She thrust the paper back into my waiting palm.

Stepping onto the Jetway, I turned to give Sully one last wave good-bye before the gate attendant closed the door on my face.

I raced down the Jetway, my backpack thumping against my body with every stride. I entered the cabin, feeling suddenly very hot in Vanessa's tight jeans. I took a deep, unsatisfying breath of the recirculated air, confining and stale in my lungs. Unable to meet the irritated faces of the flight attendants busy with last-minute preparations, I headed for my seat. Walking down the narrow aisle, I felt the weight of many passengers' eyes upon me, appearing anxious to depart on time.

I squeezed past two passengers and plopped into the last vacant spot on the entire aircraft, and crammed my backpack under the seat in front of me, wishing I packed fewer clothes since now I couldn't stretch my legs. At least I stowed my bag nearby if I had to make a hasty exit. Looking out the window, I subconsciously tapped on the double panes of glass—too hard for me to break through, and hopefully thick enough to prevent Skye from detecting my presence in her realm.

Relax, Jordan, I told myself, inhaling a few deep breaths, thinking about the details Sully recounted about flying. Skye didn't know I was here…and I'd like to keep it that way. I needed to focus on finding Pele. Nothing else.

While the flight attendants explained the list of safety procedures for this aircraft, I ran through possible escape plans in the event Skye caused the plane to fall out of the air. Unfortunately, none of my scenarios seemed encouraging to guarantee everyone's survival.

Worse, the lovesick honeymooners in the seat in front of me wouldn't stop kissing each other long enough to take a breath. I couldn't tell which made me feel more nauseous: the rattling of the airplane wheels across the tarmac, or hearing the bride call her new husband pet names like "Baby" and "Hubby" in her sugary voice during those brief moments when their lips parted.

"Flight Attendants, prepare for departure," announced the pilot's broken voice over the cabin speakers.

A nervous energy consumed my gut. The pilot's voice filled the speakers, announcing our status as next in line for takeoff. I reached for the fan on the console above my head, hoping the breeze would soothe my nerves. The plane's jets roared at maximum power. Seconds later, the forward burst of speed thrust me backward in my seat, my stomach moving in the opposite direction of my body. This was a really bad idea, but I couldn't turn back now.

At liftoff, the sudden change in the cabin pressure made my ears scream, on the verge of exploding. I imagined the view leaving the city of San Francisco edging the Bay normally would've been beautiful, if the Bay Bridge hadn't lain in ruins, its upper level collapsed upon the outbound traffic below. I looked away, another wave of guilt consuming my soul, certain it would take an awfully long time to repair the damage I'd caused. The media had attributed the damage to nature—the worst storm to smother the area in more than one hundred years. Still, the weight of the disaster weighed heavy on my soul, especially now that I witnessed its magnitude from above.

The familiar sights of the Bay Area quickly grew faint leaving the coastline. I soon saw nothing beyond the deep blue ocean that extended all the way to the horizon. A new sickening feeling filled my stomach. I glanced out the window, loathing the sea. It reminded me of how much I hated Hydros for ordering William Mills's death back in Salem Village. I did what I had to do. Now she was gone and could never again hurt anyone I loved.

A sea of clouds soon obscured my view of the ocean. Drained, exhaustion consumed me. I leaned my head against the window and closed my eyes, the light motion of the plane soon lulling me to sleep.

I woke abruptly to the pilot's warning over the intercom, requesting all passengers to securely fasten their seat belts. Violent turbulence shook the plane simultaneously up and down. My tired eyes jolted into sudden alertness. I stared out the window, frightened I might lose my last meal. Outside, a dense black cloud resembling the shape of the head of an anvil towered high above the others. Its flattened top stood massively tall, protruding into the darkness. The sky quickly shifted to the black of nightfall. Rain pelted the glass, striking the window and blowing ferociously toward the rear of the plane.

I made a mistake in entering the Air Elemental's realm. My stomach lurched as the plane shook and unexpectedly dropped through the air. I feared for the safety of these innocent travelers and clasped my hands together, praying the pilot's skill would overcome the worsening weather. The anvil-headed cloud's blackened features appeared to twist and contort until they resembled the face of Skye, but in reverse. Skye's pale features appeared to transform into their ghastly negative image similar to the X-ray of my broken arm in the emergency room in Pacifica.

While the newlyweds in front of me whispered frantic admissions of love, I scolded myself for flying at all. This flight was far riskier than I'd originally guessed. Skye still found me, even concealed inside the metal hull of the plane.

My knuckles turned white when bold flashes of lightning pierced the coal-black sky outside. Sully meant well, but his efforts were in vain. I'd never reach Pele, never complete my training, and never learn how to protect the ones I loved.

Because I wouldn't survive this trip.

A very loud *crack* — like the boom from a cannon — rocked the plane. The hurried conversations and reciting of prayers stopped instantly as the cabin plunged into absolute silence. I closed my eyes, certain that deafening sound marked the end of our time on this earth.

CHAPTER FIVE

Somehow, the pilot maneuvered us through the storm and landed safely at Hilo's airport. I wanted to apologize to him for incurring the wrath of Skye aboard his flight, but settled with a simple, "Thank you." Words alone could not express the gratitude I experienced to place my feet upon solid ground.

I stepped from the Jetway, allowing myself a deep breath before focusing on my next task of locating Pele. When I asked the gate attendant where I could find the goddess, he rolled his eyes at me and walked away, muttering something about crazy tourists. Undeterred, I continued down the open-air hall, asking everyone I saw. I questioned travelers dragging their luggage on wheels, an airport security officer, an ice cream cart vendor, a tour guide bearing armfuls of purple flowered leis, a cashier at the airport gift shop, and a couple of kids about half my age who waited for their mom outside the women's bathroom.

By the time I reached the baggage claim area, my optimism faded. Everyone I spoke to—*everyone*—dismissed me for a fool. Now I was stuck here on some wild goose chase, no closer to reaching my goal than I'd been before setting a foot on the plane. You'd think if Pele had gone out of her way to contact me multiple times in my dreams, then she'd at least seek me out once I'd reached her homeland. At this rate, I would've been better off staying back in California with Sully, rather than stuck on an exotic island where I didn't know a soul.

Heaving a huge sign of frustration, I flopped down into a chair and dumped my backpack on the ground, clueless of my next step. I slid down in my seat, exhausted, and pressed my fingers against my temples to ease the tension of the flight. From my slouched spot, my eyes drifted to the bright photographs decorating the covers of a nearby rack of travel brochures and welcome guides. *I wonder*, I thought and picked a guide off the rack. Thumbing through a few pages, I searched for anything containing a picture of a volcano or Pele. After skimming past a bunch of advertisements for shopping, art galleries, and dining options on the island, I reached the section on Volcanoes National Park, located not far from Hilo.

I only made it through the first three paragraphs about the park when I felt a tap on my shoulder. I turned to face a shriveled old woman with yellowed teeth and a spine bent from age. Her dark brown eyes were deeply set into her wrinkled, tanned face and she wore her gray hair twisted into a bun on the back of her head. To hide the folds of her soft body, she wore a long floral dress with no waist—like the muumuus I saw in the shopping section of the welcome guide.

"You looking for Pele?" the old woman asked in a weathered voice.

I sat straighter in my chair. "Excuse me?" I whispered, my eyes wide with surprise.

"The goddess Pele?" she repeated. "You wish to see her?"

I nodded, afraid to trust my voice to words. *How did she know?* Unless she overheard me asking one of the dozens of strangers I'd met since I got off the plane. In fact, everyone in the entire airport probably knew I was looking for Pele.

A smile graced her thick lips and pushed up her broad cheekbones. "My sister lives near the volcano, Kilauea. Some people believe the goddess can be found there," the old woman explained. "If you'd like, I can take you along the next time I go for a visit."

I almost fell out of my seat. "Are you serious? That would be wonderful!" I exclaimed. I picked up my bag and slung it over my shoulders. I didn't care if she sounded crazier than me, I couldn't pass up this chance. "My name's Jordan," I said and stuck out my hand.

She shook it with surprising strength for an old woman. "And you can call me Auntie Lulu."

Grateful she not only offered me a ride but gave a sense of family in this unfamiliar land, I followed the old woman out of the airport and into the parking lot. Outside, varying shades of gray clouded the sky and a warm light rain misted my clothes, hair, and skin. Everything about me felt damp by the time she led me across the entire parking lot. She eventually stopped in front of an old orange Pontiac Firebird with lines of rust around the wheel wells. The car seemed almost as aged as Lulu herself, making me think the mild climate here in Hawaii allowed cars to live well beyond their intended life spans.

I climbed in the passenger side, set my bag on my lap, and closed the door. Auntie Lulu turned the key in the ignition and the engine slowly chugged to life. "Have you ever met Pele?" I asked.

"Yes," she admitted in a voice so soft I barely heard it over the noisy car.

I spun my head to face her, my eager ears trained on her response. "What was she like?" I asked excitedly.

"It was a long time ago," Auntie Lulu said with a look that dismissed further discussion on the topic. Without another word, she threw the transmission into drive and slowly pulled out of the lot. The car sputtered a bunch of times, making me wonder if I might have better luck walking to her place.

We drove away from the airport and down the wet road

in silence. She kept her eyes trained on the road, forgetting me entirely. Certain I'd angered her with my comment, I gazed out the window, the sights of my new location breezing past. Tree limbs stretched high into the air, grappling for the scant amount of sunlight that graced this rainy landscape. Decaying fallen leaves carpeted the ground while bright orange flowers dotted the canopy.

I waited a long while before I chanced another question. "When do you plan to visit your sister?"

"Maybe tomorrow or the next day," she said in a casual tone. Her eyes never left the road.

"Oh." I sighed, disappointed I'd have to wait that long. "Well, I guess I can come back then," I added, figuring I could probably last a day or two on the beach camped out under a tree, even with the rain and my anxiety about the sea.

"Or you can stay with me," she offered. "I have an extra room."

"Are you sure?" I snuck another peek at the woman. Maybe she wasn't mad at me after all. "That is very sweet, very generous of you. Is there anything I can do to pay you back for this favor?"

"Perhaps I can think of something," she said with a gleam in her yellowed eyes.

I heaved a huge sigh of relief, ready to do whatever it took to have her bring me to the volcano so I could finish my training quickly. I could still get back to Pacifica and spend the summer with Sully.

A few miles further down the road, we passed a black sand beach and turned up a short concrete driveway lined with cracks. At the end stood a faded pink house built upon shortened stilts and capped in a corrugated tin roof. A white lattice fence sealed the space under the porch to keep out unwanted animals. The yard grew thick with all sorts of unkempt vegetation—hedges, ornamental flowers, bushes, and ferns with unfurling fiddleheads. Beautiful pale gold flowers, shaped like trumpets of angels, dangled from one tree in her front yard. I guessed ages had passed since anyone had completed the slightest bit of maintenance on the place. Still, it definitely beat a few nights alone on the beach.

She parked under a rickety shelter alongside the house that she called the carport. "Is this your home?" I asked, surprised by its neglected state. But Auntie Lulu didn't reply. *Really, Jordan, what else would she do? Borrow someone's house?*

I gave a nervous smile, knowing that was how I survived in the past, skipping from one unoccupied vacation villa to another in Pompeii, praying the Roman guard wouldn't catch onto my plan...until Gaia found me and buried the town in Mount Vesuvius's massive eruption.

I shook my head, certain a simpler explanation existed. Maybe she'd grown weary of keeping up with all the work in her old age.

Auntie Lulu shut off the car and climbed out the door, her weight shifting from one foot to the other as she staggered up the steps. "Auntie Lulu?" I called and hurriedly followed her inside.

Her voice flowed down the hall. "Make yourself at home. It's the second door on the left."

Following her instructions, I deposited my backpack on the bed and cracked open the windows to air out the spare room. Brushing away a few cobwebs, I surveyed the room, noticing a thin single bed with a worn hand-stitched quilt, an old wicker chair, a small dresser with three narrow drawers, and a pair of white lacey curtains that fluttered like a pair of restless ghosts in the incoming sea breeze. *Way better than the beach*, I thought. My lips drew into a relaxed smile, grateful for her offer to help find Pele.

Before I had a chance to unpack, I heard Auntie Lulu's footsteps outside my door. "It's time," she said in a gravelly voice.

I spun my head, a chill of familiarity in those words. "What did you say?"

She leaned against the doorframe. "I decided to take you up on your offer. So it's time to begin."

"Oh. Okay. What did you have in mind?"

She waved a soft arm, gesturing for me to follow her through the house to the backyard and handed me a rake. "How about here?" she suggested and pointed to the open space in the backyard where the grass should've been. Instead, a thick carpet of soggy leaves, decaying husks, fallen seedpods, and rotting fruits covered the entire area. So many leaves littered the ground, not a single blade of grass could grow.

"No problem," I said with false confidence. A little voice inside my head reminded me this wouldn't take long and tomorrow she'd take me to see Pele.

It took the better part of half an hour just to uncover the sidewalk that led to her front yard. When I paused for a rest, a curious creature took advantage of the cleared walkway. Toting a pointed brown and gold shell the length of my thumb, a land snail slid across the concrete sidewalk, leaving a shiny slime trail to denote its path. It craned its long neck, searching for food. I bent down and touched its patterned shell gently, but the snail instantly recoiled, tucking its eyes and tentacles inside. I understood how it felt, thinking of all the times I had narrowly avoided danger as well. Instead of having a home in which to hide, I sped across time to another place altogether, leaving forever the memories of my past.

A small part of me feared I might grow too relaxed here in the safety of Auntie Lulu's house, just like I'd done at the Trudeau's in Pacifica. But I had no other options. I needed to learn more about my foes and my powers. And so far, Pele was the only one who might provide answers to the knowledge I sought. I had to meet her.

While I raked, I considered my future training sessions with the goddess, wondering what skills and techniques she might teach me. My initial enthusiasm eventually waned. I raked the debris into an enormous pile in the middle of the yard, loathing the dank smell that filled my nostrils and the burn in my arms from the fatigue of each pull. Why hadn't Auntie Lulu bothered to hire someone to periodically clean up this mess? Why wait until the entire backyard had reached this decrepit state?

Hours passed before I completed my task. Maybe Lulu wasn't as sweet and generous as I'd initially thought. Maybe she was just a lonely old woman who needed some help with her yard. I provided free labor in exchange for a place to stay and the promise of a ride to the volcano. I assured myself it wouldn't be long before I met Pele and completed my training so I could go back to the life I missed.

My arms hung limply by my sides when I lumbered up the steps and knocked on the back door. Auntie Lulu appeared, a trace of satisfaction lining her mouth. In a weary voice, I asked, "So what would you like me to do with everything now?"

With a shrug of her shoulders, she suggested, "Burn it."

My exhaustion quickly faded as my mind drove into a state of full alert. I blinked, alarmed by her statement. Was that a typical method of removing unwanted yard waste? Or did her words insinuate she secretly knew my true identity? For a long moment, I stared at her, trying to unravel her intent. "Do you have any matches?" I finally asked in an innocent tone, calling her bluff.

The expression on her face registered slight disappointment. "There are some inside the kitchen. If you need them," she said and closed the door behind her.

I stood alone on the back step, wondering if I should bother searching the kitchen drawers for a pack of matches to keep my cover. Or start the fire with a snap of my fingers when Lulu wasn't watching.

After deciding that preserving my cover ruled over my eagerness to finish the job, I found a pack of matches in one of the kitchen drawers and an open bag of marshmallows lying on the counter. *She told me to make myself at home, didn't she?* I grabbed the matches and marshmallows, and headed back outside, ready for my bonfire.

It took me a frustratingly long time to start the fire with matches, but once I finally got it going, it crackled and sputtered, the glowing cinders shifting under the weight of the pieces above. Sparks flew while the red-hot coals from beneath appeared to wage a war against the cooling black embers from above. I pierced a stick through a marshmallow and propped it over the fire while I waited.

But the marshmallow slid off my stick and dropped into the fire. "Darn it," I muttered and watched it quickly catch flame. Only it didn't shrivel into a wrinkled black mass. Instead, hot bluish tongues of fire lapped its outside, causing it to swell and take on a frightening form. My eyes grew wide as the marshmallow's charred outer layer enlarged until it resembled a human's face. Sections of its surface caved inward, resembling sunken eye sockets and a mouth wailing in pain, devoured in flames. Suddenly, I no longer saw a white stubby cylinder of fluffy, marshmallowy sugar, but the recognizable face of Hydros seeking revenge.

Frightened, I stepped backward, stumbling over my feet. Reaching for the hose, I aimed the nozzle at the middle of the fire. *"Go away!"* I screamed at the image and turned the hose to maximum. The fire hissed in protest, sizzling upon contact with the shockingly cold water. The ground remained so hot that puddles of mud formed, instantly bubbling over in raging boils. Clouds of gray smoke choked the air, making me cough and gasp for a breath of reprieve. Luckily, the marshmallow disappeared, consumed in the flickering light. Yet the damage was done. The gruesome image had etched itself permanently in my mind.

I turned off the hose and plopped onto the ground, letting the smoking remains dwindle as I pondered the past, haunted by visions of her. She did terrible things. She posed a threat to the lives of millions of innocent people.

Was I any different? Had my act of destroying her sealed my fate to become cruel and heartless like the other Elementals? A part of me questioned my motive, wondering if I'd made a huge mistake in taking her out by the San Francisco Bay.

Still, destroying Hydros didn't solve my problem when two more threats remained at large. And until I removed them from this world, I would never be safe…nor would anyone I knew.

When the fire reduced to a pile of smoldering ash, I sprayed the hose across its surface once more, certain I had extinguished it fully, and then headed inside. I would deal with the rest tomorrow.

I went straight for the shower, letting the water run hot to wash away the reek of the bonfire and the horrors plaguing my mind. Meanwhile, a new wave of determination filled my soul, bringing new hope and encouragement. Tomorrow, Auntie Lulu would take me to see Pele. And I vowed to do whatever it took to master my powers so I could rid the world of the other Elementals forever.

CHAPTER SIX

That first night, sleep did not come readily, despite my fatigue from the long trip and hours of manual labor. Even with my magically rapid recovery, I could still feel a tug in my side from the accident, aggravated with each pull of the rake. The rhythmic roll of the waves across the street and the pings of raindrops on the tin roof kept me up for hours. I tossed and turned, uneasy this close to Hydros's realm. Eventually, I lulled myself to sleep with the small hope that Pele would have the answers I needed. I could cope with the nightmares of Hydros and the grueling work for the short time I stayed here with Lulu.

The next morning, I discovered Auntie Lulu did not intend to visit her sister by the volcano that day. My face fell with disappointment when she decided to have me clean her koi pond and rebuild its surrounding rock wall instead. I knew I shouldn't complain since she graciously provided meals and a place for me to stay. But living with Lulu differed vastly from my time with Micah's family in Pacifica. Back in California, Celia's harried pace left me pressed for time while Micah's cell phone practically dictated his every waking move. Yet here in Hilo, Auntie Lulu managed fine without those necessities.

Thoughts of how much I missed Sully filled my mind while I scooped huge handfuls of slimy water plants from the surface of the pond and dumped them in a pile on the ground. Occasionally, a fish broke the surface, its scaly white head decorated in striking splotches of orange and black. Despite the state of decay of the rest of the yard, the fish appeared healthy and well fed. Maybe Auntie Lulu devoted all her spare time to tending to her koi rather than maintaining her yard.

For several hours, I moved huge chunks of lava rock—some rounded from rolling in the sea's crashing surf, others rough and abrasive, coming directly from the volcano. Even though I had eliminated the threat of Hydros, the constant sound of water bubbling and splashing in the pond still put my nerves on end.

By the time I finished rebuilding the retaining wall, dried slime and muck covered my arms, masking the dozens of scratches I'd acquired from lifting and setting the rough, porous rocks. I walked up the porch stairs, ready to clean off the grime in the shower, when Auntie Lulu met me at the door.

She pointed to the hedge, covered in unruly scarlet hibiscus flowers and leafy branches.

I looked down at my filthy arms and sighed, guessing my shower would have to wait. "I suppose you want me to trim that back a bit for you?"

"If you don't mind," she said in a tone that insinuated I had little choice in the matter.

"Do you have some hedge clippers I could use?"

"No, but you can pick up a pair at Lipoa's Hardware in town." She handed me a twenty-dollar bill. "Tell them I sent you."

After running my arms under the outside spigot, I followed her directions into town to a small, local store whose sign on the front door boasted "Service with a Smile." The store's owners, a pair of brothers named Marvin and Gerard Lipoa, at first intimidated me with their bulky arms covered in patterned tattoos of geometric shapes and their thick black hair tied in long ponytails that stretched more than halfway down their backs. But true to their motto, they gladly helped me find everything

I needed…with wide smiles that pushed up into their cheeks when I told them Lulu had sent me.

Marvin chuckled, a deep bass type of laugh. "You mean crazy Auntie Lulu?" he said in a heavily accented voice that rose and fell like a wave at sea. "Sure, we know her. She's an old friend. Used to come here years ago, but we haven't seen her in a while."

I found the "crazy" adjective somewhat unsettling, but wasn't surprised. With the state of her yard, I didn't think she'd done an ounce of work since her last visit years before.

"See she's putting you to work already," Gerard said as he rang up my receipt and passed me the change. "Tell her we said 'aloha.'"

I left the store with a new pair of hedge clippers and a sneaking suspicion that wouldn't be my last trip to Lipoa's Hardware.

The clippers sliced through the branches easily, but the repetitious motion strained my sore arms in ways I never imagined. By late afternoon, I finished trimming the hedge and worked up quite the appetite. When I entered the kitchen, Lulu sat at the table, her eyes trained on my every move. I grabbed two slices of bread, spread mayonnaise on each, and then layered ham and Swiss cheese in between.

"It's done," I announced, needing to justify my break.

"Excellent," she replied, a small smile winding across her lips. She folded her hands across the table. "You know, I was thinking tomorrow you could repaint the lattice fence under the porch. It could really use a fresh coat of white."

"Tomorrow?" I exclaimed and wheeled my head around. "But I thought…?" I forced myself to stop mid-sentence. I had no need to sound ungrateful, especially when I lacked other options for finding the goddess.

"What is it?" she asked, oblivious to my woes.

"Nothing. Forget it," I muttered and grabbed my sandwich. I stormed out the door, needing space from Auntie Lulu and her broken promises. I began to think Marvin was right. Maybe Lulu was a bit crazy…or maybe she'd scammed me into doing all this work for free with no intention of taking me to see Pele.

I trudged down the porch stairs, my eyes at my feet. A small black lizard with striking yellow marks across its back leapt off a painted step into a nearby bush in an attempt at flight. I completely understood how it felt, hoping to fly away to freedom. Instead, I was stuck here with an endless list of chores, all in exchange for a chance to meet the fire goddess from my dreams.

I just didn't get it. If Pele was so eager to contact me before — eager enough to heal Cam and me — why the hiding game now? Wouldn't she come and find me here at Auntie Lulu's?

My feet mindlessly led me across the street to the coarse black sand of the beach. Tiny chunks of volcanic rock covered the beach, broken down over time by the relentless pounding of the ocean's waves. I settled onto the top of a picnic table with a weighty sigh and gazed across the ocean with no intention of placing a toe in the water. Fear still lingered in my mind, even in Hydros's absence.

Suddenly, I got the funny feeling someone watched me. Heavy breathing carried through the air. Alarmed, I glanced downward toward the noise. A fairly large white dog sat beside the table. It panted eagerly, its eyes glued to my meal. A string of drool dangled out one side of its mouth.

I breathed easier at the sight of the friendly dog. "Why don't you ask your owner for something to eat?" As soon as those words left my mouth, I noticed the animal's bare neck. "Oh," I said, feeling sorry for the stray. "You don't have a home?"

The dog shook its head and sneezed. I couldn't decide if that response counted for an answer or if the animal simply had sand in its nose.

"Neither do I," I admitted with a deep sigh. "No one to talk to either. Except for you, I guess."

The dog blinked, revealing fine white eyelashes along each lid. When it opened its dark brown eyes again, I detected a striking intelligence inside its gaze. Keeping my sandwich out of reach, I stretched one hand down to pet its head. "How is it you seem to understand everything I'm saying? I must be crazy to be sitting here talking to a dog." *Or lonely*, I thought, missing Sully more than ever. I made a mental note to ask Lulu if I could borrow her phone to call him later that day.

When I raised the sandwich to my mouth for a bite, the dog's eyes followed it with intense interest every inch of the way. "Or you're just looking for food," I observed, ripping off a section of crust and tossing it in front of the dog's feet. "It's okay. I don't really like that part much anyway."

The dog quickly gobbled it up and hungrily waited for more.

"Fine. Here you go," I said and tossed another section of crust to the ground. "You know, if you don't have an owner, I'll bet you don't have a name either. What do you think of Buddy?" I suggested.

The dog gave me a funny look, shaking its head as if rejecting the notion.

"Oh, you're not a boy, right? Yeah, that probably won't work. Well, do you like Girl?"

The dog's mouth closed tight in disapproval.

"Nah," I agreed. "Too generic. How 'bout Molly or Martha or Lucy?"

Bored, the dog plopped down and began scratching behind her ear.

"You know, I'm sorry I don't have a brush to clean you up. I bet under all that matted black sand, your fur must be pretty, as soft and white as snow. I wish I knew some Hawaiian words to give you a name fitting to the islands." I tried to think of an appropriate name for the stray when my eyes caught the massive peak of Mauna Kea in the distance. I remembered reading in the airport's welcome guides that Mauna Kea ranked as the tallest mountain on the planet if you measured it from the ocean floor to its top, and that in the winter months a layer of white snow generally capped the summit.

I turned back to the dog. "Do you like Mauna Kea?"

She gave a brief wag of her tail.

"You're right. It's too long and formal. So what about just Kea?"

The dog stood tall on all fours. Her tail happily swished side to side at the suggestion.

"Kea it is, then," I declared and tossed her another scrap of bread.

While I shared my sandwich with Kea, my mind wandered back to Sully. If I asked Lulu to use her phone, she'd probably find another task to complete first. So why not just set off into town on my own? Even with my limited computer background, it couldn't be too hard to find the library and contact Sully using the free online account he'd set up for me.

Kea gave a hungry whimper, so I tossed her the last scraps of my sandwich. She looked eager for more until I showed her my empty hands. "Sorry. All out. But you can tag along if you wish. Maybe we'll find something else for you to eat." And with the dog at my heels, I headed into town, eager to speak to Sully.

When I connected with him on the computer, he began with a simple, "How are things?" which I quickly spun into a litany of my current woes. I lamented about the lightning strike aboard the plane, having people think I was crazy to search for Pele, Auntie Lulu offering to bring me to the volcano and then changing her mind, and the chores...the endless list of chores. Only after our conversation ended did I regret my choice of words. I should've asked more questions about his new job.

I found Kea waiting outside when I left the library — probably looking for more food, I guessed. She followed me back to Lulu's, so I dumped my worries on her. "I don't know why I even bother telling you. You're just a dog and can't understand a word I say." Still, it felt good to vent, even if that someone couldn't reply.

My heart grew heavier when I neared Lulu's home. Kea scooted off after a bird she spotted in the road, leaving me alone again. I ran up the steps and into the house, quickly finding Lulu at the kitchen table, reading the front-page headlines of the newspaper. "Can I borrow your phone?" I asked her anxiously. "I want to call one of my friends back in California."

Lulu looked up from her paper and gave me a pointed look. "Is it a boy?"

My checks warmed. I mumbled, "Um…yes," wondering why she had to be so direct.

She leaned back in her chair, interested. "Your *boy*friend?"

"Not really," I blurted in a defensive sort of way. My face flushed hotter, recalling our parting kiss in the airport, making me think I should amend my initial response. "Well, maybe," I admitted bashfully.

Lulu shook her head, her mouth turning down in the corners. "I'm sorry, but I don't carry long distance. Everyone I know lives here."

"How about a laptop? An iPad? Or Wi-Fi?" I wondered aloud, thinking of other options.

Silent, she stared back with a blank look.

Okay, I take that as a no. I sighed. "I think I'll head back to the library and try to get a hold of him right now."

Lulu glanced at the clock. "You'll never make it. The library closes in a couple of minutes."

I flopped into the chair across from her and propped my cheeks on my hands. "Guess I'll just have to go first thing in the morning," I said dejectedly. I couldn't believe how much I screwed things up—especially on my first overseas date.

Lulu left the table to escape my pity session, I assumed. A few minutes later, she returned with a tent and a rolled-up sleeping bag and dumped them on the floor by my feet. "We'll go see Pele tomorrow," she announced. "Early." She turned, leaving me alone in the room.

I blinked, dumbfounded. I thought she'd made a new list of chores for me to complete tomorrow, beginning with the lattice fence. What had I said to make her suddenly change her mind?

Chapter Seven

I guessed my apology to Sully would have to wait. But he would understand. At least I thought he would. Pushing the worry to the back of my mind, I packed my backpack and gathered the tent and sleeping bag to set off for the volcano and complete the last leg of my journey.

We drove for the better part of an hour—past waterfalls trickling down the hills along the road. We cruised beneath long flowering vines dangling so low from the treetops they almost brushed the roof of Lulu's Firebird. The dense foliage common to this side of the island made a sudden shift to black when hardened lava flows punctuated the lush forest growth.

We reached the entrance to Volcanoes National Park and Lulu dropped me off in front of a red rustic building with a corrugated roof and a huge stone fireplace. The sign said "Volcano House," which seemed an accurate description of the structure perched on the rim of the volcano's wide crater.

I unloaded my backpack, tent, and sleeping bag from the back of her car. Lulu handed me a bag of packaged foods and bottles of drinking water to last my stay and told me she planned to pick me up in two days after she visited her sister. I figured I could meet the goddess and learn some new skills in that amount of time. Plus, if things progressed better than planned, I hoped to complete my training and return to California sooner than I imagined.

Loaded with supplies, I entered the Volcano House, unsure of my next move. My head swiveled, absorbing my new surroundings while searching for a clue. Tourists headed toward the dining room, the viewing deck, or the gift shop, all with a destination in mind. *Where should I go?* I wondered, kicking myself for forgetting to ask Lulu where to find Pele before she drove away.

Rooted to my spot, I felt the weight of eyes upon me from the adjacent room. Only when I walked over to the threshold, the room lay vacant. A couple of armchairs sat around a coffee table alongside the hearth of an empty fireplace of mortared lava rocks. In the center of the fireplace, I spotted Pele. Well, sort of. A sculptor had carved her image in relief from the black basalt of her own volcano.

I stepped closer to the fireplace, captivated by the carving. The sculptor depicted the fire goddess with her palms outstretched, whether welcoming visitors to her home or generating another eruption, I couldn't say for sure. Her short hair framed her face in a heart-like shape, so different than the long flowing tresses that melted into lava as in my dreams. Still, Pele's sentient eyes resonated with the power she had manifested to split the earth and release a molten plume jetting into the air.

I set down my gear and stood before her, my index finger outlining the contours of her rounded face. The fireplace stood unused in summer, but I felt a trace of heat radiating from the stone. The spirit of Pele resided in that very spot.

Suddenly, the carving's eyes appeared to glow, lit from within.

"She knows I'm here," I whispered.

I whipped my head around, wondering if anyone else witnessed the change, but the room remained empty. The other tourists seemed preoccupied in the gift shop, perusing the souvenirs of hand-carved wooden tikis, chocolate-covered macadamia nuts, and tropical scented hand lotions. Alone, I stood before the carving for several quiet minutes, waiting for another sign from the goddess. Her lack of a response discouraged me, so I whispered for her to show me where to go. The carving's glowing eyes appeared to shift to one side.

Now I'm getting somewhere. Her recognition of my existence brought a smile to my face. I followed her gaze out the large panes of glass toward the barren lava field. In the distance, I spotted a thin spire of rising smoke. A knowing smile wound across my face. Of course…she wanted me to visit her in her domain.

But when I looked back at the carving to confirm her intentions, another visitor entered the room. The eyes on the stone fireplace instantly faded cold and black, as vacant as if her spirit had left the premises.

I picked my gear off the floor, stuffed the food and water into my backpack, and slung the straps over both shoulders. I left Volcano House with my gear in hand and set forth toward the smoking spire, expecting to hike a fair distance. I doubted Pele would present herself until after I ventured far from the watchful eyes of any other visitors to the park.

A short ways past the trailhead, the white stray appeared by my side, her mouth opened wide as if expecting more treats.

"Kea?" I exclaimed. "How'd *you* get all the way out here?" I spun my head, wondering if she'd snuck a ride in the bed of someone's pickup to follow me in search of more food. Or maybe she considered me her new owner after I'd given her a name. Whatever the reason, the dog had amazingly made her way down to the National Park, which I suspected didn't permit pets. "We should get moving before a park ranger sees you," I advised and pressed forward at a brisk pace, the dog happily trotting at my heels.

Once the Volcano House shrunk from view, I set down the

tent and sleeping bag, opened up my sack, and pulled out a strip of beef jerky and some crackers for the dog from Lulu's stash. Kea gobbled the jerky and munched on the crackers, licking up all the crumbs that dropped to the ground. I opened up a water bottle for myself, downing half in three long gulps, and poured some into my cupped hand for her to lap with a reddened tongue.

We continued on our way for the better part of an hour. The sun broke through the clouds to beat upon us. Its heat radiated up from the black rock of the lava flow, making me roast like a rotisserie chicken spinning on the spit at the supermarket.

Kea panted heavily, her ears drooping to the sides. I stopped for another water break, giving her ample amounts to quench her thirst. I glanced around, realizing not a single tourist ventured this far in the insufferable heat. Up ahead, the smoky spire drew a gray line through the clear sky. "It's not much farther," I told the dog and picked up the gear to finish our hike.

Luckily, the trail wound near the flow's edge, cutting past a grove of shade trees. I paused for another break to wipe the bullets of sweat from my brow. But when I opened my water bottle to quench Kea's thirst again, the dog disappeared. "She probably ran off to the shade like I should," I told myself, my skin baking under the strong Hawaiian sun.

But before I could seek respite beneath the branches, a wispy white trail danced from the nearby spire and into the grove of trees. Seconds later, the fire goddess Pele emerged, her flowing black hair trailing behind her every step.

My jaw fell open. Quickly straightening my face, I congratulated myself. *I did it! I found her!* I dumped my gear to the ground and let the backpack slide from my shoulders, completely forgetting my uncomfortably hot state. "Madam Pele," I addressed the goddess with a reverent bow. "I am *so* glad to finally meet you in person. And I wanted to thank you for healing my friend, Cameron. He told me all about your visit in the hospital. You saved his life."

A small smile graced Pele's stunning face. "Sometimes I have to give a little to get what I want. Time is short and the situation has changed. It was of utmost importance you come to me right away, so I called upon a favor from a gifted healer, the moon goddess, Hina. She helped you both recover."

My hand subconsciously drifted to the thin scar on my abdomen. No wonder the pain from a wound I'd deemed fatal had faded so quickly.

Dozens more questions flooded my mind. "So you'll be teaching me personally?" I began, sorting through my thoughts.

"Yes," she replied with a simple nod. "What powers do you already possess?"

"I can create fire and use it to jump across time," I stated, thinking fast.

"Go ahead. Show me your abilities."

"Right now?"

"Right now," Pele invited, her face exuding confidence in my skills.

"All right," I said in a small voice, feeling a bit hesitant under the pressure of her watchful gaze. I opened my hand, my palm facing upward. My technique had worked in Sully's car when a flame inadvertently torched the ceiling upholstery. Not that it mattered much—Gaia did a fabulous job of totaling the rest of the car when she collapsed the tresses of the Bay Bridge upon us. But when I snapped my fingers together, nothing happened. No spark, no heat, no flame…nothing at all.

I blinked, looking at Pele in confusion. She nodded, a motion for me to proceed.

Focus, Jordan. I furrowed my brow in concentration. Biting my lower lip, I rubbed my palms together and aimed them away from Pele, expecting bursts of flames to rocket off my hands and create a wall of fire like when Gaia had trapped my friend

Lucius and me in the pandemonium that consumed the streets of Pompeii in the wake of Mount Vesuvius's violent eruption. Only the fire didn't come.

Pele crossed her arms over her chest, waiting. Her lips drew taut with disappointment.

"I don't get it," I told her, dragging my hands across the perspiration that accumulated on my brow.

"You need to feel the power within you, harness the energy from your core, embrace the strength of your element so you can become one with its source."

"How did I do all those things before?" I wondered aloud.

"Fear is powerful…and you let anger consume you. Your thirst for revenge fueled your power. Now you need to channel that energy without letting fear or hate cloud your thoughts. Be in control of your emotions and learn how to manipulate your powers on your terms. Though you use fire as your catalyst, in truth, the magic resides inside of you. But first, you must believe with every ounce of your entire body and soul."

I looked at her, skeptical. "And how do you propose I do that? Forgive Gaia and Hydros for what they did to me, who they took from me? I'll always fear them, always hate them. You can never erase the pain they caused me."

A gleam shone in Pele's eyes. "We'll see about that." She held a deliberate pause before explaining. "I have decided your training will consist of two parts. The first will expand your understanding of your powers and challenge you to use them in ways you never before imagined."

"Finally we're getting somewhere," I muttered under my breath, hopefully too low for Pele to hear.

Her small, disapproving glance reminded me I stood in the presence of a goddess. She could probably see or hear anything she wanted.

"And the second?" I asked, eager to change the subject.

"The second part will require you to understand the past."

"So you'll essentially be teaching me history lessons?"

Pele shook her head and clarified, "You will be traveling back to the past to witness these events firsthand."

My eyes grew wide. "I didn't even know that was possible! I thought I could only travel forward. At least that's what had happened to me whenever I perished and jumped through time."

"Only because you panicked. I am here to teach you an easier way to journey through time and space."

I liked the sound of that. "And you think by going to these different times, I will learn how to protect the ones I love?"

"Absolutely, child." She said this in a way that made me think she intentionally withheld information. Still, her plan seemed the best shot I had of eliminating Gaia and Skye. For a moment, the thought saddened me, remembering the days Skye and I shared. I thought of her as a sister back then, before Gaia had warped her soul, transforming her into a threatening menace that would stop at nothing to destroy me. How I longed to rid my life of fear and pain forever.

"I'm in," I agreed. "How soon can we start?"

"Like I told you before, time is short. We must begin immediately," she replied in an urgent tone. "So we will start with walking on air."

Cool! My eyes grew wide, eager to begin.

First, Pele demonstrated how to heat the air around her, making her body seem less dense and therefore able to float. The rising thermal stirred her hair, slowly lifting her feet off the ground.

"Wow," I breathed. She made it look so easy.

However, I quickly learned it was anything but. I squeezed my eyes shut to focus, believing with every ounce of my heart that I could duplicate Pele's skill. Heat coursed from my central core and pain rippled out through my arms and legs. I gritted my teeth, forcing myself to forget the pain.

"Focus your energy on heating the air molecules near your feet. Move them under you to lift you off the surface," she advised.

I pushed the heat from my palms and the soles of my feet and willed the heated molecules to collect beneath me until they fused into a single mass. Ever so slowly, I gradually felt the mass grow in size, elevating my feet off the ground.

Only it seemed about as easy as attempting to stand on a swaying mass of Jell-O.

I stretched my arms out for balance, pretending I rode Micah's skimboard in Pacifica when I zipped toward an incoming wave. Only I wobbled back and forth on unsteady legs, unable to stand upright on the shifting mass of air. A second later, I tumbled over the back side, landing flat upon the prickly surface of the rough lava rocks.

"Ow," I moaned, my body sore from the fall.

"Try again," she requested.

The sky sank low to the horizon while I continued her exercise. Repeatedly, I reformed the heated mass of air beneath my feet until I finally reached a level of competence in Pele's eyes. "Not bad," she admitted, probably as close to a compliment as I would receive. "Next time, we'll try something new."

Exhausted from the hike across the lava field and the challenge of completing Pele's task, I crumpled into a heap on the ground. Exhaling heavy breaths, I remembered the pain when fire burst forth from my palms in Old Chicago. The torture when the lava bomb collided with my skull in Pompeii. And the agony of my fiery death upon Gallows Hill in Salem Village.

"I just don't get it," I said, my brow furrowed with confusion. "Why do Gaia's powers seem painless and effortless when mine are the complete opposite?"

"When you learn to accept your Elemental name, Pyr, and become one with your true identity, the pain will disappear,"

Pele explained. Her reasoning not only seemed logical, but simple to accomplish. "Once you embrace your powers with your whole heart and soul, you will control them in ways you never previously imagined."

"Embrace my true identity?" I wondered aloud. *Was she serious?* "But I never wanted any of this. I only wished to be a normal girl named Jordan who lived a normal life, free of fear."

"No one's life is ever simple, especially not yours. You are special, that is why you were chosen for this important responsibility."

"Chosen to be an Elemental? By whom? And why?"

"The Fire Element selected you. The rest of your story must wait until you are ready," Pele said with a soft, sympathetic smile.

I frowned, frustrated by Pele's cryptic remark. I wished she could just tell me everything straight out. Right now.

But the beginnings of a scowl written across her face suggested otherwise. And I knew if I pushed her for more details, she'd probably vanish in irate silence like she had in my dreams.

Chapter Eight

Pele shook her head at the sight at my fatigued body, weary from exertion. "We will resume your training first thing tomorrow morning." She turned to leave.

A sudden thought bloomed in my head. I blurted a weak, "Wait!"

She paused long enough for me to ask, "A long time ago in Pompeii, Gaia disclosed that I was the embodiment of the element, Fire...and that if I perished, she would find a replacement. I have to know, was she speaking the truth?"

Pele said nothing for a long time. Finally, she admitted, "It is true. You were chosen for your resilience and your empathy toward others."

Without waiting to contemplate why the Fire Element perceived resilience and empathy desirable, I dared, "And if I died...?"

"The Fire Element would select a different being to embody."

"So Hydros is not truly gone," I stated glumly. "Even though I destroyed her, the Water Element will soon find another person to take her place. That's what Gaia meant. There would always be another."

Pele nodded. Guilt and confusion filled my soul. All this time, I thought I helped save innocent lives by removing Hydros from this world. Instead, the Water Element would soon manifest itself as a new threat.

The cycle would never end. My eyes drifted to the ground with the knowledge I'd never be safe. That I'd never lead a normal life.

Pele folded her hands together. "The Four Elements of Earth, Air, Water, and Fire have existed for all time, even before time itself. Each chose to fuse with a being to protect the planet from a future threat."

"But if Gaia's supposed to protect the planet, why is she so destructive? Why won't she leave me alone?"

"In time, child. I promise you will understand the full truth in time. For now, I need you to rest. Tomorrow we will continue your training so you may learn more about the past."

"The past?" My brow wrinkled in confusion.

"Rest now," she ordered and rose to her feet. Outlined in fire, Pele's silhouette glowed against the black night sky.

I buried my face in the palms of my hands, my fatigued body pushed to its limit as my brain struggled to grasp the underlying message behind her obscure remarks. But when I looked up to see if she might clarify her intent and help ease my mind, her form had already vanished.

Great. Alone again, I thought with a great dose of sarcasm. Frustrated, I dragged myself from my spot and struggled to set up the tent. The poles refused to cooperate with my wearied hands, so I settled for a lopsided, unsymmetrical version of a shelter and crawled inside, my body drugged with utter exhaustion. Tears stung my eyes. Why wouldn't Pele tell me what I wanted to know? Why must she dodge my questions, only providing the most basic of facts and hide the rest until later? Couldn't she see that I'd never be able to do this? That I'd never measure up to her expectations or meet her lofty goals?

If only I had a friend here, I could release some of the pressure from my burdened shoulders, talking late into the long, dark night. Instead, I found myself surrounded with unfamiliar sounds of nature and the steady clash of waves against the rocky shore. The lack of man-made noise reminded me of just how much I missed Sully…and how much I regretted our last conversation. I never had a chance to apologize before I left with Lulu to find Pele. And now, I couldn't say when I'd get another opportunity to speak to him.

The solitude soon grated on my nerves. Back in Pacifica, Sully and Micah would hang out in the basement for hours, playing their video game, Zombie Dominion. But here, I felt entirely disconnected to the outside world. Alone on a vast field of lava, uncertain of what tomorrow might bring.

I heard a pawing at my tent flap, making me instantly regret my desire for other sounds beyond the breaking waves. My heart leapt up my throat, uncertain of what types of large mammals lived out here. Could it be a wild pig or a goat? Would they even venture out to this desolate spot? The pawing grew louder, accompanied by a shallow whimpering sound. I suppressed a shudder and slowly unzipped the tent flap to peek outside.

In front of my door stood a fairly large, white furry creature. Its mouth opened into a characteristic grin.

"Kea," I said with a smile, reenergized by her company — even if she couldn't talk back to me. "How are you, girl?" I asked and waved for her to join me, leaving the zipper open a bit for her in case she wanted to leave before I woke. Panting happily, she plopped down on my sleeping bag. I petted her soothing fur and scratched her behind the ear. "What'd you do after you left me?"

She gave an audible yawn.

Probably slept most of the time in the shade. She quickly drifted off, but my mind couldn't relax. Grateful for company, conscious or not, I launched into a lengthy story about my hesitation and worry until exhaustion eventually overcame me.

"Time to move over," I told Kea and pushed her aside to

crawl into my sleeping bag.

Only she had no intention of budging. With a final yawn, the dog curled up into a white, fluffy ball, smack in the middle of my soft sleeping bag, her tail tucked neatly over her nose.

"Kea!" I scolded. I grabbed a corner of the bag to pull out from under her dozing form.

Though she didn't open her eyes, her disapproval emerged as a grumble from the depths of her throat.

"Oh, come on. This is *my* spot," I told her, attempting to push her off the bag.

This time, I received her full attention. Kea lifted her head, growling possessively and baring her teeth.

I leapt back, astonished by her sudden change in temperament. "Fine. Keep it," I muttered and stretched out across the floor of the tent, its weatherproof nylon surface offering little buffer from the prickly lava beneath. Uncomfortable minutes passed. I edged closer to the sleeping bag, hoping I could slide my body along one side without Kea objecting. But my plan didn't work. The dog stretched her arms and legs, sprawling her body across the cushiony surface.

I groaned. So much for wanting a friend nearby.

Inching my back toward Kea's fuzzy coat for warmth, I eventually fell asleep on my cold, hard bed only to wake the next morning, stiff and sore. An empty sleeping bag lay beside me with Kea nowhere in sight. "Stupid dog," I muttered. She'd probably left right after I fell asleep, wasting a perfectly good sleeping bag in her greedy moment of comfort.

Rubbing the sleep from my eyes, I staggered from the tent, squinting into the mid-morning sun. I stretched the kinks from my arms and back. Pele waited right outside. She held in her hands a plain woolen shirt and skirt of neutral colors, woven in dull tints of gray and off-white. "What's all this?" I asked.

"Clothing from the time period, so you'll blend in."

"We'll see about that," I said with a frown. No matter how hard I tried, somehow I always managed to draw attention to myself. "Gaia has a way of finding me."

Pele handed me a pair of leather boots with thick, cushioned soles. "Not with these, she won't...as long as you don't do anything careless, that is," she said with a meaningful smile.

I simpered, wondering exactly how many details she knew of my past.

"Go ahead," Pele prodded. "Try them on."

I ducked back inside the tent, stripping off my pajamas to replace with clothes from several millennia ago. I slipped the off-white shirt over my head, not entirely sure which unadorned side marked the front. Long, thick sleeves attached to the bodice at right angles, concealing all the curves in my chest and waist.

Lovely, I thought, heaping on the sarcasm. With fumbling fingers, I wrapped the rough gray skirt around my waist and tied it in place with a sash, and returned outside. The skirt reached past my calves, leaving no skin exposed between that and my tan leather boots. Funny—having grown used to Vanessa Sullivan's fitted clothing, I now felt dressed in a heavy burlap sack, unbearably hot and itchy in the Hawaiian sun.

I looked down at my outfit, extremely glad that Sully wasn't here to see me in this unflattering ensemble. "So this is it?" I asked uncertainly.

"Almost. You'll also need this," Pele said and handed me a small section of cord, finely braided from the golden fibers of a coconut husk and fastened into a loop with a tight knot.

I stared at her in confusion, trying to decipher her intent. She reached for a strand of her flowing black hair, holding one lock up for me to see. She twisted its molten end until a section of it broke and pooled in the palm of her hand. Reaching for the coconut husk cord, she set the fibers inside the molten material and blew on the hair to cool it. I watched in amazement as the broken lock of hair congealed into a smooth, polished rock of black volcanic glass.

My eyebrows pinched together. "An amulet? What's this for?"

"When you're ready to come back, this obsidian amulet will return you to this exact spot," Pele explained.

"But how will a necklace magically bring me back here? To this same time and place?"

The goddess smiled softly. "Like I told you before, the magic resides inside of you. All you need is to believe in yourself and feel this specific time with every ounce of your entire body and soul. Of course, this would be much easier if you'd accept your Elemental name, Pyr. But until then, I suppose I must help you along your journey." Within seconds, she produced a white tongue of fire on her palm, a dancing specter in the bright sun. I stepped closer to the intense heat of the flame, much hotter than I imagined fire could get. "It's called, 'ke ahi kea', meaning 'the white fire.'"

"Is it safe?" I wondered aloud.

"Not just safe, but faster, too," she said and closed her palm, making the white flame disappear. "You don't want to ruin your clothes or your hair, do you?" she asked with a knowing wink, making me guess she was aware of my disheveled appearance after I escaped the fire in Old Chicago.

"So this is what happened when I jumped before…and ended up in Pompeii or Bora Bora or Chicago or Pacifica?" I guessed.

Shaking her head, her long hair swayed, exposing the fiery insides of her shimmering black strands. "No. In those cases, you panicked. Your desperation to escape your current predicament sent you spiraling out of control to a new destination that seemed—in your mind—a safer place to exit the time continuum. This amulet will help focus your energy to this precise location at this precise point of time. Although you will feel like time has continued in your absence; in fact, it has not. Your life is linear, but from your perspective it is not since you are able to journey to the past and return to the present time."

I clutched the obsidian in my hand, swaying on my feet at the magnitude of her words. So my entry and exit points could be predetermined, but if I didn't focus my energy properly, I might end up in some random location at an unspecified period. Had my future become a twisted game of roulette based entirely on chance? And what would happen if I didn't do things right? I might not make it back at all, and never, ever see Sully again.

God, I hope this works. I slipped the cord around my neck and tugged on it to make sure it felt secure. "Okay. I'm ready," I fibbed, straining to keep my voice from cracking. My hands trembled by my sides, my knees turning to jelly. I balled my hands into fists, hoping Pele didn't notice the mounting fear inside of me.

"Good luck," she said in a way that suggested I would need much more than luck to return intact. I prayed she knew what she was doing.

She shut her eyes, concentrating her magic on the piece of obsidian around my neck while chanting in the ancient Hawaiian language. Soon, the glossy black amulet began to glow white-hot. Pele's voice grew deeper, the strength of her words increasing. Her speech captivated me, even though I didn't understand a single word aside from the three she'd already mentioned. Strangely, I found myself relaxing as she continued her chant, raising her hands skyward until white fire burst forth from the amulet and consumed my entire body. I focused on her words, willing myself to remember one phrase to hopefully ignite the magical amulet when it was time to come back.

But my concentration soon waned. The fire mounted, growing hotter and making me gasp for breath. The intense heat shocked me, so unlike anything I'd ever experienced in my previous jumps. From the tips of my toes to the top of my head, my body felt encased in a deadly heat that threatened to melt me to my core. Eyes wild with fright, I glared through the flickering flames at Pele, screaming at her to stop the pain. But she didn't relent, the flames growing higher and hotter until I could no longer see her through them at all.

I held my breath. Tongues of white flame licked my body, sending me spiraling from Pele and her expanse of black jagged lava rock. Soon, I entered a different sort of darkness where traces of starlight flickered before disappearing…where colors blurred into unrecognizable shapes and images. My speed increased, my stomach lurching from the incredible pace of my journey. I felt strapped into a seat on the world's fastest roller coaster times two. I wanted to cup my hand to my belly to calm my stomach, but my appendages remained pinned to my side, impossible to move, spinning out of control. Seconds later, all motion abruptly ceased. I landed atop a patch of grass and instantly doubled over, struggling to catch my breath without getting sick. Nothing drew attention like the smell of nausea.

CHAPTER NINE

Ancient Ireland, 3500 BC

Pele's white fire eventually dissipated. I stared with marvel at my clothes, pure and clean. *Now that is something I've gotta learn.* Pele's skill at helping me jump through time unscathed impressed me. Sure, the burning and nausea left something to be desired, but still, for the first time ever my skin and clothes didn't end up charred and covered in soot.

Raising my head, I soaked in my surroundings, momentarily letting my body adjust to the new environment. The approaching autumn painted a few trees with splashes of gold and auburn. Otherwise, every inch of the ground appeared blanketed in more shades of green than I'd ever seen in my life, cut only by a winding dark gray river. Thick clouds hung low, enveloping the verdant landscape in a shroud of mist.

I scanned the countryside, looking for a sign of Gaia and Hydros. Down the riverbank, I noticed a small hut and the slow movement of a few head of cattle who grazed on the thick grass. With no other evidence of villages or settlements nearby, I decided to head there. Why else would Pele have sent me to this remote emerald isle?

I inhaled a deep breath to steady my nerves, but the saturated air reeked of damp earth, providing little relief. Anxious to conceal myself from Gaia who had found me so many times in the past, I headed toward the forest's edge. *But she's not looking for you*, Pele's voice echoed in my mind. I hoped she spoke the truth and this mission would help me better understand my foes.

As I walked, beads of dew clung to each blade of grass, dampening my boots and the hem of my skirt. My movement alarmed a thin ground bird with mottled feathers and a crown striped in black. He tilted his head backward and emitted a loud *crek, crek...crek, crek* call before he took to flight. His bright wings flashed the color of chestnuts against the green vegetation as he darted to safety with his thin legs trailing behind.

I quickened my pace to distance myself from the sounds of nature, hoping they wouldn't draw attention from Gaia. The humid air stuck inside my lungs. Thick dark clouds threatened to spill their contents and soak the earth. I pressed onward toward the wide, winding river, hoping to seek shelter in the hut before the sky drenched this already sodden, green land.

I glanced up the river teeming with salmon and caught a glimpse of movement up ahead. A figure cloaked in a dark traveling cape walked urgently toward the nearby hut and herd of cows. I instantly dropped to my knees, ducking behind the reeds and took measured breaths, my heart beating rapidly inside my chest. When the person turned for a moment, unruly russet curls poked out from under her hood. I recognized her hair instantly, curled tightly in the high humidity and impending rain. A pleased smile spread across my lips knowing I accomplished the first of my tasks. I found Gaia without her noticing me.

Sloshing as quietly as possible through the wetlands, I trained my eyes on her every movement. Fortunately, between the gurgling current and the splashing salmon heading upstream, the river masked most of my noise.

This landscape appeared confusing and alien to me, but Gaia walked with confident, hurried steps. She turned up a trodden dirt footpath toward the hut nestled along the base of a steep hill. Long grasses, reeds, and straw blanketed the entire dome-shaped hut from the rooftop to the ground, protecting it from the elements. The home possessed only one small rounded entrance in the front, too low to walk through upright. When Gaia approached the hut, I ducked behind the thick trunk of a nearby oak to watch the scene unfold.

Outside the thatched hut, a tall, lithe girl—perhaps sixteen years of age—hummed to herself in a carefree tone while she gathered supplies. Her dark brown hair flowed freely in the light breeze. She wore clothes like mine, in simple shades of brown and gray, accented with a white sash around her waist and basic embroidery outlined upon her sleeves. When she glanced up at the stranger, I instantly recognized her bold blue eyes and knew I'd found Hydros—or at least her former self.

Determined, Gaia strode right up to Hydros. She threw back her hood and introduced herself to the girl.

"Shannon," the girl said, wiping her hands clean on the sash of her skirt before she extended one hand in greeting.

My eyes grew wide. She had another name, too? My throat felt tight, thinking of Gaia cradling Hydros's dying body. Was the Water Elemental much different from myself?

"It's a pleasure to meet you, Shannon," Gaia said and accepted the girl's hand. Even from this distance, I saw Gaia's eyes gleam with delight.

"I can see that you are not from these parts. Are you in need of food or drink?" Shannon offered.

"Perhaps, if I might stay and rest my weary feet awhile. Are you alone?" Gaia asked, surveying the vacant farm.

Shannon nodded. "My parents and twin are fishing. The salmon have returned to their home. Can you not hear them calling for her?" she asked and tied a rope around the neck of the nearest cow and petted its dark brown coat and white muzzle with affection. Guiding the cow toward a post near the hut,

Shannon lashed her rope in place, holding the animal steady while she prepared her for milking.

"Calling for whom?" Gaia wondered aloud.

Shannon pointed to the embroidery upon her sleeves. Squinting, I could barely make out the forms of fish swimming against the river's current. She explained, "Sionan, the woman who dared to eat the forbidden salmon from the well. Legend says that when red berries from the Rowan trees fell into the well, the fish that ate the fruits not only gained red spots but incredible wisdom. The men worked very hard to collect these salmon, but woman were prohibited from joining in the work. One day a woman named Sionan caught a red spotted fish and ate it, wisdom and all, when suddenly the waters rushed forth from the well and swept her into the sea."

I peeked out from behind the tree, grateful neither Gaia nor Shannon seemed to notice me eavesdropping. Preoccupied with her work, Shannon paused her story to grab a hand-carved stool and a bowl of pottery. The cow lowed softly and chewed her cud, her large cheek muscles grinding from side to side. Shannon set her earthen bowl and milked the cow.

"Every year the fish return by the thousands," Shannon continued dreamily. "When they pass on their journey upstream, I think I hear them whisper her name. It's like they're talking to me. My parents named me after Sionan and the river that shares her name," she said. "Almost like they knew we had something in common."

"Or that you both seek knowledge. A knowledge that I alone can provide," Gaia added. She set her hands upon her hips, appearing delighted with the course of their conversation. She couldn't have scripted it better herself.

Shannon pinched her eyebrows together. "How so?

"You said you hear the salmon whisper your name, correct?" Gaia began.

"Yes…" the girl answered with hesitation.

Gaia's mouth curled up on the sides. She flashed Shannon a knowing look. "But those are not the only creatures who listen to you, are they?"

Shannon stood up with a jerky motion, sloshing some of the fresh milk out the side of the bowl. "I don't know what you're talking about," she said with a shaky voice and started for the house at a quick pace.

In that moment, I realized that unlike me, Shannon was already aware of some of her powers. How Gaia knew this fact remained beyond my level of understanding. But Gaia wasted little time in arguing her point, wishing to take Shannon and leave this pastoral existence. She stepped in line behind Shannon to press her point. "The salmon, the river otter, the waterfowl — they all respond to your wishes, do they not?"

Shannon cast a nervous glance over her shoulder before squatting through the door of her hut. With Gaia preoccupied, I quickly scampered to hide behind a closer tree, eager to hear the rest of their conversation.

"And it's not just them, is it?" Gaia goaded through the narrow entrance of the hut, "but the Cata monster, too. Am I right?"

Shannon returned outside, empty-handed. "Don't be ridiculous," Shannon replied with a nervous laugh. "The Cata is nothing but a tale. No one has ever seen it."

I peeked at Shannon, trying to discern her true intentions. Did she sound nervous this stranger knew too many of her secrets? Or did the girl fear for the safety of the Cata monster Gaia mentioned? I couldn't say for sure.

"Do not worry. Your powers are safe with me," Gaia replied unconvincingly. Her lips curled into a cunning smile — one I knew all too well. I had learned from experience that Gaia would say whatever necessary to sway someone to her side. "But others may not treat you so kindly. If you come with me, I can teach you to stretch your abilities and learn the greatness of your powers. You are capable of much more than communicating with simple creatures that live within your realm."

"My realm?" Shannon asked. Her hand trembled, reaching for a clean pottery bowl. "I'm afraid I do not understand what you are talking about."

A fly buzzed by my ear. I shooed it away, desperate not to miss a single word.

"Oh, don't be so naïve," Gaia retorted. "You are aware you possess powers that others do not. Do you not see that the river ebbs and flows with your command, helping to irrigate your family's crops from one season to the next."

Shannon shook her head. "I only tried to save time from carrying the water myself. I meant no harm."

"And why do you think your mother sent *you* to collect shellfish for supper?"

"Because I always return with a full bucket?" Shannon proposed.

"No," Gaia explained, "it's because you alone can halt the tide's advances."

"That's preposterous. I simply gather the limpets and mussels when the tide pools are low."

"Yet their levels remain low far longer than naturally possible whenever you go near the shore." Gaia gave the girl a meaningful stare. "Still you do not believe," Gaia pressed, taking a step closer to Shannon. "Tell me you have not noticed that the weather seems to mirror your very mood?"

"What are you suggesting?" Shannon shrugged. She wrapped her arms tensely around the empty bowl. "It rains here often, regardless of my moods."

"But haven't you noticed that the skies share in your pain, letting their heavy contents fall whenever you grow sad?"

She thought about this for a moment and dismissed the connection. "It's merely a coincidence."

"Yet you don't question why you often feel sad?" Gaia pressed.

Shannon looked at Gaia in silence, waiting for her to explain.

"It's because you are not challenged to meet your full potential. That is why I am here," Gaia declared. "To show you your destiny."

"And to do this, I must leave my family?" Shannon asked, her lip quivering. "Leave this life?"

"Of course," Gaia said and crossed her arms over her chest. "A small sacrifice for the greatness you may achieve."

"I must decline," Shannon admitted with a tone of finality. "I like my life, love my family. I have no need for anything more, regardless of what you may think."

A pang of jealousy gripped my heart. Why didn't I have the same foresight to distance myself from my family before Gaia turned my fire powers against my defenseless parents and little sister?

Gaia unwound her arms and placed both her hands on her hips. She clicked a disapproving *tut-tut* with her tongue. "Foolish child. There is so much more waiting for you than this mundane life. Come with me and I will show you precisely what I mean." Gaia walked a few paces from the hut, expecting Shannon to follow. Yet the girl remained rooted to her spot.

Gaia turned. "You don't need to make this difficult. Surely, you understand you have no future here. Your only option lies with me."

"No. I will not leave my home." Shannon stood defiantly by her front door. But her lips trembled when she added, "This is all I know."

I watched the girl shake, sharing her fear. Strangely, I found myself sympathizing with Shannon, the girl who became the despised Water Elemental.

Anger flooded Gaia's face, making her eyes grow thin. She skimmed the farm, seemingly searching for something to sway Shannon's mind. In that instant, I realized with Shannon's family conveniently absent, Gaia lacked sufficient motivation to instill fear through her powers. It was different with me when my family lay trapped inside our burning home.

"Foolish, stubborn girl," Gaia muttered to herself, her nostrils flaring like a charging bull. "Only concerned with the moment. She lacks the foresight to look beyond the boundaries of her sheltered world. Still, without her..."

Shannon studied her with trepidation, waiting for her to finish her thought. Yet instead of speaking, Gaia closed her eyes, focusing her anger and frustration inside and released it with a sudden stomp of her foot. A tremor rocked the earth, loosening the soil along the hillside and sending a shower of pebbles tumbling down against the base of the hut. The milking cow gave an alarmed *moo*, trying to distance herself from the commotion.

Shannon screamed. Her bowl dropped from her hands, shattering into jagged fragments upon the ground as the landslide intensified. Gaia ground her foot into the earth, concentrating and directing her power toward the loose material at the top of the hill before sauntering back down the trodden path, leaving Shannon terrified and alone.

A loud rumble followed. Rocks and boulders bounced down the steep slope, aimed directly at the roof of the hut. The cow's eyes grew white with fear. She jerked at the rope digging into her neck, desperate to escape from her milking post.

Biting her lip, Shannon faltered, torn between returning to save the unfortunate cow or fleeing for her life. Her face wrought with conflict, Shannon turned from the hut, racing down the path after Gaia. I ducked behind the tree trunk when she passed, then peeked out the other side, my eyes trained on her form.

The rumbling increased, more rocks piling about the flattened hut. I pressed my fingers to my eardrums, unable to block the clamor. Luckily, Shannon's family could not suffer the same fate as mine who lay trapped inside our home as the burning roof collapsed upon them. Despite the pain she currently endured, I envied her fortune.

When Shannon caught Gaia and tackled her to the ground in anger, the noise finally ceased. Shannon panted as she pinned Gaia to the muddy path and watched the cloud of dust settle from the falling rocks. Nothing remained of Shannon's home except a mass of rubble and debris. Her face reddened. She stared at Gaia with hostility.

"What are you doing? Why are you doing this to me?" Shannon cried and pointed to the ruins of her home and farm. As if on cue, a light misty rain dripped from the low, gray clouds.

Gaia's hair turned frizzy in the soggy weather, tightly framing her face. She squinted into the dreary sky. Her lips twisted into a sly smile, watching the droplets fall with timed precision. Inside her calculating mind, I imagined her envisioning the possibilities of Shannon's untapped powers, once she could properly control them to do her bidding.

Gaia's face changed, masking her thoughts. With a rehearsed sigh of feigned exasperation, she looked back at Shannon and said, "I told you before. You are the one who manipulates the element of water, from the sky, lakes, rivers, and ocean. Like me, you are one of the Four Elementals. It makes perfect sense that you join me and learn to use your powers as they were intended. In fact, there is no other choice."

Shannon's brow creased, filled with enmity. "And if I don't?"

"Perhaps your twin will be easier to convince," Gaia threatened.

"Leave my family alone," Shannon said. A determined look filled her tear-stained eyes. "But if you want me, you'll have to catch me." She lifted her skirt to her knees and darted toward the sea, her leather boots splashing through the marshy land.

Gaia frowned, appearing frustrated with Shannon's unexpected obstinate behavior. With a heavy sigh, she tore after her prize. The Earth Elemental's dark cloak trailed behind her, flapping on the breeze with each long stride.

I allowed Gaia a short lead before I left my hiding spot to follow, taking a slightly different course along the side of the hill. I hoped they consumed each other's attention and failed to notice my movement against the rich autumnal colors. I picked up speed, my heart pounding inside my chest, searching for suitable cover to witness the last moments of their altercation. I remembered Shannon's story about her namesake being swept into the sea for her newfound knowledge. I feared a similar outcome for the girl who should one day accept her Elemental name, Hydros.

Shannon glanced over her shoulder and quickened her pace, nearing a full sprint. She raced toward the precipitous rocky cliffs that rimmed the cold, dark waters of the Atlantic, unbroken to the horizon. Up ahead, I saw her hesitate along the cliff, just above the River Shannon's delta — a fanning triangular mass of brackish water where the fresh water current mingled with the salt of the sea. The wind whipped the girl's flowing brown hair in fluid waves. Her head jerked nervously from left to right. She glanced behind her, seemingly displeased with Gaia's rapid approach.

Suddenly, Gaia stopped in her tracks, her eyes glued to Shannon's trembling form. In her moment of distraction, I passed her unnoticed and stole ahead toward a rocky field. I ducked behind a boulder, periodically peeking out from my protective spot.

"You don't need to do this," Gaia shouted over the strong wind off the sea.

But Shannon didn't respond. Instead she peered over the edge, contemplating her next move.

"You have so much potential, you must believe me," Gaia continued in her most persuasive voice. "I can teach you to use your powers in a way you never dreamed possible."

Shannon took another step toward the edge. Her toes curled over the side like a diver on a platform, preparing for the leap.

I gasped, realizing her intent. "She wouldn't," I whispered to myself, inching higher over the boulder. I craned my neck for a better view.

"Don't take the chance," Gaia said, coaxing her from the edge. "Come, step away and join me. I'll show you a world you never before imagined."

But Shannon resisted. With a fierce look at Gaia, she spat, "*Never.*" She looked across the sea where the surface churned, darkening beneath the patter of raindrops. Cupping her hands around her mouth, she screamed. "Cata! Help me!" Shannon folded her hands together. Her lips moved, reciting an unspoken prayer. Despair filled her face as she stood by the sea cliff, waiting.

Far below, the water began to boil. I heard a sound similar to the blow of a giant whale surfacing from a dive. My eyes instantly turned toward the ocean where a shadowy form rose from the dark depths of the frigid sea. Gasping, I fell backward onto my hands, startled by the immense size.

Water spilled off the shiny, charcoal black head and humped back of a monster easily a dozen feet in length. It swiveled its regal head proudly upon its long neck, like a graceful swan gliding across a pond. A low wake fanned behind its webbed feet. Its eyes focused on Shannon on top of the cliff, communicating with her in an unspoken language.

With a deep breath and a last, spiteful glare at Gaia, Shannon leapt off the cliff side and plummeted into the sea, tucking her appendages into a tight cannonball to protect her from the impact. Seconds after, Shannon disappeared into the dark water with a tremendous splash. I heard the serpent suck in a gulp of air before it dove, likely in search of its new meal.

I crawled to the edge of the cliff and peered through the rain for a better view. Far below, the bubbles dispersed, but Shannon didn't return to the surface. I reached for the golden cord of the coconut husk that bore Pele's amulet and pulled it out from beneath my shirt.

"What a waste," I grumbled, realizing this mission was pointless. No one could survive a fall from that incredible height or escape the jaws of the beast. I hadn't found the Hydros I defeated by the San Francisco Bay Bridge. I kicked myself for misinterpreting Pele's directions. Now I must start over and search for Shannon's identical twin instead—hopefully before Gaia convinced her to join the wicked cause.

I reached for the amulet to return to the Big Island so Gaia wouldn't detect my presence here and redirected her rage upon me when I heard an unexpected noise below. Forgetting Gaia completely for a moment, I scrambled toward the edge of the cliff and peered into the dark waters below. In a tremendous splash, the serpent resurfaced with Shannon clinging to his slippery neck.

"Wow!" I breathed. My eyes bulged to the point of bursting. Maybe she was tougher than I'd thought! Secretly, I cheered for Shannon's fortitude and skill in eluding the Earth Elemental. Gaia stood at the rim of the cliff as the tail of the serpent disappeared. I glanced back at the Cata monster's head rising from the dark water. Shannon's long brown hair flew freely behind her and her face beamed with pride. As suddenly as it had begun, the rain faded.

The monster dove with his rider, his body undulating into the distance until it disappeared into the inky sea. A flurry of bubbles appeared. With a great gust of exhalation, he shot a spray of mist high into the air. Amazingly, Shannon remained glued to his back, like a kid at a theme park, enjoying the ride.

Water poured off her face when she turned to Gaia balanced on the edge of the cliff far above. Shannon laughed — a deep, smug laughter — flaunting her skill in evading Gaia.

Gaia's face flushed red with fury. She ground her teeth and stooped to grab a handful of dirt. Pointing one hand in Shannon's direction, she muttered something too low for me to hear and released the dirt, letting it scatter in the wind. Then Gaia turned on her heels, marching back toward Shannon's crushed home. *Would she wait for the twin to return?* I wondered. *Did she expect to have better success in converting Shannon's sister to her cause?*

I gazed across the ocean, scanning the surface for the serpentine motion of the resurfacing Cata monster. His form grew more distant, but one thing remained certain in my mind — Shannon had vanished as well.

Moments after Cata's tail silently slipped beneath the murky water with a small splash, the faint colors of a rainbow appeared, stretching from the sea cliffs all the way to the middle of the Atlantic, touching the exact location I last saw Shannon strapped to the magnificent beast. The rippled surface of the squall line moved further out to sea and the colors of the rainbow intensified into brilliant bands arcing across the sky.

I stood to follow Gaia, but noticed she had vanished. I blinked in confusion. She was just there a second ago…how could I have lost her so quickly? I sprinted back toward Shannon's flattened hut, my mind racing with possibilities to explain Gaia's sudden disappearance. Yet when I returned to the landslide, the area remained vacant.

Questions crowded my mind, vying for my attention and begging for resolution. Did Shannon escape? Had Gaia set out in search of Shannon's twin sister? Or did Gaia return to a different time altogether? I never saw her wearing an amulet similar to mine, so how did she manage to jump from one point to another? Perhaps she had already mastered the ability to use her own magic to travel across time that Pele had mentioned. Regardless, I decided I needed to know more about her powers in order to better understand my foe.

Unable to track their movements on my own, I realized I must return to Pele, hopeful she would answer some of these questions for me. I placed my hand to my chest, feeling the weight of the amulet tucked safely beneath the bodice of my woolen shirt. With a careful glance to ensure I was indeed alone, even in this desolate section of countryside, I aimed my hand at a nearby bush, already dead and devoid of leaves. A spark zoomed from my palm toward the bush, but its damp branches couldn't hold the flame. With a frustrated sigh, I created a flame from my palm once more and tossed it into the air above me. Clutching the amulet, I wished with every ounce of my flesh and soul to return to the very spot from which I first came.

The amulet glowed brightly, transforming my ordinary flame into a burst of white fire that consumed me, rocketing me through time and space. I returned to the familiar setting of Kilauea's fields of lava, basking under the hot midday sun and a sky of the brightest blue. I shielded my eyes, surprised by how quickly I had left the sodden skies and verdant hills of Ireland to return to this lava field, sparsely adorned with resilient ferns and red lehua blossoms. Pele stood in the same spot as when I'd left, awaiting my safe return.

"So, what did you learn?" she prompted.

I related my entire tale to Pele—from the moment Gaia introduced herself to Shannon's monumental leap into the sea—before voicing the one question that burned foremost in my mind. "Why'd Gaia let Shannon go so easily?" I asked the goddess.

"Let her go? Whatever do you mean?"

"Well, I saw Gaia mumble something just before Shannon vanished."

"Go on."

"And she sprinkled a handful of dirt into the air, letting the wind catch it while she spoke."

"Ahh," Pele said, nodding with understanding. "Gaia used her own internal magic to manipulate Shannon's jump to a new location of her choosing."

"So Shannon didn't disappear on her own accord?"

"Not at all. I believe in this circumstance that Gaia let her go, hoping to entice her more easily the next time."

I pondered her words for a moment, thinking that maybe I hadn't been so lucky to escape Gaia after all. Is that why she let me go the first time? She knew she'd find me again by picking my exit spot in advance, conveniently located in the unassuming town of Pompeii at the base of an active volcano. "So Gaia set me up. She knew all along…" I began aloud, without expecting a confirmation from Pele. I closed my eyes, a new sense of dread filling my soul. Poor Lucius and the townsfolk of Pompeii. I never had a chance to make it to the Oracle in Delphi. Not when Gaia had already strategically planned my future, regardless of the cost of so many innocent lives.

"So what do I do next? How can I determine her next move?" I questioned the goddess.

"I think you already know the answer to that question, child. Search your heart."

I produced a ball of fire in my palm and rested the back of my hand against the ground. I listened with all my heart, remembering Pele's suggestion. Closing my eyes, I searched my soul for the pulse of their hearts that inherently locked Gaia and me together. For a long time I heard nothing beyond my own heartbeat and the pulse that throbbed in my veins. But I detected a different sound, a distant, muted sound from a time and place so very far, far away. When I slowly opened my eyes, I looked at Pele, feeling torn.

"You've found her?" she asked.

"Yes. She's in Atlantis," I declared. Conflicting emotions warred across my countenance. A part of me felt proud of myself for locating her on a small island in the Mediterranean, yet the other part of me felt profound disappointment in discovering this new truth. I didn't need Pele to say a word to grasp the realization that my training was far from complete. Meaning my call to Sully must wait a while longer…because I had to travel back in time again.

CHAPTER TEN

"Hydros probably can't track you down...not yet, at least," Pele advised and handed me a white linen tunic for this trip. "But promise me one thing. You won't do anything foolish, like chance a swim in the ocean again, will you?"

"You know about that?" I gasped, remembering how quickly the superstorm descended upon the Pacifica coastline after my little skimboarding episode. I only meant to impress Micah and Sully, but ended with a short dip in the ocean that enabled Hydros to pinpoint my precise location. "You really don't think I need to worry about Gaia?"

"No, but just to be safe, you should wear these." The goddess handed me a pair of sandals with extra thick rubber soles.

I slipped on the shoes and stepped inside my tent to change into the new outfit she'd provided. The cloth hung loosely around my body, so I tied a section of cord around my waist and adjusted the folds. Luckily, this tunic felt far more comfortable than my clothes from the last trip.

"And now for your hair," Pele said when I emerged from the tent. Her fingers deftly wove my hair into a braid down the back of my head, adorning it with lovely jeweled barrettes. She plucked a handful of velvety white flowers and tucked them carefully into the folds of my braid. I imagined I looked so different compared to my escape from the burning streets of Old Chicago that landed me in modern day Pacifica. Feeling surprisingly beautiful, I wished I had a mirror…or better yet a phone to take a picture to send to Sully.

"Ready?" Pele asked. She stood back to admire her work.

I took a deep breath. "As ready as I'll ever be."

Her lips turned up in a smile. She closed her eyes in concentration and chanted in Hawaiian. The obsidian amulet around my neck glowed a brilliant white. I recognized a few words of her chant—like *kea* meaning *white* and *ahi* for *fire*—before the amulet's flames engulfed my entire body in a blinding, oppressive heat. My body whisked away from the familiar lava fields through the dark tunnel of time and space to the precise destination I had chosen.

All the while, I prayed to God I hadn't made a huge mistake.

Atlantis, 1260 B.C.

After I landed, I surveyed my arms and garments, once again amazed to find the white linens of my tunic remained intact. Even the delicate flowers in my hair felt as fresh as when Pele had plucked them from their stems.

"Amazing," I marveled with a low whistle. I concentrated and snapped my fingers together, mimicking Pele's actions. But to my disappointment, only a small yellow flame appeared within my palm. I made a mental note to ask Pele to reveal her trick once I completed this mission.

My eyes left my fresh garments to marvel at the unparalleled beauty that unfolded before me. A range of toothed mountaintops surrounded the valley of patchwork fields teeming with a wide array of crops. Above the peaks, long beams of sunlight poked through the downy clouds, casting a brilliant glow upon the earth. But in the center stood the most spectacular sight of all: an island set like a solitary gem in the middle of a sapphire sea. A tall peak rose alone from the heart of the island, its summit capped with a monumental temple of sparkling stone pillars that supported a great roof of glittering gold. Canals encircled the island in concentric circles, with a single road bridging the mainland with the island's center.

"My destination," I assumed and set forth down the path leading toward the resplendent city of Atlantis. The obsidian amulet bounced up and down with each step, its glassy black surface gleaming in the intense rays of the tropical sun. I tucked Pele's amulet beneath my tunic to avoid unwanted attention. Nearing the bottom of the hill, the path widened into a cobbled street and led through a series of gates and towers. I slipped into the flow of pedestrians entering the city, secretly glad my straight black hair and olive skin helped me blend in well with the native Atlanteans.

I passed columns of soldiers marching in formation, parading down the magnificent city streets where buildings glittered in the sunlight. Judging by the conversations of the crowd around me, the troops readied for battle against their rival city of Athens. Each soldier wore shiny armored plates with a trident emblazoned across his chest and a helmet decorated with plumes dyed a brilliant shade of aqua to honor the sea god, Poseidon. Spectators assembled to cheer the city's protectors with fanfare and flags waving on high.

I slipped through the boisterous crowd, searching for a sign of Gaia and Shannon. Just inside the second gate, I spotted Gaia's russet hair falling in long waves down her back. Slowly, I inched closer, hiding behind the carts in hopes of overhearing their conversation unnoticed.

"But it's so unbearably hot here," Shannon complained and plopped down along the side of the curb, mopping the beads of perspiration from her forehead.

"Try this," Gaia insisted. She presented Shannon with a gift wrapped in paper and string.

Shannon ripped open the parcel and held up an elegant tunic of indigo silk, pressed flat.

"What do you think?" Gaia prodded.

"It will suffice." Shannon said in a bored tone. She stood, holding the tunic against her body and stepped behind a privacy curtain near one of the carts to change. Her face wore a fixed frown when she emerged, even with the wind rippling through the folds of her airy silk.

"And now for your hair." Gaia presented an ivory comb and smoothed out her strands, tying them off her neck in a loose bun. "Better?" she asked.

"I suppose," Shannon replied unconvincingly.

"Just wait. You will learn to love this land," she said, eager to entice the scared girl with the power and glory of Atlantis. She led Shannon through the crowd. I waited until they were further up the street before leaving my hiding spot. I followed at a safe distance, weaving between midday shoppers, my eyes trained on Gaia's every move.

Suddenly, Gaia paused, spinning her head in a suspicious glance over her left shoulder, sensing someone followed.

Frightened she had spotted me, I stopped in front of the nearest cart filled with glass vials of various shapes, my back turned toward Gaia as I pretended to make a purchase. Feigning interest, I picked up a vial containing a ruby colored liquid, turning its contents over in my hand while I prayed Gaia hadn't noticed me.

"That's Dragon's Blood," declared a little girl, not more than ten years of age. Her deep brown eyes studied me intently, urging me to make a purchase. She stood behind her cart in a simple toga. Her plain clothing didn't detract from her inherent beauty. A pronounced widow's peak and silky black hair framed her heart-shaped face. Her mouth turned down. I wondered why she seemed so sad for someone so young.

I blinked and looked down at her frail form. "Dragon's Blood? But I thought dragons didn't exist." Then again, I never imagined a serpent like the Cata monster existed either.

In an instant, the girl's frown erased into a wide, knowing smile. Her white teeth gleamed bright against her dark skin. "It's not from *real* dragons," she corrected me with a chuckle. "It comes from the Dragon tree." She pointed across the street to a large tree that towered nearly fifty feet above the vendor's carts below. Its upper branches wove together into a complex network to support the broad, fan-shaped canopy above. "Dragon trees make good medicine," she continued. "And when I break off the bark, I collect the red Dragon's Blood."

My gaze returned to the girl, mildly impressed with her knowledge and skills for someone of her age. "You sure know a lot for a little girl."

She stood straighter, her dark eyes filled with conviction as she crossed her arms over her chest. "I'm not a little girl anymore. I'm old enough to take care of myself."

I peeked over my shoulder to ensure Gaia and Shannon remained within view. "I'm sorry," I began. "I didn't mean to assume—"

A hardened look formed in her eyes.

What a little spitfire, I thought. My smile widened. "What's your name?"

The girl proudly puffed out her chest. "My name is Monifa, daughter of Aziza."

"Monifa?" I repeated. "That's a pretty name."

The girl's chest slowly deflated. "It means *lucky*," she stated, her voice softer. A faraway look filled her eyes. "But I don't feel very lucky."

"Really? Why's that?" I asked in a distracted tone and snuck another glance at Gaia and Shannon. They had moved a bit farther down the street, stopping briefly as Gaia directed Shannon's gaze up the hill toward the peak of the magnificent Temple of Poseidon. The bright midday sun reflected brilliantly off the golden rooftop and pure white pillars, like a beacon calling to Gaia.

"I am an orphan," Monifa continued as her dark eyes glazed with a coating of tears. "My mother, precious Aziza, died in childbirth, so my father chose this name since I was lucky enough to survive. But now he's gone, too."

"Really?" I asked, my voice filled with sincerity for the girl who shared my pain of losing her entire family. For a moment, I completely forgot my concern of Gaia detecting my presence in this ancient island and focused on the girl's tale.

Monifa nodded. "When the Atlanteans attacked our Egyptian town, my father went to fight against them." She heaved a deep, saddened sigh before finishing in a small voice, "He never returned."

"I'm so sorry to hear that," I said, placing a gentle hand upon her shoulder. "How did you end up here? Were you adopted?"

She shook her head and took a step out from behind the cart. Hearing the jingle of metal chains dragging against the hard ground, I instantly regretted my question. My gaze traveled down her small frame toward her ankles where a pair of metal shackles bound her dusty bare legs together. How foolish of me to remind her of her unfair situation.

Monifa squeezed her eyes shut to block the horrors. "They took all the survivors," she explained, "and made us into slaves. That was four months ago now. Four months since my luck went away and I was sold to the old widow Vallejo."

"I am truly sorry," I said again, meaning every word. I remembered the pain I felt when Gaia collapsed the roof of my house, trapping my family inside, before manipulating my fire to ignite the structure. The screams of my little sister, Sarah, still echoed in my ears.

So captivated by her story and lost in my past, I contemplated the unfortunate turn of events that bonded this stranger to myself. When I clasped my chest to share in her pain, my fingers grazed Pele's amulet. *Oh my God.* I'd forgotten all about the importance of my mission!

My head spun wildly, searching for a sign of Gaia and Shannon, but I'd lost them from view. "I'm sorry, but I have to go," I quickly apologized to Monifa and placed the vial back on her cart.

A look of disappointment filled her heart-shaped face. She hung her head and sniffled. "If I don't sell at least five more vials today, Señora Vallejo threatened to beat me again." She lifted up her plain toga, exposing the backs of her calves, covered in mottled bruises of faded yellows and greens.

With a shudder, I reached deep into my pockets, praying Pele had the foresight to give me something to use for bartering. But my pockets were empty. *What did I expect — she'd actually have access to ancient coins from a lost civilization? That's asking a lot, even for a goddess.*

Then I got an idea. I unclasped five jeweled barrettes from my braids, letting my plaits loosen until my black hair spilled around my face. "I'll take five," I declared, and placed the barrettes on the top of her cart.

Monifa's face brightened. "Maybe my father was right and I am a little lucky. Lucky to have met you today, at least," she said and passed me five vials of Dragon's Blood. "Thank you —" she paused, searching for a name to put with the kind customer who spared her from another beating.

"Jordan," I replied, returning her smile. "My name's Jordan."

"Thank you, Jordan," she repeated, her dark eyes twinkling with delight. She turned the barrettes over in her hand, letting the gems sparkle in the sunlight.

I gave her a quick wave and stuffed the vials in my pocket, though I did not intend to put something called Dragon's Blood on my body, regardless of her claims. Turning down the street, I quickened my pace, furious with myself for getting so distracted. The girl's tale was compelling, but not worth losing sight of Gaia and Shannon, despite my intentions to help Monifa. I frantically scanned each side street for Gaia's distinctive crown of hair. The glass vials jingled in my pocket with every step, undoubtedly attracting unwanted attention to myself. I couldn't abandon the vials now, not while in sight of Monifa and her wares.

Passing a main road, I caught a startlingly clear view of Poseidon's temple perched on the top of the hill and instantly paused in my tracks. *That's it*, I thought, changing my course to head up the street. *Gaia's definitely taking her there.*

Sure enough, far ahead on the steep street, I spotted a tiny red head bobbing up and down with each step. Gaia.

Certain that Monifa had lost sight of me, I removed all but one of the vials from my pocket and dashed up the street, hoping Pele's thick-soled sandals would silence my heavy footfalls.

I reached the temple, short of breath, my heart pounding against my rib cage. Inside, I heard the deep echoes of a pair of voices from within the great hall. I stole across the entryway, hiding behind a giant column, trying to catch bits of Gaia and Shannon's conversation.

Imposing statues towered above me, fierce expressions carved into their ivory faces to instill terror amongst the citizens of this island. Their vacant eyes stared down at me, questioning my worthiness to intrude upon this magnificent temple. In the center loomed a statue of Atlas, the first king of Atlantis and son of the sea god, Poseidon. He bore a commanding presence in the room with his sculpted muscles, chiseled jawbone and prominent chin framed in flowing tresses of hair. The exquisite detail the artists used in displaying every feature from his manicured toenails to the sinews and bulging veins in his arms and neck astonished me. His eyes remained intentionally blank and foreboding, appearing cognizant of everything that occurred in his worldly domain.

I shuddered, suddenly afraid my unwelcome presence here might rile the anger of the gods and unwittingly bring destruction to Atlantis. Gaia's voice interrupted my thoughts. I slipped behind one of the statues, craning my neck for a better view.

"Like I told you before," Gaia boasted strutting with pride across the marble floor as she gestured to the statues surrounding them, "*this* is what you were destined for — not your old, mundane life. With my help, people will soon be carving statues of us to honor our greatness."

"If you say so," Shannon replied with a disinterested nod. A wistful look filled her eyes, preferring her former agrarian existence along the banks of the river in ancient Ireland that shared her name.

Gaia's excited voice rose an octave when she continued, "Opulent jewels, unimaginable power, and worldly fame can all be yours. Imagine them constructing an entire temple like this in your honor!"

"Don't presume anything about me. I don't want any of this," Shannon cried.

Gaia's eyes gleamed as she gazed down upon the city, the golden rooftops sparkling in the sunshine. "It begins now," she stated with confidence, ignoring Shannon's hesitation. Gaia reached into her pocket and pulled out a shiny gold necklace. I squinted for a better look of their figures, backlit by the bright outdoors. Gaia slipped the necklace over Shannon's head, sliding her long brown hair to the side while she fastened its clasp.

"What's this?" Shannon asked. She held up the golden charm inlaid with precious jewels that sparkled in the light with diamonds, rubies, and emeralds.

"It's a nautilus shell," Gaia answered, "to represent the power you share with the sea. Think of it as a precursor of things to come. But for now, let me show you what else lies in store."

Gaia strode across the great hall, beckoning Shannon to follow.

The girl resisted, rooted to her spot as she examined the nautilus shell with reservation.

Suddenly, everything made sense to me. My hand instinctively crept its way toward Pele's obsidian stone tucked beneath my tunic. Did Shannon's nautilus shell carry a similar power? Would it allow Gaia to control Shannon's jumps through time, essentially guaranteeing her entry and exit points?

"It's beautiful on you," Gaia said. Her lips turned up into a smug, calculating smile, making me presume it indeed served the same function as my amulet.

"I suppose," Shannon replied in a meek tone. At that moment, I was convinced that Shannon would never join Gaia, just like I vowed never to fight by her side.

"It's perfect," Gaia continued, oblivious to Shannon's hesitation. "We can begin training here, on the outer ring of the city where you are nearest the sea."

Shannon shook her head, a frightened look consuming her thin face. "I don't think I'm ready. I don't want to make the commitment." And without another word, she turned and walked out of the temple. Gaia followed at her heels, trying to persuade her to change her mind.

I swallowed hard, fearful of what might happen next should their tempers flare. Giving them a safe head start, I ducked behind buildings periodically. Gaia and Shannon soon reached the bottom of the hill and exited the first gate. From their facial expressions and mannerisms, I knew the argument had escalated by the time they passed through the last set of gates to enter the outer ring of the island. I inched closer, eager to witness how their altercation developed.

Suddenly, Shannon defiantly stopped in her tracks. Adamant, she refused to take another step. "I've had enough. Take me back now. I want to go home."

Gaia's eyes narrowed. Her cheeks flushed hot with rage. "How can you be so insolent?" she screamed, turning on Shannon. "I offer you power and prestige—more wealth than you ever imagined growing up in your pathetic Irish hut—and *this* is how you thank me?" She planted her foot on the ground to emphasize her point. The earth responded with a mild tremor that made everybody shift suddenly on unsteady feet. I braced my body against the side of the tower and craned my neck.

"No. I only want to go home. Leave me alone."

Gaia reached for her wrist. "You will join me," she declared, her anger mounting.

"No. I won't." Louder she yelled, "*Leave me alone!*" with the intention of making a scene.

Soldiers' heads turned, ready to act. Gaia stomped her foot with greater force, rattling the earth once more.

Tears streamed from Shannon's face. She struggled to stay upright. "Stop it!" she cried, her lower lip quivering. Her eyes turned steely cold. A frightening, determined look ruled her face. I saw her hand reach behind her to summon reserves. I glanced toward the ocean, watching with disbelief where the sea began to recede. Fish flopped helplessly on the reef and Atlanteans swarmed with baskets, eager to collect this unexpected feast.

I've got a bad feeling about this. All that water had to go somewhere. And chances were, it would be returning here to Atlantis all too soon, just like the superstorm in Pacifica. Only there, I had a car to escape the surging water. And here...I glanced over my shoulder where Poseidon's temple gleamed in the bright sun. No longer caring if Gaia saw me, I turned on my heels and sprinted back toward the center of the island, seeking higher ground.

Running as fast as I could, I dodged the crowds of unsuspecting townsfolk, when I found myself on a familiar street once more. *Monifa! I have to help her*, I thought, quickly spotting the little girl by her cart of vials. "There's not much time!" I shouted and dashed toward her cart. "Quick! Come with me."

The girl's face registered alarm. "But my cart…" she began.

"Leave it. We must hurry." And without another word, I grabbed her hand and dragged her down the street, her shackles clanking with each labored step. I glanced over my shoulder, spotting the fast approaching water.

Pandemonium reigned when the first wave approached shore. It surged several stories in height before barreling up the city streets. My eyes filled with fear as I watched the monstrous wall of water head straight for Atlantis. *That's the scary thing about tsunamis*, I recalled from the last one Hydros set on Pacifica to slow my escape. *They just keep coming and coming and coming, flattening everything in their path and dragging it all out to sea.* And with everything in its path gone, the subsequent waves found less resistance, sweeping further inland with every pass.

We'll never make it to the temple at this rate, I thought grimly, sorry for the little girl forced to sell Dragon's Blood daily on the streets.

Dragon's Blood. That gave me an idea, remembering the Dragon Tree stood nearby. I hurried her up into the safety of its branches with me in close pursuit, just as the waters surged up the street and reached Monifa's cart. "You're almost there," I encouraged her. "Keep going."

She struggled up the branches as the water reached the base of the tree. Monifa whimpered with fear, but kept climbing upward. Once or twice, her wide eyes glanced downward, startled by the power of the water beneath. We reached the top branches of the canopy, but the water continued to rise.

"I don't know how to swim," Monifa admitted through trembling lips.

"It's okay. You'll be safe here," I said, comforting her. Soon the water nipped at our ankles, our calves, and our waists, before covering our shoulders.

Suddenly, the rushing current changed directions and sucked the screaming civilians and debris back to sea, including us.

"I can't hold on much longer," she cried. The water dragged her body from its spot.

I wound my arm around the stiff branches. "I've got you. I promise," I said, battling the raging waters with an outstretched hand.

Monifa reached for me, but her fingers slipped through mine.

"No! Grab hold, Monifa!" I exclaimed and stretched my arm as far as I could reach. Still, it wasn't enough. With great despair, I watched her fingers slide through mine, the current ripping her from the tree.

"*No!*" I screamed madly. Weighed down by shackles bound to her ankles, her head sank beneath the waves, soon lost from view. My tears mixed with the salty water, polluted with all sorts of debris while I clung for life within the branches of the Dragon Tree.

The waters soon receded under Shannon's control. I scrambled down the tree, crying the entire way. But the time I reached the bottom, my tunic was tattered and my arms covered in red scrapes and cuts. But when I wiped away the blood, I realized it wasn't my own. *It's Dragon's Blood*, I thought, missing Monifa even more. A pang of despair filled my heart that I couldn't save her life.

I knew there wasn't time to mourn, not when another wave would soon return. Calling upon all my strength, I forced my legs to move faster uphill.

Nearing the Temple of Poseidon, I reached for Pele's black obsidian amulet, no longer caring if others might notice. My secret would remain safe since I doubted a single soul would survive this violent day. Afraid Shannon would soon unleash her full fury, I needed to return to the present before the worst of the disaster struck.

When my hand sought the cord of coconut fibers around my neck, I touched nothing but skin. "Oh my God," I gasped, frantically searching the folds of my tunic, praying it stuck inside the folds of white linen. I found nothing. I dropped to my knees, consumed with grief. I realized my worst fears were confirmed…

The amulet had disappeared.

I panicked, my throat tight with fear, wondering if I should retrace my steps to search for it. The sea had swept away everything behind me. Did it rip off when I climbed down the Dragon Tree? It had happened so fast, my first instinct was to try to help Monifa and escape the oncoming wave rather than leave Atlantis altogether. And now I must pay for that choice.

"I don't want to die," I whispered, forcing myself to my feet. There must be another way. I glanced over my shoulder, my eyes growing wide at the new rush of water surging inland. "Just survive this next wave," I told myself, "then you can figure out a way to return." Thinking fast, I slipped the rope cord from around my waist and bound one section to a stronghold of the temple below me, the other wrapped tightly around my wrist. As a precaution, I grasped the cord inside my fist, vowing I would never let go. Once again, the waters rose incredibly fast, covering my ankles, my knees, and my waist.

I clung to the roof of the temple, having nowhere else left to climb. In the distance, I spotted Gaia and Shannon, supported on pillars of rock Gaia had thrust upward to lift them high above the incoming rush. In that moment, I envied Gaia's earthly powers. My fire proved no match against this volume of moving water. The swift current beat against the edges of her domain, but did not erode the dense rock. And when the waters continued upward, Gaia extended their pillars, creating a land bridge all the way to the mountains of the mainland.

The sun dipped below the mountain peaks, bathing the sky in

a brilliant shade of bronze, despite the destruction that unfolded before it. I caught one final glimpse of the clouds backlit in bright golden hues before the rising waters reached my neck. The rope stretched to its maximum length. I fought to tread water above the stronghold of Poseidon's temple, my only connection to the land far beneath my feet.

Traces of the distant clear pale sky flickered above my head. I held my breath underwater, praying I wouldn't drown. I could not escape through fire this time, not here beneath the water with my sole means of travel lost forever in the deep blue sea.

Just before the water consumed my head, I puffed my cheeks full of air, hoping the supply would last me long enough until the wave diminished. But the water swelled higher and higher and I feared my luck had reached its end.

I do not want to die here! I reminded myself, the waters swirling about my head. I forced myself to think of Sully, and to find strength in the slim chance I would see him once again. The air inside my cheeks escaped in a slow trail of gurgling bubbles, depleting my last reserves of oxygen. My cheeks drained flat and I gasped, choking on the water, desperate for another breath of air.

Only there was none.

I closed my eyes, ready to succumb to my inevitable fate. I would never see Sully again. Never live a normal life. Never complete this mission and return to Pele. I had failed…and not just in saving Monifa, but in saving myself.

My fingers slipped from their grip on the cord, no longer concerned about maintaining my last connection to the temple. My body felt heavy, lacking the will to survive. I sunk lower in the water column, my weary feet landing on the roof in their final resting place. Nothing mattered anymore because I had failed. I drew small comfort in reuniting with my loved ones who had passed before me.

Just when I'd abandoned hope, the wave receded. The water level descended below the top of my head, exposing my skin to the soft ocean breeze. A shock enveloped my body, surging new life into my fatigued limbs. I struggled against the outgoing current and gasped on the fresh air.

A second chance! I shouted inside my mind, forcing my body to alertness. And if Shannon called another wave upon the city, this might indeed prove my last chance to escape.

I remembered Pele's words: *"Though you use fire as your catalyst, in truth, the magic resides inside of you. All you need is to believe and feel this specific time with every ounce of your entire body and soul."*

"Kea, ahi, kea, ahi," I repeated in a low voice, committing my entire heart and soul to believing in the Hawaiian words Pele had used to summon the white fire. I focused my full attention on the stamp of time from which I had departed, hoping and praying to return to that very spot. The warmth inside me grew stronger as my anger mounted. "I don't want to die here," I repeated with conviction. Blood ran hot through my veins. I felt the familiar burn alight in my eyes, like orange firelight consumed their ebony color, until they gradually shifted into the blinding whiteness of Pele's fire. Despite my drenched clothes and hair, the fire burst forth from within me until I spiraled into the darkness of space.

CHAPTER ELEVEN

I hunched over my knees, coughing like crazy to hack up seawater from my lungs. I thought about the citizens I saw take to their boats, hoping to ride out the current. I remembered the soldiers, dressed in full regalia, struggling to save their fellow civilians. And I recalled my last view of Gaia's land bridge to guide her and Shannon to safety. It was possible others had found it...if they had made it that long.

"Did any Atlanteans survive?" I squeaked through my parched throat, burning from the mouthfuls I'd swallowed of the salty sea.

"Very few," Pele said grimly. "Even fewer believed their tale. Still, the survivors passed down the story orally, eventually transforming it into a lesson for future generations about the inherent dangers of excessive wealth and power. Little did they realize the actual cause for the city's destruction."

"See...that's what I don't get," I told the goddess. "When I was in Pompeii, I once overheard people talking about the lost city of Atlantis, only it sounded like it had been swallowed into the sea nearly ten thousand years before. But my method of locating Shannon dated the catastrophe at a much more recent time period. How could there be that much of a discrepancy? Had I messed up the date? Did Shannon actually drown the real Atlantis? Or was it just another city that shared the same name and tragic fate?"

"I might have had a hand in that," Pele admitted, blush rising high in her cheeks. She wound a lock of hair around her finger in a sultry way.

"What do you mean?" I said, aghast. "*You* changed history?"

She shrugged. "It didn't take too much work to convince one of the ancient storytellers to alter the facts…conveniently before he related the story to the classical Greek philosopher, Plato, of course," she said in an innocent tone. "So when Plato documented his account in 360 BC, nine *hundred* years had already passed since the destruction of Atlantis. My friend, the storyteller, stated the event had occurred nine *thousand* years before. He simply added an extra zero, that's all. But that minor change helped keep the great island shrouded in mystery and served as the perfect excuse to protect the general public from understanding the powers of the Elementals."

"So you intentionally changed history," I repeated, my shock turning into awe. "Why would you bother to go through the effort? Just for us?"

"I do enjoy a challenge from time to time," Pele said dreamily. "Besides, I see great potential in Elementals. You simply need a little help and direction at times."

"But if you changed history, why can't I? Why can't I go back in time and reverse these events? I could prevent Shannon's tsunami from sinking Atlantis or Gaia's volcanic eruption from burying the town of Pompeii. I could save the ones I lost—like my parents, my sister Sarah, my friends Lucius and William, and the poor little girl Monifa."

"When the Four Elements first bestowed their powers upon living beings to create the Elementals, they feared the temptation to abuse those powers and alter the course of history," Pele explained. "As a condition to limit the Elementals' control, you can travel through time within the realm of your element, but could not revisit any specific period. Once you entered a portal, it would seal itself off, preventing your future reentry.

"Think of it as your time continuum represents a really long hallway filled with doors, each opening into a different time period. Once you pass through a door, it locks from the other side, never reopening to you again. That's how you can return here to the same time and place you had just left, but never a minute sooner. This limitation guarantees you will not encounter your former or future self in any of your travels through time."

"Like a backup clause written in fine print?" I said, disheartened.

"Exactly. It's for your own safety. Otherwise, the temptation to right the wrongs of the past would be too great to overcome. You would spend your entire existence trying to fix the past, and in the end only create unforeseen problems."

My shoulders slumped forward from the weight of her new insight. "So what's done is done," I said in a solemn tone.

The goddess nodded. "I'm afraid it is."

I had to look away, unable to believe how much death had occurred from a single act of fear and defiance. Worse, there was nothing I could do to change the past. Nothing, no matter how hard I trained or how many new skills I learned. Nothing could bring back the ones I had lost. I could only look forward, only hope to save others from suffering a similar fate in the future. Still, that knowledge did little to ease my heavy heart.

"Now, for your next skill." She glanced at the sun, sinking toward the horizon. Pressed for time, the goddess began, "I want to teach you how to create a flash blast."

"A flash blast?" I asked, pushing the stabbing pain to the back of my heart. I forced myself to concentrate on the future to prevent the horrors from repeating themselves. "What's that?"

"It's a powerful weapon when used correctly," Pele explained. "If you focus your energy within your core, you can turn your entire body white hot like the sun. This allows you to melt through everything you touch by radiating the intense heat to your extremities. Or you may momentarily blind your opponent by containing your heat within and permitting only an intense beam of light to escape. Whichever you deem necessary at the time."

For a second, I flashed back to my dream in the hospital where I had melted everything within my reach. Seconds before I stretched my deadly fingers toward Gaia's helpless arm, I had woken in a pool of sweat. "I don't know if I can do that," I admitted, both skeptical and nervous at the same time. "You ask too much."

"Of course you can. The magic is inside of you. All you need to do is accept your Elemental name, Pyr, with your whole heart and soul."

I shook my head. "I can't. It's not me. I'm tired of running, tired of living so close to death. I want to be Jordan and only Jordan."

"Why bother training at all?" she challenged.

"So I can protect my family and friends from the other Elementals, that's why. My powers also represent the curse I bear. I'm tired of having others suffer because of me. I only wanted to learn how to defend myself from the other Elementals so they'd leave me in peace."

Pele's face turned down in pity. "Unfortunately, that is not your lot in life. You must understand that you won't progress until you believe in yourself."

"I know," I sighed. "I just wish things were different." I couldn't stop dwelling on my failure to save so many innocent lives from their untimely fates.

Worse, a small part of me had actually begun to pity Hydros. I had destroyed her without realizing all Shannon wanted was to protect her family. The Irish girl who eventually assumed her

Elemental name of Hydros wasn't any different from me, was she? I had started to believe I'd taken out the wrong person and should've gone after Gaia instead. The way I saw it, Gaia was the root behind all my issues and the center of all my woes. Yet there was a problem. Like Pele had said, no matter how hard I tried, I couldn't change the past—instead I could only live with the consequences that burdened my soul.

"Since you lost your amulet and still managed to find your way back here, I believe it is time for you to master the use of white fire," Pele declared, snapping me from my thoughts.

"I was thinking the same thing," I muttered in a melancholy tone, reminded of the surging waters of Shannon's tsunami covering my head.

"Jordan, you must commit your heart and soul fully, and believe you can do this with every ounce of your mind."

"I'm not so sure about that," I replied halfheartedly.

"You did it before, you can do it again," she reminded me.

I shook my head. "But things are totally different right now. At the time, I was scared, desperate, out of options. I didn't want to die."

"Sometimes that desperation proves a valuable ally," Pele explained. "Besides, you'll need to master this skill before venturing on your next mission."

I gulped. "There's more?"

"Surely you didn't think you were already done!" Pele guffawed. "But since you have your doubts, I will intentionally skip you ahead in time. So while you had a respite from Gaia and a chance to settle into your new life in Pompeii, Gaia followed Shannon through time. All the while, Shannon created maelstroms, ice storms, flash floods, and mudslides in her own desperate attempt to avoid Gaia." Pele handed me yet another outfit for my upcoming trip and a wad of outdated foreign currency.

115

"In this new mission, you'll travel to England, about a decade after the turn of the century. This time I anticipate you will notice a change in the dynamics of their flawed relationship—a change that will provide crucial insights into understanding Shannon's past and Gaia's motives," she added, and I slipped into the clothes she had provided—a long skirt, high-collared blouse, and a plain pair of boots.

"Now all you must do is believe that you are one with the fire," the goddess finished.

I sighed. "Okay."

She gave me a reproachful look. "No. I mean it. You must truly believe."

"Okay. I will," I repeated with more confidence than I felt.

Pele nodded. "That's better. Listen carefully and commit each and every word to memory."

She began to chant:

Ke ahi kea
Ikaika o 'uhane
Lawe mai a a'u a ku'u 'aina hou.
White fire,
Strong of spirit,
Bring me to my new land.

"Now say it with me," Pele requested.

The first two lines weren't too bad, but my tongue twisted in multiple knots when we reached the last verse. "I'll never be able to remember this," I admitted with a heavy sigh.

"Of course you can. You only need to try again."

And so we did while dusk then darkness descended upon the land. Over and over until the words permeated the depths of my memory, infiltrating my body until I could feel them grow as steady and strong as the beats of my heart.

"Ke ahi kea, ikaika o 'uhane, lawe mai a a'u a ku'u 'aina hou."
I hadn't realized Pele's voice had stopped guiding me until I

116

reached the final word.

I blinked at her with surprise. "I did it! And you know something, I think you're right...I actually felt a little different inside."

"Eventually you will sense the power of these words so you can achieve this feat without uttering the chant aloud. But for now, you should know them by heart. And the more you believe, the less pain you will feel until the entire process becomes as effortless as Gaia's. Now, try it for real."

"The white fire?" I asked, doubtful I could accomplish this feat regardless of knowing the chant.

She nodded. "Begin."

I took a deep breath, accessing my bottled-up frustration and sorrow for the growing list of lost lives. As my lips repeated her chant, I channeled that power outward from my core, devoting all my strength to the growing heat inside of me.

"You're close," Pele said, giving me a rare smile of satisfaction.

I felt my eyes glow from a warm orange to a blazing white. An agonizing scream strangled in depths of my throat as I forced the last of my reserves outward. I couldn't wait until this whole process became as painless as she claimed. Still, her methods worked and my hands began to glow a brilliant white.

"Now that you have reached this stage, all you will need to do is envision your new destination, commit to it, and you will be there. Think of Southampton on the tenth day of April in the year 1912."

I replayed her words in my head as my lips muttered the chant, softly at first, then increasing in strength. White flames licked my body with intolerable heat. Before I knew it, Pele's form disappeared as I rocketed back through time.

CHAPTER TWELVE

Southampton, United Kingdom, April 10, 1912

I landed in the alleyway near a busy street, crowded with people scurrying in every direction. An impressive passenger liner stood docked in the harbor, with four smokestacks towering over the bustling street. Long lines of people prepared to board the ship. I had only made it a short ways when I spotted Shannon's lithe form across the road, her head spinning back and forth, watchful of Gaia. She paused, her gaze fixed on a couple locked in a strong embrace. The woman had tears in her eyes when she reluctantly left the arms of her boyfriend to depart on her voyage.

Shannon's hand reached for the nautilus shell around her neck and marched toward the woman, confident in her decision. Too far away to hear their exchange, I saw Shannon's lips move hurriedly to explain her proposition. She looked from the woman to the ship and back. Shannon reached behind her neck, unfastened the clasp, and presented the jeweled charm.

"She's making a trade," I whispered, realizing her intent. "She's desperate to get on that ship to get away from Gaia."

The woman wrung her hands nervously, glancing from her boyfriend toward the ship and the future that awaited her. Biting her lip, the woman handed Shannon her ticket and suitcase in exchange for the nautilus shell necklace. Once freed of her obligation, she ran back into her boyfriend's waiting arms.

Shannon lugged the suitcase toward the boarding ramp, eager to distance herself from this town before Gaia reappeared. In her haste, she stumbled over the weight of the bag. A polite young man dressed in britches and a vest entered the line behind her. He offered her a hand, helping Shannon to her feet. She blushed when her eyes met his. He spoke a few words in introduction before they walked up the boarding ramp together.

At that moment, I realized she had sealed her fate, bound for a new destination far from here. But in order to complete my mission for Pele, I must find my own way onto that ship. I dashed up the street, searching for someone with an extra ticket to sell. Soon, I spotted a man in the center of a crowd of commoners who claimed they were eager to try their luck in New York. I burst through the crowd right up to the front, offering him double his asking price. A satisfied grin wound across his face as he pocketed my bills and handed me a third class ticket. I bolted toward the ship, making it onto the outer deck moments before the crew raised the boarding ramps.

Passengers lined the ship's sides, enthusiastically waving to the gathering crowd below as the ship set off from port. After the town of Southampton shrank from view, people returned to their cabins, buzzing with talk of a new life in America, the land of opportunity.

I lingered by the railing longer than most, watching the shoreline shrink from view. I didn't know why Pele needed me here, but felt certain her reasoning would present itself in time. When I finally returned to my deck, I passed a ring buoy looped around a hook on the railing. It read, White Star Line, *RMS Titanic*. Why did that name sound vaguely familiar? I racked my brain, trying to remember if I'd read about this ship in Mr. Tabor's class, the day I'd flipped through the history book and discovered my unintentional role in starting the Great Chicago Fire. Unable to recall a single detail, I let the thought fade from my mind, dismissing it as a mere coincidence.

I tried to remain inconspicuous throughout the trip, unlike the first class passengers I noticed on the upper decks, wearing fine garments when they strolled after dinner. The men dressed in tuxedo-style suits and tailcoats, white bowties, top hats, and polished shoes and the women in the latest fashions of inlaid lace dresses and oversized hats with ornate plumes. Instead of parading my clothing, I wore my hat pulled low, pretending to be engrossed in a book on a nearby lounge chair. Sometimes I'd hide in the shadows at a third-class party below deck. Other times I'd casually pass Shannon in the hallway, showing no sign of recognition. All the while, I watched her relationship blossom with the man she met at boarding. A man I had come to learn was named Bradley Burke.

Those first few days of the voyage, Shannon appeared blissfully happy at Bradley's side, until the fourth evening when Gaia suddenly appeared. She dressed in an opulent evening dress of emerald green that matched her eyes and a woolen scarf around her neck to ward off the cold. Tucking her russet curls beneath a stunning, wide-brimmed hat, she strode right up to Shannon. No wonder I hadn't seen Gaia yet this trip. With expensive clothes like those, she must have traveled the entire time in first class.

"Go away," Shannon hissed upon recognizing the Earth Elemental. She locked her fingers firmly inside Bradley's hand. "I don't need you. I don't want your life."

"This is not your destiny," Gaia declared. She stepped between Shannon and Bradley, forcing their hands apart. "You are meant to come with me."

In that moment, I realized Pele was right. The battles I had missed between the Water and Earth Elementals throughout the course of time had shattered Shannon's levels of patience. In an instant, Shannon's face clouded with fear and anger. An icy stare glazed her countenance while her fueled emotions manifested themselves in the form of uncontrolled power.

My eyes grew wide, watching Shannon's irrepressible fury toward Gaia freeze the water into massive chunks of ice that protruded from the inky sea. The cracking crystallization of her element rang clear in the crisp night air. "I said, 'Go away,'" she repeated in a chilling tone.

I heard the panicked voices of crewmembers alerting the bridge, "Iceberg! On the starboard side!" Loud noises from below carried through the ship. A first officer ordered the engines in reverse to change course. Despite their frantic attempts to avoid the obstacle, Shannon's iceberg grazed the side of the hull. A grinding metallic sound rattled my nerves when the iceberg collided with the starboard side, buckling the ship's hull. Fragments of ice scattered across the deck.

All too late, I recalled the passage in Mr. Tabor's textbook that stated the supposedly unsinkable ship had hit an iceberg, sending over fifteen hundred passengers to their watery graves on its maiden voyage. I swallowed hard, realizing this unfortunate and, according to Pele, unpreventable fate.

Bells rang across the ship, warning people to return to their rooms and don their life jackets and warm clothing to prepare for an evacuation. Gaia and Shannon joined the flow, but I stayed put, afraid to miss them boarding the lifeboats. After a long while navigating the crowded hallways and stairs, they appeared on deck and waited in line with Bradley to evacuate. I noticed an expression of profound guilt written across Shannon's face. She wrung her hands together nervously with each step closer to the front of the line.

"Women and children only," the officer announced, motioning for Gaia and Shannon to board. Shannon's face wrought with worry. She gazed at Bradley, reluctant to leave him behind.

"It's time for us to go," Gaia said, placing a strong hand on Shannon's wrist and dragging the frightened girl onto the lifeboat.

"No!" Shannon screamed and reached out for Bradley. Gaia and one of the ship's officers forced Shannon into the boat seconds before it dropped suddenly into the water far below. I heard the panicked screams of women and children carry over the melancholy tune of a stringed quartet playing on the outer deck.

From his spot, Bradley watched her lifeboat hit the water. Making a quick decision, he climbed over the railing and plunged after her, hoping to join her inside the boat once at sea. I ran to the railing, squinting to discern the scene below. The icy water quickly sucked the breath from his lungs and seized his limbs.

Shannon turned her head toward Bradley, struggling in the frigid water beyond her reach. The lifeboat drifted farther from the ship. When the life jacket impeded his stroke, he unbuckled the vest, freeing himself from its bulk and splashed through the water after her. *"Bradley, no!"* she shrieked, but he didn't heed her warning. The weight of his waterlogged pants and jacket soon pulled him downward.

"Why wait so long? Why won't she act?" I muttered to myself. After all, this was her realm. What did she care if others discovered her powers? Was she afraid they would blame her for the accident?

Shannon rose from her seat, preparing to go in after him when Gaia placed a restraining hand on her arm to keep her safely in the boat. My heart heaved with sorrow, reminded of my personal pain of losing my friend Lucius at Gaia's hand in the tragedy that engulfed Pompeii when Mt. Vesuvius erupted.

Unable to swim any further, Bradley gurgled, struggling to stay afloat in the inky water. Shannon wrestled herself free of Gaia's grasp and leapt from the lifeboat.

Gaia watched, a look of frustration etched upon her face. Shannon sprinted toward him with confident strokes. When Bradley slipped beneath the surface, Shannon dove after him.

I studied the water anxiously, expecting them to break through seconds later. Only neither reappeared. Soon, the trace of her bubbles vanished, leaving only a still patch to mark her last tie to this world.

Why didn't she use her powers? Why vanish with him? I wondered, at a loss for answers. *And why didn't Gaia pursue her?* Those questions bounced around my mind as I saw Gaia sink to her knees in the lifeboat, showing an uncharacteristic measure of defeat. In this precise moment, I could tell the strain of this futile pursuit wore on her. Between battling both Shannon and me to support her cause, Gaia's resolute determination had begun to fade. However, Gaia — a talented actor — masked her true feelings in front of us, so neither Shannon nor I would realize her internal struggle. I suspected that unless she changed her motive, she couldn't maintain this pace much longer.

Secretly, I feared my newfound empathy toward the Earth and Water Elementals made me susceptible. Not just to bend under the mounting pressure, but to break into irreparable pieces. Someone had to give, that much was certain. But who would lose her determination first? Gaia, Shannon…or *me*?

However, I had little time to ponder the answer to that question. The captain shouted, "Release the last lifeboat!" With those few words, a new terror rocked my consciousness…the crew had deployed all the lifeboats.

Leaving me trapped, stranded on a sinking ship.

And to make matters worse, only I possessed an alternate means to escape, even though I could not risk using it here in full view of others where I would cause more alarm. Pangs of loss gripped my heart, remembering Pele's words. There was nothing I could do to spare the inevitable loss of life in the tragedy at sea.

Or was there? One of the first officers began tossing deck chairs overboard in an effort to buoy those already in the water as the ship sunk bow first. I joined his crusade until we had exhausted the supply. Praying I had helped save at least a few lives, I decided I must leave this ship before I joined the list of names of those who perished.

Struggling against the flow of frantic passengers in life jackets, I fought my way below decks, down several staircases, until I entered one of the boiler rooms where discarded shovels for moving coal lay strewn across the floor after the workers fled to safer grounds.

I felt a sudden lurch, like the ship had snapped in two. "It's now or never," I told myself grimly and uttered the chant Pele had taught me, "*Ke ahi kea, ikaika o 'uhane...*" The floor beneath my feet tilted at an incredible angle, reminding me of how little time remained before the hull sank to its final resting place upon the frigid bottom of the North Atlantic. Tears of guilt streamed from my cheeks. The white flames sputtered, unwilling to take hold in my conflicted state. I braced myself against one wall and attempted the chant again. But loud cracking noises of the ship's demise filled my ears, breaking my concentration. The words of the chant lost their meaning and drained my power. With no other options, I dove headfirst into the fiery boiler, my body consumed in flames. I prayed with all my might I would somehow return to Pele.

CHAPTER THIRTEEN

The next morning, Pele opened my tent flap and let in the bright rays of the sun. I shielded my eyes and rolled over on my side, unwilling to leave the safety of my sleeping bag. Surprisingly, I had returned to my precise destination, though my body and clothes were covered in soot from using my conventional method of travel. It took me forever to scrub my face clean with some of my precious supply of water, but it was worth it. Still, I lay awake in my tent most of the night, reliving the horrors from Atlantis and the *Titanic*. After everything I had endured, I couldn't dare to imagine what would happen next.

"Why didn't Shannon save Bradley?" I asked weakly. "I don't get it. She could've saved him...she could've saved everyone if she wanted."

"I believe the guilt of causing another accident was more than she could bear. My understanding is that she did indeed save Bradley Burke and brought him safely to New York. Yet he served as a constant reminder of the destruction she had caused. She didn't want to be viewed as a monster, not even in her own eyes. So when Gaia found her once more, she abandoned her feelings for him and left without protest."

Her answer made sense, but it did little to ease the hurt inside my own heart. "I couldn't do anything to help them, just like you said," I told Pele, my voice choked with tears.

125

"That's not true," she corrected me. "You saved some from the frigid waters, providing them with a chair to rest upon until a lifeboat returned."

"Still, there was so much death," I moaned helplessly. "So much death."

"I assume you'll be happy to hear this is your last mission," Pele said.

I grunted an unenthusiastic reply, my body numb with loss.

She grabbed my hand and dragged me from the tent. My legs wobbled beneath me as I rose to my feet. "You'll be headed to Central Colorado, to a small town on the slopes of the Rocky Mountains," she added as she handed me a long coat lined with fur around the hood and cuffs.

I muttered a bleak, "Whatever."

"You'll be at a much higher elevation, so stay well hydrated and try not to overexert yourself. If you feel dizzy or nauseous, you may have something called altitude sickness and should find the town's doctor. He can help."

I gave a disinterested nod.

"Perhaps you don't understand," Pele explained. "When I say 'small town' I mean literally, it is only one block in length, so you will need to use caution to—"

"Yeah, yeah. I got it. Stay out of sight. Don't get caught," I snipped. "And don't die."

Snatching the coat from her hands, I threw it on over my clothes. Regardless of what happened next, at least things would be over after this. I could catch up with Sully for the rest of the summer. The promise of spending time with him again refreshed my soul as I focused my energy on the task. My last mission. *Thank God*, I thought, careful not to voice my opinion aloud lest I rile Pele's temper. Shedding the grief from my mind, I dismissed all feelings of reservation and accepted her last request.

Central Colorado, January 2, 1949

Having grown more accustomed to Pele's preferred method of travel via *ke ahi kea*, my nerves steadied quicker this time. It only took one deep breath to prepare myself for what lay ahead as white tongues of fire shot me through space and time.

Still, a problem surfaced foremost in my mind. I wasn't entirely certain of Gaia's next move. She seemed close to breaking Shannon...but almost closer to breaking herself. I imagined the strain Gaia felt, attempting to coerce both Shannon and myself to join her quest for domination wore on her patience and endurance.

"I can't do this alone," Gaia had told Shannon. "You were destined for this."

The white fire flung me through the portal of time and space and I wondered if I, too, were destined for this. Destined to live a life devoid of true love and companionship when the fear of death and destruction remained so close. Destined to lead a solitary existence, tracking my foe through history in a feeble attempt to learn more about my own past and powers. Because at that particular moment, I would've given anything to abandon my search and my destiny altogether.

Especially when the magical tongues of white fire landed me smack in the middle of a snowstorm. And I wasn't talking about a few-flurries-dusting-the-roofs-of-houses type of snowstorm that created a winter wonderland outdoors. I meant a full-on blizzard where obnoxiously fat snowflakes descended like swarms of white locusts from the leaden sky. Through the heavy storm, I spotted a small town up ahead, cozied up along the base of a mountain range whose towering serrated peaks wore thick caps of snow.

But to make it to the security of the town was another story. The biting wind howled through the trees, whipping snow high into the air in swirling vortices that spiraled down the snowy street. A wintry gust blasted through my hair and lashed stinging flakes of snow against the raw flesh of my cheeks. A spasmodic shiver wreaked havoc on my spine. I pulled the coat tightly around my body to ward off the cold. I couldn't imagine how long it would take me to walk even that short distance in this type of weather.

But you can't stay in this spot, either, I reminded myself. My fingers and toes turned painfully numb with cold. Uncertain if this storm proved the work of Shannon or Mother Nature, I realized my needs for shelter trumped the search for the other Elementals. Squinting into the icy wind, I spotted the warm golden lights of a tavern sitting on the corner of the town's storefront. I made slow progress trudging through the deep snow, my boots sinking into the drifts that already reached well past my knees while plenty more fell from the sky. Boxy old models of cars — far less streamlined than the fancy sports cars I had seen in present-day California — sat abandoned along the sides of the roads, their exteriors swamped in several inches of fresh powder.

I didn't detect a single sign of life in these severe conditions, imagining every living creature besides me had the common sense to hunker down in safety to wait out the storm. The town appeared vacant, aside from the faint sound of the tavern's cheery music that battled the whistling wind. I headed there, desperate for reprieve from the storm before I froze as solid as the iceberg Shannon drove against the hull of the *Titanic*.

What's the harm in waiting things out in there? I shuffled faster through the thick drifts. I could always search for them once the storm ended.

I aimed my feet toward the tavern. Pillars fashioned from knobby pine buckled under the weight of the heavy snow that covered the roof like a dense layer of whipped cream. Clumps of snow clung to the irregular whorls and knots along each pillar in bizarre patterns, giving the impression of distorted faces of trolls and goblins that made the hair on the back of my neck stand on end. Beneath the new accumulation of snow, the boardwalk creaked with my every step. I trudged up to the door, eager for a respite from the eerie resemblances to frightening faces and the storm itself.

The blustery wind and snow followed me through the door. I quickly swung it shut behind me and brushed off the snow from my sleeves. When I turned, a small gasp escaped my lips, grateful I had not shed my coat or hood. I instantly spotted Gaia and Shannon tucked into a wooden booth with a pair of brothers as similar in appearance as a set of bookends. The fatigue and anguish had disappeared from Shannon's lean face, replaced instead by a rosy glow, making me surmise that the storm indeed seemed the work of Mother Nature alone. A giddy smile wrapped around Shannon's lips, apparently from one brother's interest in her. I knew how she felt. Sometimes you just needed a distraction to dull the stabbing grief of lost love.

She stroked her long braid over one shoulder, blushing when he whispered softly in her ear. He planted a quick peck on her cheek and tipped his cowboy hat toward her before rising from his spot to make his way across the room. Fearful she might detect my presence, I ducked behind a coat tree, heavy with discarded garments. Her eyes followed his path across the room, but she fortunately appeared blinded by attraction and noticed nothing aside from him.

A middle-aged waitress approached me. Her lips painted a deep scarlet, she wore a wide streak of blush to accentuate each high cheekbone and bright blue eye shadow above each lid. Though soft around the middle, her arms appeared strong from carrying huge trays of food and drinks. "Haven't seen you in these parts before," she said. "Name's Hazel, and this here's me and my Hughie's place. Come on in. You won't have much fun standing there all alone, now," she scolded, beckoning me out from behind the coat tree.

"Do you have anything in the back?" I whispered, just loud enough to be heard over the music. "I don't want to draw attention, if you know what I mean."

She gave me a knowing nod, accustomed to similar requests from other patrons who snuck out to visit this location. "Say no more," she said, motioning for me to follow her. I kept my head low, the hood obscuring most of my vision, including my sight of Gaia and Shannon for a moment.

"Right this way, ma'am," she directed, pointing to an empty bar stool in the back corner before she left to attend to another table's needs. "Hughie," she said to the beefy bartender behind the counter, "can you help her out for me, please?"

"Sure thing, sweetheart," Hughie replied and gave Hazel a wink. He set his elbows on the bar and leaned toward me. His bushy mustache concealed his entire upper lip when he asked, "So, what'll it be?"

Passing him a handful of coins Pele had provided, I replied, "Just a soda pop, please."

"That's it?" he asked, somewhat surprised.

I nodded. "That's it."

He rolled his eyes and mouthed the word, "O-kay," before preparing my drink from the fountain. While I waited, I glanced around the room, scanning the area for the nearest means to escape this confined space. Besides the front door, I noticed only three other exits: one to the restrooms, one I presumed led to the kitchen, and one out the back should I need it.

Between intermittent peeks in Shannon and Gaia's direction, I surveyed the tavern's walls dressed in bold floral wallpaper. The colorful print contrasted sharply with the other décor in the room. Framed photographs in faded, sepia tones hung only inches apart, depicting the Old Wild West where hardened men and women alike posed for portraits with their rifles and revolvers. Trophies of mule deer, coyotes, and wolves peered down lifelessly from their wooden mounts. And on one side, a large bearskin pelt of thick cinnamon fur lay tacked to the wall, each paw ending with a set of long slashing claws.

Eager to look at something besides the prematurely silenced lives of those unfortunate animals, my gaze shifted to the patrons of the bar. I noticed most individuals wore cowboy hats like the brothers that sat beside the other Elementals, plus holsters buckled around their waists. I prayed Gaia avoided a scene with Shannon inside the bar where others might be in danger. And if she didn't wait, I decided I should devise a back-up plan, even if I used my powers in a desperate attempt to save these strangers.

I began working through my strategy when a gust of arctic air rushed in as another patron entered the bar. Instinctively, my eyes turned to assess the stranger standing in the doorway. Wearing a pair of noticeable red gloves, he pulled his hands from his pockets and dumped the snow off his ten-gallon hat. He looked only a year, maybe two older than me, despite the thin layer of patchy stubble coating his chiseled jaw and stark cheekbones. He had eyes the color of roasted almonds set wide on his face. He removed his snowy leather duster and added it to the tree. Beneath, his button-down plaid shirt, sun-bleached bandana, and faded jeans appeared stained from the sweat and grime of working long hours in the field.

Hazel rose to meet him and readily motioned to an available table. But he didn't immediately accept her offer. Instead, he gazed across the room and paused. His eyes seemed to rest on my face, gauging me with sudden interest. One side of his mouth turned up in half a smile. He shook his head at Hazel and gestured toward the empty spot by me at the bar instead.

I whipped my head around, sinking lower into my seat, wishing I could disappear into the flowery wallpaper to camouflage myself from Gaia, Shannon...and him. *What had*

Pele gotten me into this time? I worried and hid my face and hair behind my hood. How could I possibly hide from them in this tiny room?

Afraid Gaia might spot me, I watched from the corner of my eye. The guy pulled out the bar stool next to me and settled into the seat. The stool creaked under his weight as he turned to face me. Ice crystals dotted his thin, scraggly beard and dampened his face in a layer of moisture, melting in the welcoming warmth of the tavern. "Howdy, miss," he said and shifted his stool a little closer to mine. He slipped off his red gloves, dropping them onto the bar, then extended a thick, calloused hand in front of my face, waiting. Embarrassed I might draw more attention to myself should I refuse, I reluctantly stuck my palm in his. He lifted it to his mouth and placed a gentle kiss upon the back of my hand. Despite his gruff appearance, his demeanor seemed startlingly polite. A part of me felt surprised when my cheeks grew warm.

"Tate Meachum's the name. It's mighty fine to meet you, Miss —" he said with a deliberate pause, as if expecting me to complete his sentence.

Hesitant to disclose my identity with Gaia so near, I snuck a quick peek over my shoulder at Shannon's booth, relieved to find them absorbed with their company. I looked back at Tate and whispered the first inconspicuous name that popped into my head, "Bethany."

"I reckon I haven't seen you in these parts 'til now, Miss Bethany. You ain't from around here, are you?"

I felt the blush rise higher into my cheeks. Wasn't there someone else he'd prefer to talk to so I could focus on this last mission? "Oh, I um...no, I'm...um...just passing through," I stammered distractedly and chanced another glance at Shannon and Gaia from beneath my hood. Fortunately, they looked quite preoccupied. Shannon laughed lightheartedly from her perch on one brother's lap. Meanwhile, the other brother wrapped his arm possessively around Gaia's shoulder. I rolled my eyes, certain neither understood the inherent dangers Shannon and Gaia posed.

"The usual, Tate?" Hazel asked him, interrupting my thoughts.

"Make it two," he replied, nodding his head in my direction. He scooted his bar stool closer to mine.

Understanding his intent, I quickly piped up, "That's okay. I'm good." I held up my soda glass and inched my stool away from his. "Besides, I need to get going soon."

"Well, Miss Bethany, before you leave this here tavern, I s'pose I might interest you in a dance?" Before waiting for my agreement, he turned and hollered across the room, "Eh, Billy Joe. Ain't you got your banjo on you?"

"Yeah? What's it to you?" A scraggly man in overalls replied.

"Well, how 'bout you play us a tune?" Tate asked. He ran his fingers through his shaggy hair. Another table enthusiastically echoed his request, begging for Billy Joe to entertain them with their favorite song.

As Billy Joe struck up his banjo, Tate turned toward me, holding out his palm. I saw lines of dirt embedded deep within its creases, evidence of the hard labor he endured day after day, regardless of the weather. Still, my pity for his small joy of entertainment didn't outweigh my fear of having Gaia notice me in this tavern.

I resisted, shaking my head resolutely. "Thanks, but I think I'm afraid I'll have to pass—"

"Aw, c'mon now," he said, grabbing my hand firmly in his. "I ain't gonna bite. Just one quick dance."

I shot Hazel a pleading look when she set his drink in front of him.

"Hush now, Tate," Hazel said and placed a strong hand on his shoulder to stuff him back onto his seat. "She ain't wanting you to be botherin' her all night. Why don't we find you a new spot?"

"I don't need no new spot," Tate objected. "This one serves me just fine."

Behind the bar, Hughie's ears perked up. "You givin' my woman a hard time?" he said, jabbing a thumb in Hazel's direction.

"I ain't giving no one a hard time. All I done was ask Miss Bethany for a dance. Ain't no harm in that now, is there?"

"There's more to it than that. You got no right talkin' to my woman that way," Hughie threatened with an irritated twitch of his thick mustache. Ready to settle this on the spot, he puffed out his chest and rolled his sleeves halfway up his arms that looked as thick as tree branches.

"Hughie! Let it go," Hazel scolded. But I could tell from his biceps flexing beneath his flannel shirt, that he had no intention of heeding her advice. His face reddened as he leaned over the bar and invaded Tate's personal space.

My eyes flashed from Hughie to Tate and back again. This was not going to end well, I feared. I pulled my hood tighter around my head and sank into my stool. I contemplated the prospect of venturing back outside. Would I fare better waiting out the storm? Or surviving another minute inside this tavern where a potential fight brewed?

Before I had a chance to answer my own question, Hughie pulled back his fist, aiming right for Tate's broad nose. *Uh, oh,* I thought and slid off my stool to safety.

Hughie took a huge swing, but Tate safely ducked out of the way. Surprised his fist made contact with nothing but air, Hughie's momentum carried his weight forward and his torso sprawled across the counter of the bar. He knocked over our drinks, spilling their contents. The glasses crashed to the floor.

Hughie's nostrils flared. He scrambled back to his feet and

cocked his arm for unleashing another punch. This time, his fist connected with Tate's left eye. The blow threw Tate from his stool. But from the look on Tate's reddening face, I had a suspicion the hit bruised his ego more than his eye. He quickly scrambled to his feet, eager to finish the scuffle.

Within seconds, the other patrons in the tavern left their seats to support their friends (or to engage in the simple thrill of the brawl, I couldn't be certain). As fists flew across the crowded room, I suspected the pair of brothers who sat with Shannon and Gaia had also joined the tussle. I glanced across the room, wondering how the other Elementals fared in the midst of this mess.

Only Shannon and Gaia's booth sat empty.

"Oh my God! I don't believe it," I muttered to myself. "They're gone!" But when? How? Why? Kicking myself for losing contact during that brief moment when Hughie's temper had flared and Tate's obstinate behavior had left him with a pretty shiner, I hurried through the commotion surrounding me, ducking a few falling bodies en route, and slipped outside.

The snowfall had lessened considerably during my time inside the tavern, but the shock of the biting wind hit me the second I stepped out the door. Pulling my coat tightly around me to ward off the cold, I spun my head from left to right, hoping to catch a glimpse of them despite the frigid gusts that drove the flakes against my cheeks.

Squinting into the shards of snow, I spotted a dark mass about halfway down the street that potentially resembled four bodies huddled closely together to block the intense wind. I headed in their direction, wading through the deep snow, trying to reach them in time. Fortunately, they made slower progress than I did through the thick powder that buried the street. I trudged behind, noticing the mass divide in half, like Gaia and Shannon had split, each on the arm of a brother. But when I got closer, I realized I had made a mistake. Instead, the brothers had separated from the girls, heading back to their home I assumed. Meanwhile, Gaia dragged Shannon in the opposite direction, to her great disapproval. Her cries of heartache carried over the wind. I ducked behind a pillar on the boardwalk to hide. Shannon's rising anger made every word she uttered come out as a yell. I listened intently, eager to see the outcome and complete Pele's final mission so I could return to Sully and normality.

Just a little further, I told myself and pushed my longing to see him from my mind, forcing myself to focus on this moment in time. Only a few yards away, I kept my eyes trained on the girls, trying to predict their next actions. Gaia looped her arm through Shannon's to lead her out of town.

However, Shannon refused to go easily. Pushing Gaia away, she screamed, "No!" as tears leaked from her eyes. "Not this time. I don't want to leave again!"

"But you must, Shannon. It ends now," Gaia told her. A final bout of determination refueled her tired emerald eyes. "I won't pursue you any longer, but you still have a choice."

"A choice?" Shannon exclaimed, her voice cracking with disbelief and exasperation. "Not once have you let me choose anything about this life!"

"You have always had this choice," Gaia declared. A wicked grin toyed with her mouth. Looking straight into Shannon's eyes with a powerful conviction, she explained, "You can either join me or I will destroy you and everyone you love." Without waiting for Shannon's answer, she gave a clear reminder of her resolve. Her eyes flickered toward the towering peak before she pounded her fists into the snow with all her might.

"No," Shannon breathed, following Gaia's gaze up the steep slope.

Seconds later, a frightening noise emanated from the mountain in a booming *whoomph* that echoed throughout the valley. I peered at the source of the sound. A terrified gasp escaped my lips when I realized her intent.

Gaia's forceful blow to the ground had generated a massive avalanche.

While noise of the bar fight spilled out the door of the tavern halfway down the street, I could only gape in awe, watching the snow shift on one portion of the mountain. The rumbling continued, triggering the avalanche to wrap from one side of the mountain's bowl to the other. It began its speedy descent directly toward the town.

I sucked in my breath. "Oh. My. God," I whispered, helplessly watching the billowing mass of white careen down the slope.

Suddenly, I didn't care what happened to Gaia or Shannon or the brothers. I turned on my heels. I made slow progress through the drifts that smothered the street. My muscles burned from exertion and my mind raced through a short list of options to ensure my escape.

I planned to slip into an alley to avoid the rushing snow when I spotted Tate exit the tavern up ahead, staggering from the abuse his body withstood.

"Tate! Watch out!" I screamed. Changing my mind, I bolted straight for him, trying to reach him in time.

He spun in the direction of his name, squinting with his good eye. His face turned ashen at the sight of the approaching avalanche. I glanced over my shoulder, surprised at the speed of the rushing snow. At the end of the street, buildings funneled the snow through the street with surprising force, quickly swallowing everything in its path.

Including *me*.

Engulfed in a roiling wash of white, I lost sight of the world around me. The barreling mass of snow drove my helpless body forward. I swore under my breath. *No! This can't be happening. This was supposed to be my last mission!*

Furious, I swam toward the surface, desperate for air, fearful I wouldn't make it in time. I forced heat to build inside my core, letting it radiate outward from my palms in a frantic attempt to melt the snow.

Eventually, I reached the surface, gasping for a breath and climbed from my hole to search for survivors.

The whole street lay covered in white except for one recognizable object. A red glove punched through the snow.

Tate's glove.

"Tate!" I screamed and dug furiously through the snow, grasping huge handfuls. I unburied his arm, hoping I'd uncover his head before it was too late. I willed more heat into my hands in a frantic attempt to melt the pile on top of his body. My hands clawed at the snow until they reached his ten-gallon hat. I yanked it from his head, making a small pocket of air. Still I heard no sound.

"C'mon, Tate. You can make it," I encouraged him and scooped out the space in front of his face. I hoped the snow covering him had held enough air for him to breathe. If I'd left him too long, his own exhalations could become poisonous.

I was thrilled to hear him sputter on the wickedly cold air, erasing my fears.

"Are you okay?" I asked, panting from exertion. I lay on my belly in the thick snow, my face only inches from his, eager for his response.

"You...did...it," he gasped between staggered breaths. His head popped up through the hole I'd melted. Thick white flakes coated his hair and lashes. His skin looked several shades paler than it had in the tavern, making me tremble at his narrow brush with death. Slowly, the color returned to his cheeks as he sucked in deep breaths of fresh air. "You did it," he repeated. The corners of his mouth turned up into a grin of relief. "You saved me."

I did, I thought and smiled back. I scooped large handfuls away from him, helping uncover his shoulders and torso, grateful I had not lost another soul to the fury of an Elemental. My family, Lucius from Pompeii, and Monifa from Atlantis may have all suffered cruel, unfortunate deaths, but I managed to save Tate. His words repeated in my mind, making my smile widen.

But before I could utter a word to express my profound relief he had survived, he kissed me firmly, deeply, right on my surprised mouth, his stubbly beard and mustache scratching my lips. For a moment, I couldn't move, paralyzed by the shock of his action and the exhilaration of his good fortune. While his lips lingered on mine, I thought of Sully and how much I missed the sweet, soft kisses we had shared. I suddenly felt a dire need to return to his time and tell him how much he meant to me, even if I had to confess to Pele I was done with my training. What was the point of all of these dangerous missions, anyway? Was she deliberately trying to get me killed? Like Gaia, I felt myself near the point of breaking. I had absolutely no patience left for these life-and-death situations.

With renewed determination, I broke away from Tate's kiss. "Let's get you outta here," I said, letting my hands grow hot once more.

I helped him wriggle free from his spot until he could stand on the surface. Shivering in the blustery wind, I pressed my heated palms to his clothes, melting the snow in an instant.

"How are you doing that?" he wondered, astonished.

"Don't ask," I replied, knowing I shouldn't use my powers in front of him, but so little time remained to prevent him from overexposure and hypothermia in this type of weather.

"Come on, we need to find the others," I told him once I finished my task. Together, we walked back and forth, crisscrossing our tracks to make sure we'd covered every inch of snow in front of the tavern. We uncovered Billy Joe with his banjo and one other patron with a thick, bloody lip from the brawl. The banjo had seen better days, but both men seemed perfectly fine. Confident we had scoured the area completely, I realized I had not found Gaia or Shannon.

"Are you sure you're okay?" I asked Tate before I left to search for the other Elementals.

He nodded. "Never better."

A warm smile filled my face, knowing my role in securing his safety. "I'm sorry to do this, but I've gotta go," I admitted and turned up the street.

"Miss Bethany?" he called, but I kept walking, focused on my target. I felt his calloused hand slip inside mine. "Miss Bethany," he repeated, reminding me of the pseudonym I'd used to hide my identity.

I whirled around and glanced into his wide-set eyes, the left one beginning to swell shut from Hughie's punch.

"Thank you," he whispered and swept me into a final kiss farewell. Pangs of missing Sully flooded my heart, mixed with guilt and confusion. *Is it considered cheating,* I wondered, *if I didn't initiate the kiss?*

"Glad I could help," I told him and walked away. And I meant every word.

I plodded across the snow for the next half hour or so, searching for others but finding none. When I rounded the corner of town, I heard a soft weeping and stopped suddenly in my tracks, pressing my back against the building. Shannon knelt beside the bodies of the brothers, inert upon the ground. I stared at their pale faces, deprived of oxygen for too long. A grim realization struck my heart. She hadn't made it in time.

Gaia stood beside the weeping girl. "I can't do this alone," she admitted. "You are destined for this. And I believe deep inside, you know it, too. You have seen the marvelous powers you wield and understand the vast untapped potential you still possess. Now is the time for you to channel your energy and focus it for a single cause.

"I can't," Shannon said. Her lips trembled, exhausting her strength in this final act of defiance. "I won't."

Gaia's eyes flickered. I knew that satisfied look. With Shannon fading in resolve, Gaia had almost won.

Gaia threatened, "Perhaps your twin will be more receptive to my invitation." And with a dramatic show of her threat, she raised her hand high into the air, poising it above the ground for effect.

"No," Shannon sobbed weakly. "Don't."

With her spirit broken after her tragic loss aboard the *Titanic*, plus here after the avalanche, I knew Shannon couldn't bear to lose another person she loved. Her shoulders heaved with unspoken sorrow. She clutched her knees, rocking on her heels as if contemplating her decision. Would she willingly sacrifice her twin sister or accept the role of Hydros herself?

Cold, wet, and defeated, Shannon begged, "Leave my family out of this. This is only between you and me. Do I have your promise?"

I swallowed hard. She had made her choice.

"My promise?" Gaia asked. Her lips drew into a cunning grin that made my insides churn. So close to giving up, now Gaia grew in strength, feeding off the sweet taste of victory.

Shannon continued, her voice faint from exhaustion, "Yes, that as soon as we're finished with your quest, I can go back home. You'll leave me alone. That you won't touch my family."

"Agreed."

"Fine," the girl relented in a small voice, her shoulders slumping forward. "Let's get this over with. So where do we begin?"

"First, you need training to control your powers," Gaia announced. "Then we need Fire and Air."

I gulped, knowing at that moment they had decided to come

141

after Skye and me.

CHAPTER FOURTEEN

During the journey back to the present time, the entire hike to Volcano House, and the whole return trip to Hilo in Auntie Lulu's Firebird, I thought of little beyond the cave in Bora Bora where Gaia and Hydros had found us and tortured Skye, eventually breaking her spirit until she agreed to join their cause. Now, she seemed a mere fragment of her former self, as twisted and evil as Gaia because I had failed to prepare her for the encounter. Unfortunately, like Pele had claimed, it was too late for me to change the past.

But when Lulu pulled up in her driveway and I noticed the chipped paint of her white lattice fence, the reality of the present rushed back in full force. I had never finished that project, had never apologized to Sully...all because Lulu had spontaneously decided to visit her sister.

It seemed like forever since I'd last spoken to Sully, like ages had passed instead of the couple of days I'd spent working with Pele. Without a word to Lulu, I threw my bag on the bed and dashed to the public library, anxious to get there before it closed. Trails of sweat streamed down my brow while I logged into the computer, hoping he'd still want to speak to me after my unexplained avoidance, even if the computer terminal seemed about the least private place for us to talk.

When the video link fed through, Sully looked surprised and

slightly upset. I figured he had every right to be mad after I'd unintentionally blown him off. But I never suspected there was more.

Not until it was too late.

"Nice to hear from you," he said, his voice unnaturally sarcastic.

"Ohmigod, Sully! You wouldn't believe what I've been through." I sighed, launching into a lengthy explanation of my recent problems. In hindsight, I probably shouldn't have begun our conversation with complaints about wasting my time and accomplishing next to nothing. I should've asked about *him*, doted on *him*, and mentioned how much I missed *him*. But I didn't. And I'd live to regret that mistake.

"Worse, Pele's hiding something from me. I know she is," I said, drumming my fingers on the tabletop, dwelling on my own concerns. "If only I could get her to reveal everything to me. But how?" I wondered, like I held a discussion with myself.

When Sully emitted a heavy, bored sigh, I realized my error. "So enough about me. How are things with you?" I asked, focusing my attention on his pale blue eyes.

Sully shifted uncomfortably in his chair, appearing distracted. He ran his fingers over his light brown hair and fidgeted with his hat, like its every position felt awkward upon his head. I blinked, reading his moves. This wasn't him trying to focus, like the time he revealed the fire goddess's identity to me. Something weighed on his mind, something I suspected he'd rather I didn't know.

"Something's up," I told him. "I can tell, so don't try to hide it."

His eyes looked everywhere but at my face on the computer screen. After an unusually long pause, he replied in a falsely casual tone, "I don't know what you're talking about."

I snorted. "Whatever, Sully. Out with it. Tell me what's bugging you."

"Huh?" A nervous expression passed across his face, feigning ignorance.

My stomach flipped upside down. Why hadn't I seen this earlier? I cursed myself for getting so wrapped up in my own unsolvable issues. "You're acting weird. I know something's bothering you, so just tell me already. What is it? Did something happen to Micah or Cam?"

Sully shook his head silently.

"Then it's *you*, isn't it? C'mon. What happened? What's your big news?" Maybe I'd misjudged him. He obviously had something important to share. Was it something about his new job? Or his plans for the summer?

Summer…that was it! My eyes brightened and I perched excitedly on the edge of my chair. "You finished final exams, didn't you?" I guessed, irritated with myself for forgetting something that important. "I completely forgot to wish you good luck!"

"Well…yeah…I did," he stammered. "But that's not it."

"Oh, come on, Sully. I don't have the energy to play this guessing game. The past few days, I've spent most of my time spying on my mortal enemy and the girl I destroyed, talking to an ancient woman who loads me with chores, trying to decipher the cryptic messages of a temperamental goddess, and stealing my sleeping bag back from a stray dog who's always looking for treats." Subconsciously, I peeked over my shoulder, wondering if anyone overheard our conversation. Fortunately, the librarians appeared absorbed with their tasks of helping patrons locate particular books and use the self-checkout machines.

"Seriously," I prodded, flashing him my most convincing smile, "I could use some good news to ground me for a change."

Sully pinched his eyebrows together in confusion, pausing for a moment before speaking. "Y'know, Jordan, I don't pretend to understand who you are or what you've been doing." His voice carried a cool, distant tone. Even his words sounded a bit too formal for Sully. How long had he rehearsed this speech?

I flinched, my optimism suddenly fading. An unsettling discomfort filled my gut and I held my breath, waiting for him to continue.

He sighed. "I don't know what I expected when you left, but I guess I thought you'd actually miss me while you were gone. Instead it seems like…" He was reluctant to finish his thought.

"Seems like…?" I prodded.

"I dunno exactly. It's just different now. You've got loads of your own stuff going on and it kinda seems like we're drifting apart."

"So what are you saying?" I asked in a flat tone. I bit my lip to keep it from trembling.

"Look, Jordan. Distance relationships are hard. I just thought we could beat the odds and make things work, but I guess I was wrong."

"Sully, please. Don't do this to me. I haven't been gone that long."

"Still, Jordan. You say you're so busy, but really, how hard is it to make a little time to talk to me every day? I'd understand if you met someone else—"

"But there isn't anyone else," I interrupted. For a second, I thought about Tate's kiss after I dug him free from the avalanche, but decided that didn't count. It was a spontaneous, incidental act to express his profound relief and joy that he survived. Nothing more.

"It's not that I don't like you, because I do," Sully explained slowly, carefully choosing every word. "It's just that part of me expected you'd only be gone on a short vacation. This'll be the summer before our senior year, and I thought you and I would… well, you know…"

"Spend it together?" I wagered. My heart sank deeper within

my chest.

"And with you in Hawaii," he continued, having difficulty meeting my gaze. "I know you're busy with your stuff, but it doesn't sound like you'll be coming back anytime soon. If at all."

"Let me ask you one thing, Shayne," I said on one of the few occasions I'd actually used his real name. "Is she someone I know?"

He blinked. "What?"

"Oh, please. Enough with the formalities already. You met someone else, right?"

It took him an awfully long time to respond. "Um...yeah, I suppose."

"So, is she someone I know?" I repeated.

"I...uh...guess so."

"It's Karli, isn't it," I said, thinking fast. Chances were, once I'd left he'd gotten back together with his ex pretty fast. I knew from the first time I'd met her that she didn't like me, especially not when her boyfriend had shown a little too much interest in helping me meet his circle of friends at the lunch table.

"No, it's not Karli," Sully admitted. "She's still with Justin."

Well, that's good at least, I thought, remembering the smug smile she wore after Mr. Mendoza flunked me from Driver's Ed for my stint of panicked driving. It was an honest mistake—I'd simply thought I had spotted Skye standing alone on the hillside in the rain and needed to escape immediately. Mr. Mendoza hadn't found it the least bit funny, however, so he took over the wheel instead. In the back of my mind, I was relieved to hear Sully hadn't chosen Karli. He deserved someone nicer than her, someone who appreciated his good points instead of always putting herself first.

"Not Tessa. She's probably still with Micah," I said, thinking aloud. "Is it Isa?" I could see him attracted to her pretty, typically soft-spoken personality. I'd bet she'd be really sweet if she didn't spend so much time hanging around with Karli and Tessa.

"Nope," he replied, his expression growing more uncomfortable.

I scrunched up my nose, surprised I could think beyond my jealousy to guess who else he'd like. "Hmm, don't tell me. I bet it's…"

Suddenly it hit me, the truth striking me right between the eyes. "It's not *Bethany*, is it?"

"It just kind of happened," he explained, apologetically. "We were at a bonfire at the beach and we kind of ended up together, I guess."

"Kind of?"

Sully frowned. "I know what you're thinking—but she's changed. She said she didn't mean to hurt you, it's just that she's—"

"Available," I interrupted. "And I'm not." I heaved a deep, disappointed sigh.

Sully might have claimed he liked danger, but that word described the polar opposite of Bethany Donovan. So, when it came down to it, Sully really wanted someone who was around. And perhaps that was exactly what drew him to me in the first place—I was always there. At Micah's, at school…and now I wasn't.

I got it. But that didn't mean I liked it.

"Don't do this to me, Sully. Not now. You don't understand what I've been through lately. I just got back from Atlantis."

"Yeah, I went there once, too," he admitted casually, almost like he forgot that he'd broken up with me. "But I went so fast through the tube that I missed seeing all the sharks."

I blinked, completely baffled. "What are you talking about?"

"Atlantis, right? The hotel on Paradise Island in the Bahamas. Did you get to try the water slides through the shark tanks?"

"No, Sully, the *real* Atlantis. Before it sunk beneath the sea.

Sully, I almost *died*."

"I know. It's a pretty intense ride, isn't it?"

I shook my head, baffled that after all he'd witnessed, all he knew I'd been through, he still didn't fully understand. "And I went on the *Titanic*."

"Huh," Sully said, scratching his head. "Didn't know they released it again in theaters."

I was tempted to say it wasn't a movie but the real ship when I decided my point was irrelevant. Things were over between us. I'd had a second chance with him and blew it. And despite the ordeals I'd endured, he didn't believe me, didn't believe the reasons I messed things up between us, and probably never would.

"So I guess this is good-bye," I admitted with regret. Tears built in the corners of my eyes.

Sully frowned. "Just remember, if you ever need anything, Jordan, anything at all…"

A sad, crooked smiled crossed my face. Even when he was dumping me, he still acted helpful.

"Good-bye, Sully," I whispered before I logged off, afraid I couldn't keep the tears at bay much longer. This whole breakup would be worse if he actually saw me cry.

After Sully hung up, I laid my head on my arms across the keyboard and sobbed until the librarian kicked me off the computer five minutes before the building closed.

Chapter Fifteen

In a daze, I strolled aimlessly from the library, confused and alone. Part of me hoped Kea would turn up so I could unload the myriad thoughts plaguing my mind. Instead, I only had myself to argue with.

It's not like you didn't do the same thing to him before, my conscience told me in a bossy tone.

"That was different," I objected aloud, not caring if anyone heard or regarded me as crazy for talking to myself. "I did it to protect his life."

And Micah? Of course my conscience had to bring up that topic again.

"I thought I liked him," I admitted.

It's better for Sully this way. Now he can be with a normal teenage girl.

I snorted. "Like Bethany is normal?"

More so than you.

"Thanks for the reminder," I said, bitter.

Hoping to rid my annoying conscience's voice from my head, I plugged a finger into each ear and hummed a catchy tune as my feet carried me back toward Lulu's house. But instead of going inside, I turned for the beach and ambled across the sand, out amongst the lava rocks until I'd ventured far from everyone. Satisfied I was alone, I plunked down onto the rocks and cried until my tears ran dry.

Guilt clouded my decisions. Before, I watched my family, Lucius, and William die simply because of their association to me. And I couldn't save the poor slave girl, Monifa, from the drowning of Atlantis or the doomed passengers aboard the sinking *Titanic*. All those innocent victims had experienced the wrath of the other Elementals.

But Hydros perished at my *own* hand after I had manipulated the fire tornado toward The Three in an attempt to silence her destructive wave from reaching shore. I remembered the grim scene all too well, the wooden spike protruding from her thin abdomen. I remembered how Gaia had held her protectively, lovingly cradling her injured body as Hydros faded from this world.

True, I had saved many lives in the Bay Area that day. But the despair of taking another's soul outweighed all the joy I'd felt for the briefest of moments.

Why bother with my responsibilities and obligations? Where had it gotten me? Absolutely nowhere. I'd lost everyone I ever cared about in one way or another—all because of the other Elementals. All I wanted was to disappear, to go someplace where I could actually feel wanted, needed. Someplace besides here. Maybe I wasn't cut out for this...maybe the whole world was doomed because deep down I wouldn't commit my heart and soul to my role and refused to accept my Elemental name, Pyr.

But you managed to save Tate from the avalanche, my conscience chimed in.

I blinked. "You're right." A small smile filled my face, recalling Tate's enthusiastic thank you when I dug him out of the treacherous snow. With his help, we managed to save a few other people from the tavern as well. I wiped the tears from my eyes, saddened I hadn't reached Shannon's pair of brothers in time. But I wasn't a superhero; I couldn't save everyone. Still, the relief and happiness of finding Tate alive proved a valid reason to press forward.

That's it! Why hadn't I realized this before? Hadn't Pele made some offhand comment about wanting me to figure this out by myself? My smile widened. Maybe some good could still come from the pain of losing Sully.

I rose to my feet and wandered further across the lava bed that protruded into the water, far from the locals and tourists who milled around the beach. Suddenly, Kea appeared by my side, panting happily. She brushed her body against my leg so my fingers strategically touched her fur, most likely to scratch an itch between her shoulder blades.

"I'm sorry, Kea," I apologized to the stray, like she could understand my every word. "I'm going to go away now. To a place where I'll actually be of some good. It's time for a new beginning for me." I sighed, almost second-guessing my choice. "Which means I doubt I'll ever see you again."

She stopped panting to study me pensively with alert eyes, like she not only understood me completely, but approved of my decision.

"Thanks for the support," I said and bent down to wrap my arms around her neck. She pressed her chin snug across my back to return my hug. "I'll miss you," I whispered. "You've been a good friend. I'm sure someone else will think so, too, and want you to be a part of their family."

Kea pulled her head back and licked my cheek with her rough tongue. Her jaw dropped and she began to pant again, letting her hot dog breath hit me full force in the face.

"Bye, girl," I said with a final scratch on her head. I quickly stood, eager to place some distance between my nose and her mouth.

Seconds later, her eyes left mine and focused on an object in the distance. *Probably that bird again*, I mused, watching the dog bound across the lava rock and out of sight.

"It's time," I told myself and heaved a deep breath, realizing I forgot to thank Auntie Lulu for everything she had done for me before I left. Something in the depths of my heart told me that she'd understand.

Consuming myself with white fire, I cleared my mind and recited a single thought: *Take me to where I'm needed.* I wanted to feel normal, needed, loved. And that could only happen if I distanced myself from Pele and let my heart dictate my next move. I'd had enough of her dangerous excursions to past destinations—this time I planned to go wherever the magic chose to send me.

The heat inside of me spread through every cell within my body. A feeling of contentment swelled in my core, radiating as soothing warmth to the tips of my appendages and into my mind.

"Take me where I'm needed," I spoke the thought aloud in a clear voice, letting the desire consume every cell in my entire body until I believed it with all my heart. I repeated Pele's *ke ahi kea* chant again and again. The warmth of contentment spread throughout my body, easing the pain of Sully's breakup, allowing me to focus on my new direction in life.

A direction of my *choosing this time*, I thought with pride. Tongues of white fire lapped at my heels, spinning upward, and consuming every inch of my body. The black lava rock beneath my feet and the vast ocean stretching to the horizon faded from view. The magic spun me from this land into a fresh, exciting future.

CHAPTER SIXTEEN

A warm tropical breeze brushed my cheeks and the bright rays of the late morning sun hit me with their full intensity. I did it! I rolled over on my pillow, letting my head sink into its downy surface. I actually felt rejuvenated now that the pain from Sully's breakup had dulled. "A new time, a new place...a new beginning," I whispered merrily to myself. Happiness spread to every part of my body, contemplating the novel future of my own creation.

Yet when I opened my eyes, all the joy I'd felt upon awakening vanished in an instant. I flew up in bed and rubbed my eyes, unable to believe what I saw. Nothing had changed.

Nothing.

Every feature of Lulu's spare bedroom looked identical as when I had left—the sheets, the curtains, even the flimsy little dresser. Not a single object stood out of its designated place.

I wanted to cry, realizing my ineptitude. What did it matter if I could engulf my body in white fire, if the flames didn't actually transport me anywhere? Or worse, what if I couldn't produce white fire at all? What if everything I'd lived these past few days had merely been a dream?

Take me where I'm needed. Who'd have thought I'd end up back at Auntie Lulu's doing more chores? Or be stuck here tending to her frail, sickly aged form until the doctor eventually confined her to bed? I gulped, unable to imagine the long years that lay ahead.

I stumbled out of bed and staggered to the kitchen on lethargic, weak legs. Lacking the energy to do anything, I plopped in a chair by the table and let my head fall into my hands. Depressing thoughts consumed my mind.

A few minutes later, Lulu entered the room with a spring in her step. She pulled out a chair and sat across from me at the table. "I'm thinking purple," she said in a cheerful tone.

I lifted my head off my hands to glance at her. Aside from the carefree look painted across her face, she seemed the same as yesterday. She'd even worn the identical shirt two days in a row to save on laundry.

"Excuse me?" I grumbled, confused.

"Well, *light* purple," she clarified.

My head dropped into my hands again. I muttered, "I don't get it," And to be honest, I didn't care, either. The magic had failed. What a waste Pele's training had been.

"I think it's time for a fresh coat of paint. With all the improvements you've made around here, pink just doesn't seem to fit this old place anymore. Besides, Lipoa's has a sale on outdoor paint colors. A new look, a new color…a new beginning. What do you think?"

My heart stopped. "What did you say?" I managed, wondering if she'd possibly overheard me from my bedroom. But that was impossible…especially when I'd whispered the thought to myself!

"Could you be a dear and start on the house for little old me?" Lulu warbled and pushed some bills across the table.

I scratched my head, convinced I'd simply misheard her. "Now?"

She nodded. "The sale ends today."

It didn't matter that I hadn't eaten anything yet. I doubted I could've kept the food down in my unsettled stomach anyway. After stuffing her money deep into my pocket and jamming my feet into my sandals, I trudged out the door, purposefully letting it slam loudly upon its hinges behind me.

"Take me to where I'm needed," I grunted, kicking a stone off the sidewalk and into the grass as I tramped down the hill into town. By far, that had to have been the stupidest idea I'd dreamed up in a long time. Like I didn't have anything better to do than more chores around Lulu's cottage. A part of me felt like she just used me for free labor to fix up the place before selling it for a bundle so she could move into one of those retirement condos down by the beach.

I began to wonder why I even bothered coming to Hilo in the first place. Things would've been so much easier if I had simply stayed in Pacifica near Sully. I hadn't realized exactly how much I missed him until he was gone. It might've been a challenge to avoid Micah for the rest of the school year after Celia made it abundantly clear that she didn't want anyone in her family to go anywhere near me. But I'm positive I would've found a way to fare better than I did here.

I envisioned Sully at the party on the beach, sitting around the bonfire, talking to Bethany. She laughed at something he'd said and casually slipped her hand inside his. She batted her eyelashes at him and Sully swallowed hard, unable to turn away from her gaze. For a long moment, they sat in silence with their foreheads almost touching. She moved closer until their lips…

Get over it, Jordan, I chastised myself. *It's done.* Still, those words did little to erase the pain and hurt clouding my heart.

After rounding the corner into town, I paused in front of the sign for Lipoa's Hardware Store, a sign I expected to see all too often in the future.

"Service with a Smile," the sign on the glass door proclaimed. Too bad I don't have anything to smile about. Dejected, I kicked myself for unintentionally driving Sully from my life.

With the image of Bethany kissing my ex still fresh in my mind, I furiously threw open the door and barged into the store. In that same instant, I heard a loud yelp when the door met resistance, only opening halfway.

I quickly realized why.

On the other side, a tall teenage boy hunched over on the floor, clutching his gushing nose. Crimson drops splattered his hardware store apron. His bold blue eyes flashed with anger, making a wave of guilt wash over my whole self.

"Oh, God! I am *so* sorry," I said and covered my shocked mouth with my hands.

He blinked, the anger quickly dissolving from his eyes, like my heartfelt apology somehow surprised him.

I dropped to my knees beside him, the image of Bethany and Sully quickly vanishing from my mind. "I totally didn't see you. Is there anything I can do?"

Blood pooled in his hands. He shot me a pleading look.

"Got it. Tissues, rag, ice…whatever works, right?"

I guessed he would've nodded if it hadn't been for all the blood. I stood up and called loudly to the back of the store. "Hey, Marvin? Got a bit of a problem here. Can you bring some tissues up front? And how about some ice?"

Marvin readily appeared, shaking his head as he surveyed the scene. "That'll leave a shiner," he declared and handed me a box of Kleenex before leaving for more supplies.

I pulled out four or five tissues and wedged them into the boy's bloody hands. When the tissues quickly stained, I yanked out another half dozen.

Marvin returned with a Ziploc bag of ice and a trash can. "Just make sure you don't get any on the floor or you'll be cleaning the floors at closing tonight," he said in a joking manner.

"No breaks for the injured?" I wagered, handing the boy the

bag of ice.

The boy shrugged. "I was scheduled to clean floors tonight, anyway." He held the ice to his nose with one hand and the wad of tissues with his other.

I watched him, trying to think of something helpful to say. "Do you think you should go to the emergency room?"

"I'll be fine." He tossed his clump of bloody tissues in the trash can and held out his hand expectantly.

I passed him another stack of Kleenex. "Maybe it's broken," I suggested. "Can I see it for a second?"

He removed the bag of ice obligingly.

"It looks kind of crooked," I noted, resisting the urge to cringe.

"It's always been crooked," he said, flashing me a quirky smile that curled up on one side. He reapplied the ice.

"That much?" I said.

He shot me a fierce look.

I bit my lip. "Sorry. Not helping."

"Seriously, I'll be fine. You don't need to worry about me, Jordan."

A lump stuck in my throat, making it difficult to breathe. "You know my name?" I managed in a squeaky voice. How could he when I hadn't introduced myself yet?

He shrugged. "It's a small town. News travels fast," he said, stating the obvious.

"Oh, right," I said, feeling like an idiot. How hard could it be to learn the name of a single new person? Especially when I was the only teen female in the store.

I sat back on my heels, still puzzled. Had I seen him around town or at the beach before and simply hadn't noticed, my thoughts too preoccupied with my training and Sully? I studied his features, searching for a sign of familiarity. The boy's sun-kissed brown hair flopped forward, except for the cowlick above his forehead, just a little to the right of center. Not that I could actually see his full face with a wad of tissues covering his nose, but I guessed he was about my age—sixteen, seventeen at most. Even hunched over, he appeared tall and lean, but not scrawny. And his eyes were the most amazing shade of blue, reminding me of the shallow cerulean waters surrounding the reefs in Bora Bora where Skye and I had fished for dinner.

I stared back, perhaps for a moment too long, convincing myself I'd never actually noticed him before. When I handed him a stack of tissues, he gave me a short, confused look and tilted his head forward, pinching the bridge of his nose to help stop the bleeding.

"Are you sure you're okay…?" I paused, realizing I hadn't learned his name yet.

"I'm Liam," he said through the tissues. "Liam Innis Reilly."

"Really?" I replied, wondering how many other teenage boys I'd ever met had actually spoken their middle name. What a dork.

"Not *Real-ly*. It's pronounced *Rye-lee*." He stuck out his hand and then reconsidered. "Maybe some other time when my hands aren't quite so messy."

I crinkled my nose. *Yeah…or maybe not*, I thought, wondering when my guilty feelings would subside. But for the moment, I felt compelled to stay by his side, at least until the bleeding settled down. "So, how long have you been working here?" I asked, but for lack of anything better to say.

"Today's my first day."

"Ouch. Not off to the best start, are you?"

"I'll manage, I s'pose."

I twiddled my thumbs and looked around the store, my mind drawing a blank on other topics of conversation. After what seemed an appropriate amount of time to politely wait for his bleeding to stop, I said, "Well, I should probably get going. Hope your nose feels better, Liam." I left him with a tissue jammed up one nostril.

The entire way home, I kicked myself for hurting him…all because I hadn't looked before I threw open the door. It was so much easier to deal with Marvin and Gerard at Lipoa's instead of their clumsy new employee. "Liam Innis Reilly," I muttered to myself. Now would I feel obliged to apologize to him every time I entered the store? How could I be so careless?

Not until I got all the way back to Lulu's faded pink house did I stare down at my empty hands. "Oh, I don't believe it," I groaned.

I'd forgotten all about buying the paint.

Turning on my heels, I ran down the hill, my sandals flopping beneath my feet, anxious to get things over with as soon as possible. I wiped the beads of sweat from my brow as I reached the hardware store and placed my hand on the door to step inside. Only the door moved from the inside.

"Saw you coming this time," Liam said, propping the door wide open for me. His bleeding seemed to have stopped, but I noticed some discoloration and swelling around his crooked nose.

Splendid. Now I've got my personal greeter, I thought with a bundle of sarcasm. I gave him an awkward grin. "How'd you know?"

"It wasn't that hard. You must've come here for a reason, other than making the door become acquainted with my face."

I winced. "Sorry about that."

"When you left empty-handed, I figured it wouldn't be long before you'd be back. Only this time, I thought I should be ready," he finished with a joking smile and reached for the last Kleenex in the box. "So, what can I help you with?"

I pointed to the advertised "On Sale" sign posted above the rainbow of paint samples.

"Right this way," Liam pronounced, eagerly trotting toward the display.

I rolled my eyes. "Service with a smile, right?" I whispered to Marvin and reluctantly followed his new employee.

"Don't expect anything less," Marvin replied from behind the cash register. He flashed me a wide grin that showed all his white teeth.

When I caught up to Liam, he said, "To start, I'll need to know a little about your project so I can gauge the volume of paint you'll need."

Liam's nerdly words echoed in my head, *Gauge the volume of paint*. I didn't know anyone actually talked like that. Funny to think that Micah had once considered *me* a nerd, just because I thumbed through the pages of the history text during Mr. Tabor's lecture. But he didn't understand that I only wanted to catch up on everything I had missed in my jump from the Great Chicago Fire to the present time.

I rolled my eyes again, wishing Marvin could have helped me instead. "I've got to paint the house," I replied with a heavy sigh.

"Just the trim?"

I shook my head sadly. "No. The whole thing. Auntie Lulu says she wants the house to be purple now, not pink."

"Purple?" he asked, giving me a sideways look.

"Well, light purple, I guess."

"The whole house, huh? That's a pretty big job."

"Thanks for the reminder," I mumbled. Crossing my arms over my chest, I pondered how long it would take me to finish. Days. Weeks, perhaps.

Liam scanned the paint samples in front of the display. I noticed he slouched over a bit, like he'd just finished a growth spurt and wasn't yet comfortable with his new height. "Light purple, you say? Well, we've got a bunch of options: Exotic

Orchid, Mystical Lavender, Intimate Violet, Luscious Lilac, or Pandora's Box." He spread a bunch of paint samples across the counter for me to peruse.

Who comes up with these names? I wondered, trying to figure out how Pandora 's Box of evils from Greek mythology was even associated with a particular color. "Oh, I don't know. I guess that one," I said in a lackluster voice as I randomly pointed to one of the nearly identical shades of light purple.

"Luscious Lilac it is," Liam grinned.

I blew the hair from my face. "Whatever. Can I get two gallons?"

Liam furrowed his brow. "I don't think that will be enough."

"Maybe not, but it's all I can carry back," I replied.

Liam set the two gallons of light base paint under a machine and added the tints. He said, "You know, painting the whole house by yourself sounds like a pretty big job. Do you have much experience?"

"Nope," I muttered coolly, wondering when I'd ever have the time to learn how to paint a house between training to use my fire powers or running for my life from the other Elementals. Oh, and don't forget finishing all of Lulu's chores.

He moved the gallons into a different machine that agitated them vigorously to uniformly mix the paint. "Could you use some help? I'm off tomorrow morning." He reached under the counter to grab a couple of paint sticks, placing them on top of the gallons of Luscious Lilac paint.

"Yeah, right. Like you'd want to help me after I broke your nose."

"I told you before, it's not broken," he said, giving me that quirky smile again.

I scrunched up my face, certain he was lying just to be nice. There was no way his nose had looked that crooked before.

"Plus, I'm pretty good with a brush," Liam added. He

reached for a three-inch paintbrush lying on the counter, twirling it between his fingers like a baton in a parade. But after the third spin, he lost his grip and the brush sailed across the counter, dropping to the floor with a clatter. Liam's face turned red. He scrambled to pick up the brush before Marvin or Gerard noticed. He ran his fingers through his hair in an embarrassed sort of way. His hair parted by his cowlick before flopping back into it original position.

My eyebrows floated up my forehead. "If you say so," I replied with a low whistle. "I can't pay you for your work," I declared, certain this would change his mind.

"That's okay," Liam replied obligingly. "Lulu's an old family friend. I know she can use a little help."

"*You* know Auntie Lulu?" I asked incredulously, completely forgetting his comment about small towns. "So you know her place."

Liam smiled. "It's looking a lot better now."

"Thanks," I sighed, my eyes glazing over. I thought about the long hours I'd labored cleaning up her overgrown yard before she took me to see Pele, and wondered if things would've been different if I hadn't complained to Sully about all the work Lulu gave me. Not that I could go back and change my past actions, especially when he'd made it abundantly clear that he seemed perfectly happy with Bethany—an involuntary shudder traveled down my spine at that thought—and had lost all interest in me.

"So, what do you say?" Liam said, snapping me from my pity session. He removed the gallons of Luscious Lilac from the machine and handed me a couple of paint sticks. "Meet you at eight?"

I blinked. "Huh?"

Liam leaned across the counter, his face uncomfortably close. His eyes sought mine. "I'll bring my own brush."

"Oh, right." I took an uncomfortable step back from the

counter. Could someone please remind me why this guy actually volunteered to help me paint the house on a morning off from work? Still, having him there would cut my work considerably so I could get on with my life.

"Eight sounds great," I agreed with a nervous grin and paid for the two gallons of paint. I prayed I hadn't made a mistake in accepting his help.

"Here, let me get the door for you," Liam offered and bolted ahead to open the door wide for my exit.

"Suit yourself," I said, lugging the paint off the counter and out the door. "I think your new help is a little too helpful," I muttered to Marvin as I passed, trying not to grimace under the weight of the full cans. Marvin gave me a funny smile, but I hadn't meant for my comment to sound like a joke. The last thing I needed was for Liam to offer to carry the paint back to Auntie Lulu's place for me.

Maybe I'd made a huge mistake in accepting his help. Or maybe I should suggest that he start on the back while I paint the front. That way I could avoid spending another minute with him.

CHAPTER SEVENTEEN

I didn't get very far on the house that afternoon. Anxious about the magnitude of Lulu's chore and having to see Liam again, I had difficulty falling asleep that night. In my dreams, the job lasted for what seemed an eternity, the walls of Lulu's house magically extending for entire city blocks. Just when it seemed I had reached the end, a new section of wall appeared, constructed within minutes. Soon, the chore stretched from months into years, with Liam appearing every morning, eager and willing to help.

"Aaarghh!" I screamed and rolled onto my belly, stuffing the pillow over my head. *What is it with him?* Deep inside, I suspected he had another reason for wanting to help me. If only I could decipher his motive.

Tossing and turning in bed most of the night, I finally drifted off only a few hours before sunrise and didn't wake up until five minutes before eight the next morning. "Oh my God!" I gasped. My eyes flew open with shocked alertness. "He'll be here any second!"

After throwing on a junky shirt and an old pair of cutoff shorts, I ran to the bathroom and splashed water over my face, forcing my mind into a state of coherent consciousness while hoping I could wash away the dark puffy bags under my eyes. Unfortunately, neither actually worked. Still groggy, I set a speed record for brushing my teeth and dragging a comb through my hair—pulling out a handful of snarled tangles in the process—and darted into the kitchen with less than a minute to spare before eight o'clock.

Just as the second hand of Lulu's kitchen clock marked the hour, I heard a prompt knock at the front door. *Breakfast will have to wait,* I told myself. I strode to the door and opened it widely, reminding myself to thank him right away for his help, even if I didn't entirely want it.

Thoughts of appreciation immediately fled my mind when I gaped openmouthed at Liam on the front stoop. Well, my attention didn't fix on Liam himself, rather his nose.

"How is it?" I asked hesitantly, my gaze glued to the white noseguard taped over his puffy bridge and the pair of nasty purple bruises that traced the bottom of each eye.

"It doesn't hurt too much…anymore," he admitted, though by his expression I thought he withheld the full truth to avoid upsetting me.

"It looks straighter," I said, for lack of anything else to compliment about its improvement. In reality, I thought it looked about ten times worse than it had yesterday when blood gushed into his hands.

"Yeah…I decided to take your advice and go see the doctor. You were right," Liam continued. "It wasn't *that* crooked before." He chuckled and then reconsidered, like laughter itself caused unnecessary pain.

"What did they do?" I asked, remembering the hot pink cast the doctor had wrapped around my broken arm at the ER in Pacifica.

"Only reset it," he said with a nonchalant shrug. "No big deal."

"Ouch." I flinched, thinking it seemed a much bigger deal than he let on. "Sorry about that."

Liam tilted his head to one side, like my apology surprised

him. He shook his head to refocus. "I brought a few brushes, just in case you didn't have extras. And I wasn't sure you'd gotten enough paint, so I mixed another two gallons for you."

"That was nice of you," I said, speaking the truth. By the time I'd gotten home from Lipoa's yesterday, my arms burned from the strain of carrying the heavy gallons all the way back up the hill. "But you didn't have to go to all the trouble."

"It wasn't any trouble. Things slowed down a bunch at the store after you left."

"I'll bet. Nothing like starting off your first day of work with a broken nose."

"That's not what I meant," he said, almost apologetically.

I looked back at him awkwardly, unable to think of anything to say in reply. Anxious to put some distance between the guy who aimed too high to please and myself, I mumbled, "Well, then, ready to get started?"

"No time like the present," Liam replied with enthusiasm.

"I thought I could start in the front and you could start in the back," I suggested.

His smile faded. "Oh, okay. If that's what you want." I detected a hint of disappointment in his tone.

Liam disappeared behind the house with a gallon of paint and a wide brush, and I set to work, opening my own can. After swooshing the stir rod until the paint turned a uniform shade of light purple, I dipped in the brush and coated the top half of the bristles. Starting from where I'd left off yesterday, I moved my hand in big sweeping motions from left to right and back again.

Drips of paint splattered off the brush, coating my forearms with a fine speckling of purple. Though I tried to stay clean, my shirt and shorts belied my attempts. Dots of Luscious Lilac flecked the ends of my black hair. I couldn't imagine what the rest of my face looked like as the brush whimsically ejected paint with every stroke.

Dip, sweep, sweep. Dip, sweep, sweep. At first, I found pleasure in the work, watching the bright new color mask the old faded pink. However, the rhythmic motions quickly dissolved into mind-numbing tedium when I repeated the process over and over and over again. The minutes lagged, the muscles in my arm burning. Back and forth, back and forth I continued until my shoulder also turned numb. By the end of the first hour, my wrist ached with every slight movement and my fingers tingled with thousands of needles simultaneously stabbing my flesh. Even switching hands did not increase my productivity or stamina for long. Soon, the wall of house seemed to lengthen before me. I imagined it extending out to the end of the yard, over the road, and across the beach. Only it didn't end there. Instead, the faded pink siding stretched into the sea, all the way to the horizon. I cringed, recalling my dream where an overly helpful Liam returned, morning after morning, as if haunting my very existence.

I hoped if I let my brain wander, I could block the pain raging through my arms. It figured my mind quickly settled on images of Sully. And the more I thought about him, the more my blame for losing him fell upon Pele's shoulders. By sending me off on all those missions, I missed my opportunity to apologize to him. Worse, her magical training seemed largely ineffective. Sure, I could get back on my own from Colorado after the avalanche, but a simple request of sending me where I was needed went entirely ignored. With renewed determination, I decided I would weasel more details about my purpose from the goddess on my next visit. There had to be a real reason she called me back. Why else go through the trouble of healing Cam and me?

Unless I abandoned her training altogether. Did I possess enough skills to protect myself from the Elementals in the future? I couldn't be sure. Skye's powers had grown since she located me in Old Chicago. Quite possibly, her skills now exceeded the powers she had possessed then. Was it worth taking the risk and leaving my training incomplete?

While I contemplated my desire to return to the volcano at all, Auntie Lulu called Liam and me to the porch where she had laid out a mid-morning snack — steamed white rice with two slabs of fried Spam each. Before I could ask why anyone would elect to fry meat from a can, I realized something. Lulu was acting uncharacteristically pleasant — she'd never whipped up a snack for me before, regardless of how much time I'd devoted to her chores. Could she be putting on a show for her old friend Liam? Or did she seem grateful simply for the improvements to her home?

In between bites, Liam chattered amiably with Lulu. I focused on my food to avoid looking at his bandaged nose. *Bandaged*, I reminded myself with a heap of guilt, *because of my carelessness*.

Before Liam inhaled his final bite, he asked Lulu, "Do you have a ladder?"

My brow pinched with confusion. *A ladder?* I thought, wondering how far he'd gotten already if he couldn't reach a spot with his tall frame.

She led him into the carport to take one down from the rafters. I cleaned up my plate, lacking the enthusiasm to paint. Still, the sooner I completed this project, the sooner I could find Pele and demand an explanation for my magic's failure.

While my brush slid from side to side along each panel of pink wooden siding, I reached the conclusion that I definitely had too much time to think. Unresolved issues plagued my mind, accompanied by tragic scenes of lost lives of those I could not save. And here, I'd thought my new purpose would change all that. Instead, I painted the side of a house. Some help I was, dwelling on the failures of Pele's near-death missions and the hurt from Sully's break-up.

Suddenly, Liam appeared behind me. "I finished the back of

the house."

I quickly mopped my face with a clean square of my shirt, not wishing him to see me in my pitiable state. "You what?" I exclaimed, certain I misheard him.

"The back's all done," Liam repeated. He licked his thumb and rubbed it against my cheek. "You've got a spot on you," he explained.

I glanced down at my speckled arms and splotchy clothes. "More than a little," I admitted, surprised he had stayed perfectly clean.

"Sorry, I can't help you finish," he apologized, "I've gotta go to work now. If you'd like, I can swing by and check on you later."

"Sure," I said, kicking myself for sounding opportunistic. There were probably a hundred thousand things he would've rather done on his morning off from work than painting...and not getting paid for it. "Did you really finish the whole back?" I asked with a hint of disbelief.

His lips stretched into a proud smile. "Let me show you," he offered and headed toward the back of the house.

Following close behind, my jaw dropped in an instant. "Wow," I exclaimed with a low whistle, honestly impressed with how much he'd accomplished. While I struggled on the front, leaving faded pink on one half and crisp Luscious Lilac on the other in its current two-tone state, he had somehow managed to complete the entire back of the house, just like he'd claimed!

"How'd you do that?" I wondered, awestruck. Had I really been that distracted by my own thoughts?

"Told you I was pretty good with a brush." Liam joked and flashed me a friendly grin.

Speechless, I stared at his work, feeling pokey and inadequate. "You know, I'm really sorry I can't pay you."

"No big deal. Like I said, I owed Auntie Lulu a favor."

I blinked. Actually, I *hadn't* heard him say that before. I merely thought she was an old family friend. Was there something more he hadn't disclosed?

He continued, "And maybe you can help me out with a favor some time? Just to call it even."

"Maybe," I said, noncommittally. True, Liam had saved me at least a full day's worth of work—especially at the rate I was going. So it made sense I should owe him big. Still, the prospect of being indebted to Liam made my stomach churn. Why did he have to be so nice it made me sick? I already felt bad enough about the whole nose thing. And now he'd heaped another huge serving of guilt on my plate from painting the house. Regardless of what Liam had in mind, it would have to wait. I needed Lulu to get to Pele so I could find out how I had botched up my magic. The last thing I wanted was another task to delay my visit to the goddess.

CHAPTER EIGHTEEN

When painting the house stretched into the next two days, my sore shoulders and fatigued arms were grateful Liam had completed the back on his own. I had to admit, Lulu's place looked entirely different in its fresh coat of Luscious Lilac. In fact, with all the improvements I'd completed so far, I figured she ran out of excuses to bring me to see the goddess again.

Apparently, I thought wrong.

"The house is finished," I declared as my purple speckled arms practically dragged along the ground. "So can we go to the volcano now?"

Without offering a comment on its appearance, Lulu handed me a bucket. She requested, "Gather the plums, then we'll go see Pele."

My eyebrows shot up my forehead. "Plums?"

"My sister asked me to bring her some jellies," Lulu explained.

When will this ever end? I thought with a groan, suspecting there was another reason besides plum jelly that delayed my return to the goddess's domain. I thought her task sounded reasonably easy, plucking ripe fruits from tall, sweeping branches. However, Lulu referred to an entirely different type of plum—one that didn't grow on a tree. The natal plum grew like a landscaping hedge along one side of her yard and appeared much nicer than it really was. From afar, its delicate flowers—shaped like perfect

172

stars of snow white—matured into seductively tempting red fruits against a backdrop of contrasting deep green leaves like a Christmas scene in July. But the natal plum held a few nasty secrets to defend its luscious fruits. They were surrounded by toxic leaves and sharp, stiff thorns. *Lots* of thorns.

A heavy sigh escaped my lips when I spotted the abundance of red fruits nestled safely amongst the chaotic tangles of branches. I'd never make it to the volcano today...or ever at this rate, would I?

"Fine," I muttered to myself. "Might as well get started." I carefully reached deep into the bush, twisting my hand between the thorns to grasp a fruit. "Ow!" I shrieked, a thorn scraping my flesh. With the fruit securely between my fingertips, I pulled my hand back quickly, but the thorns scratched me on the way out as well, leaving a pair of long gauges across my wrist and forearm. Fresh blood oozed from the cuts as I dropped the plum into the bucket. It hit the bottom with a hollow, empty sound.

"Auntie Lulu, do you have any gloves?" I called.

Aside from the slam of the screen door as it shut behind her, I received no response.

"Auntie?" I called louder, watching the front door expectantly. When a few minutes passed and she didn't return, I figured she deliberately chose to ignore me. True, I could have run down to Lipoa's Hardware to pick up a pair myself, but I'd risk bumping into Liam again. What if he decided to call in that favor?

A handful of small olive green birds landed in the nearby bush, happily chittering and darting amongst the branches. With pale bellies and white rings around each eye, they paused for a moment to study me curiously. I'd probably have better luck carrying on a conversation with *them* than with Auntie Lulu herself. I sighed. Dwelling on misfortunes wouldn't improve my situation one bit. If keeping Lulu happy was my only ticket to see Pele, and Pele was my only link to mastering my powers and

173

manipulating them to destroy the threat of the other Elementals, then I might as well stop grumbling and get started.

To say my arms took a beating every time I reached far within the hedge to pick the ripe fruit was a massive understatement. After gathering a bucket full of natal plums for Lulu to make into jellies and jams, I scrubbed my battered arms in the sink. The water turned pink as it washed away the blood, spiraling at the bottom of the basin on its way down the drain.

Auntie Lulu appeared behind me, surveying my scratched and bloody hands and forearms.

"So now we can go see Pele?" I asked in a weary voice.

But instead of answering my question, Lulu spoke with reproach. "Why didn't you go to Lipoa's and get some gloves?"

I released an exasperated sigh. "I didn't want to waste the time to walk all the way down there." Not like Lulu ever offered to give me a ride.

"And this is saving you time now?"

I winced as the warm water seeped into my open scratches. "No," I said, certain she didn't have enough Band-Aids in the medicine cabinet to cover all my wounds.

"Stubborn child," Lulu said with a frown. "Use your head. That's why God gave you brains, to make good decisions."

"It's not just that," I muttered and grabbed a tube of antibiotic ointment from the medicine cabinet.

Auntie Lulu leaned against the doorframe, waiting for me to continue.

I untwisted the cap and sighed again. "I know you're friends with Liam's family, but it's just that…"

She raised her eyebrows higher, expectantly, waiting for me to elaborate.

I began to liberally spread the ointment over my cuts. "I didn't want to go back to the store and risk bumping into him again."

For a fraction of a second, Lulu's face warmed. A hint of a knowing smile pushed up her bronze cheekbones. Her expression quickly faded into a hardened look set in her deep brown eyes. "Stubborn. Just plain stubborn," she said with a shake of her head. She walked down the hall muttering something in Hawaiian that I couldn't understand.

As it turned out, I'd have to wait to visit Pele until Lulu finished canning the fruit. "In the meantime, my car could use a good wash," she told me with a pointed look. She handed me a few bills and directed me to Lipoa's since she didn't have any car wash gel in the house.

With heavy feet, I slumped down the hill into town, wondering how I'd gotten stuck in this endless cycle of errands and chores. Now I owed Liam too, making me doubt I'd ever find the time to finish my training. Fortunately, Liam was busy helping another customer when I entered the store. He noticed me right away and greeted me with a friendly wave. I nodded, my eyes settling on his discolored, puffy nose. I steered toward the car section to scan the shelves in search of a product that matched Lulu's description.

Before I could decide on my purchase, Liam turned up beside me and asked, "Need some help?"

Startled by his sudden appearance, I jumped back a step. "Um, okay," I said. "You don't have to wear it anymore?" I asked, pointing at the spot where his white noseguard used to be.

"Nah. I decided I didn't need it anymore."

"It looks better," I added with a convincing smile. The swelling had subsided and the purplish bruises begun to fade into a greenish-yellow color instead. I also noted he pulled his shoulders back further now, possessing more confidence than when we first met. Which made me wonder...had he acted oddly that first time because I had accidentally broken his nose, or was I too wrapped up in my despair from losing Sully to notice the true Liam?

"Did you get in a fight with a feral cat?" Liam inquired, interrupting my thoughts.

"A feral cat?" I crinkled my nose. "Where'd you get that idea?"

He pointed at the multitude of short red scratches that covered my forearms.

"Oh, right," I said, wishing I had long sleeves to yank down to my wrists. "I had a run-in with the plum hedge in Auntie Lulu's front yard. Anyway, she wanted me to pick up some car wash gel today."

"For another chore?"

I blew the hair from my face, letting my lips fall into a frown. "How'd you guess?"

Liam's eyes softened. He glanced at me sympathetically and focused on the shelf, readily selecting a bottle. "Here's one," he said and carried it up to the cash register in the front.

"How much?" I asked, eager to get this job done.

But before Liam rang up the item, he rested his elbows on the counter. Leaning toward me until his face hovered even with mine, he asked, "Why don't you just tell Lulu you're busy? That you have a life and can't spend every minute of it doing her chores?"

I looked into Liam's bold blue eyes for a long minute, surprised by his suggestion. Had I totally misjudged his character the first time we met? His eyes gauged mine with concern, like he genuinely cared about how she treated me.

When I didn't reply right away, Liam prompted, "So, why don't you?" His eyes held mine, searching for the real answer.

In that moment, I found his gaze unexpectedly captivating and difficult to resist. Afraid I might reveal my dangerous secrets if I stared back much longer, I forced myself to turn away.

"It's complicated," I muttered, feeling more confused

than ever. How could I explain that Lulu represented my sole connection to Pele? That I needed a goddess to prepare me for taking on the unforeseen threat of the remaining Elementals. How could I explain the truth about my existence when I did not fully understand it myself?

"Well, if you need anything else, you know where to find me," he said with a deep breath. "Meaning, I'll probably see you later."

"Probably," I agreed, somewhat touched by the concern in his gaze. Despite my noncommittal front, a small part of me decided the prospect of seeing him again didn't sound as unpleasing as I'd originally thought.

Chapter Nineteen

I thought about Liam and his comment the entire way home and while I gathered supplies to clean Lulu's car. By the time I slipped into a black string bikini and an old pair of cutoff shorts, I'd convinced myself to follow Liam's advice the next time Auntie assigned me a chore. But at the moment, I needed to complete this last task before I could talk to Pele. I exited Lulu's house, my arms laden with sponges and a bucket of soapy water, when a friendly tabby cat plopped onto the ground right by my feet. Stretching out both arms and legs, he rolled onto his back, as if asking for a belly rub. With my hands full of supplies, I could only oblige with a free big toe.

"Well, hello there," I cooed and slipped off a sandal. I balanced precariously on one leg to scratch its belly.

Satisfied, the feral cat rolled back onto his feet, graciously thanking me by rubbing his entire body against my leg. His long tail twisted around my calf like a coiling snake as he strolled past.

Suddenly, Kea leapt from behind Lulu's car with a sharp bark. Her ears cocked forward and she bounded toward the cat. The tabby's yellow eyes registered fear. He flinched, his fur bristling along his arched back. He hissed menacingly at the dog. When his behavior did not deter Kea's advances, he turned and darted away, scaling Lulu's fence in an effortless leap.

"Kea," I scolded her, "he wasn't doing anything wrong."

But Kea stood alert, vigilantly watching for the cat's return. When he showed no signs of reappearing on Lulu's property, Kea trotted over and sat by my side. She wagged her tail triumphantly and opened her panting mouth in what appeared to be a huge, satisfied grin.

"Look at you," I said and laughed, shaking my head. "Now you're a watchdog, too? I don't get it. All this for a scrap of bread? That doesn't make me your owner, you know. So why are you so protective of me?"

Dropping the sponges in the grass, I knelt next to Kea, slinging my arm around her neck to scratch her shoulder blade. The dog gave me a fast lick on the cheek before trotting under a shade tree to take another nap.

Ready to begin, I grabbed the hose and aimed its nozzle toward the hood of Lulu's burnt orange Firebird. I was about to turn on the water when Liam pulled up in his royal blue Hyundai Tiburon coupe with the sunroof propped open.

Kea's ears perked at the sound of him turning off the ignition. Forgetting her nap, she bounded over to the car, her tail swinging widely from side to side.

"Thought you might like a little help," he said with a wide grin. Liam climbed from the car and greeted Kea with a good scratch behind the ear. Her hind leg thumped the ground uncontrollably, like he'd found the perfect spot.

"Thanks. I would." A surprised smile filled my face, realizing I actually felt glad to see him. After all, he had occupied my thoughts since my visit to the store that afternoon. Careful not to let my eyes linger on his for too long, I focused on Kea's happy expression instead.

See? Even Kea likes him, I told myself.

Just then the tabby cat reappeared on the fence. Kea's attention instantly trained on the feline. She scooted out from under Liam's hand and darted behind the fence into the neighbor's yard,

179

barking fiercely. "Silly girl," I told her with a roll of my eyes.

Liam chuckled and shut the door behind him, leaving his keys in the car so he could turn up his music. A rock ballad piped from the car's radio, carrying a slightly romantic tune. Liam ripped off his Lipoa's Hardware shirt and tossed it onto the front seat.

I blinked, forgetting all about lingering eyes and revealing thoughts as I studied Liam's tanned form. Although the tops of his shoulders looked slightly pink like they'd seen too much of the strong Hawaiian sun, the rest of his body wore an even shade of bronze, clearly defining the muscles of his chest and arms. And his surf shorts — printed in swirling designs of varying shades of blue — rode low across his hips and hung down just past his kneecaps to accentuate his tight calves.

"Here, let me get that for you," he said, taking the hose from my hand and giving the car a thorough rinse. Once finished, he tossed me a sponge, dunking his into the bucket. When he dribbled his soapy sponge over to the car to start on its tail end, I found it surprisingly difficult to look elsewhere, unsure if the music had begun to influence my thoughts. *Cut it out*, I scolded myself. *You've seen plenty of shirtless guys at the beach.* Still, something about his physique — long and lean, yet surprisingly strong — captured my attention. I belatedly soaked my sponge in the bucket and set to work on the opposite side of the car, sneaking interested glances at him, hoping he hadn't noticed.

He couldn't have changed that fast, I reminded myself. *Remember how annoying you found him just a few days ago?* True, but I'd been in a particularly annoyed mood at the time.

Absorbed with my thoughts, I absentmindedly reached behind me to immerse the sponge in the bucket again when my hand brushed Liam's on accident.

Surprisingly, I felt my heart leap inside my chest at his unexpected touch. "Sorry," I mumbled a bashful apology and continued with my work, chiding myself for getting distracted.

"No worries," he admitted, though his cheeks turned a fast shade of pink, noticeable even past all his bruising. With a quick shake of his head to compose himself, he went back to soaping the car's roof.

That's not helping. I forced myself to stop looking at Liam or trying to interpret his thoughts and finish the job. Sure, it was nice of him to offer to help, but I couldn't risk involving him in my life. So far, I'd been lucky the Elementals hadn't found me since my arrival to Hilo. But I figured it was only a matter of time before my luck ran out. A part of me found relief in the fact that I no longer had to worry about Sully getting hurt. Still, I didn't have time for a new distraction.

While I busily kicked myself for getting sidetracked by Liam, I heard him mutter under his breath, as if he was waging a similar discussion with himself. I pretended not to notice as I casually strained my ear in his direction under the ruse of cleaning the driver's side door. At one point I thought I heard him say, "Just finish the job. You don't have time for anything else," in a way that suggested his behavior somehow displeased him.

Did he think he'd devoted too much time trying to be nice to me and help with all these chores? But it didn't make any sense. Why would he even care what I thought? He knew nothing about me.

Or was it to please his old family friend, Lulu? Well, if that was the case, he might as well give up now. Since I'd arrived, I'd learned pleasing that old woman seemed an impossible task.

Curious to know how a guy as overly nice as Liam could ever be mad at himself, I leaned a little closer, eager to hear more. A few minutes later, I thought I caught something that sounded an awful lot like, "Time's running out."

"Did you say 'time is running out'?" I asked, unable to contain my curiosity. "Before what happens?"

His face paled as he caught my gaze, his hand pausing on the

181

sponge in mid-stroke. "Never mind," he said, looking away and vigorously sponged down the car's roof once more. Instead, he began chattering on about a lady who wanted a specific match of paint and nothing he mixed seemed exactly right before he ended his shift and handed her problem over to Marvin. His words blurred together, my mind drifting from his story. Deep inside, I couldn't help but wonder what thoughts really plagued him, and what topic he purposefully chose to ignore. But most of all, I wondered what would happen when the time did indeed run out.

Confused by his actions since he obviously didn't want to elaborate, I tried to focus on my work instead and perched on tiptoes to lean across the car. Heated by the sun's hot rays, the steaming metal burned into my bare belly when I raised each of the wiper blades. With fingertips fully extended, I stretched for the spot in the exact middle of the windshield, the one place that seemed impossible to reach for someone of my height. Sure, I could've asked Liam, but had tired of playing the role of a damsel in distress. I could handle this, even if I fried my belly in the meantime. I had barely managed to coat the area in soap when a blast of water from the hose squirted me directly in the spine.

"Oh my God!" I screamed in shock. I spun around, noticing the hose lying on the ground near his feet. "What was that for?"

Instead of replying, a guilty smirk snuck across his face. I instantly understood his intent.

"You did that on purpose, right?" I asked, glaring at Liam.

With a shrug of false innocence, he reached into the bucket. Before I could react, he lobbed a soapy sponge at me, hitting me right in the belly button. "You *so* did not just do that!" I exclaimed.

I glanced from him to the frothy bubbles that clung to my skin and narrowed my eyes. Ready to retaliate for that stunt, I grabbed the hose off the ground and aimed it at Liam, preparing to unleash it at full strength. Only when I pressed the trigger, nothing came out. Confused, I peered down the nozzle. Out of the corner of my eyes, I noticed him nudge the hose with his foot to release a kink in its length. A blast of water hit me at maximum force, straight in the face. I immediately dropped the hose, its errant flow spraying the kitchen window by mistake on its way to the ground.

Liam took one look at me before clutching his stomach and doubling over in hysterics.

"Not funny," I grumbled and mopped my stringy wet hair from my face. My anger quickly dissolved into laughter, thinking of how ridiculous I must've looked to Liam. He had the whole thing planned all along. I just couldn't believe I fell for it.

Lulu walked out her front door. With arms crossed over her chest, she flashed me a disapproving look.

"Sorry," I mumbled an apology while Liam and I tried to contain our laughter.

But instead of criticizing my work, a crooked smile twisted across Auntie Lulu's lips. She leaned toward me and whispered in her raspy, wizened voice, "I like this one." She jabbed a thumb in Liam's direction.

My face instantly flushed, probably to the color of crimson, I guessed. Not that I should care about Auntie Lulu's opinion toward a guy, a part of me couldn't help but agree. Despite the fact that my bikini top, shorts, and hair were drenched from our water fight, I had to admit, Liam's playful nature intrigued me. I wouldn't necessarily say I *liked* him, but I definitely teetered on that edge between finding his behaviors either frustratingly irritating or delightfully humorous—and my desire to spend more time with him equally puzzling.

I grabbed a rag to help Liam dry the car. Starting on the grille and headlights, I dried them spotlessly clean, moving onto the hood. My rag swooshed back and forth across the surface, attempting to reach every inch of its surface.

But when I looked up to note Liam's progress, I saw him give me a disparaging look. "Jordan, you've left huge streaks everywhere," he said, disappointed.

"So?" I asked. "At least it's dry."

"Ugh. You're such a girl," he grumbled. "Lulu's not gonna want to drive a car that looks like that."

"Why not? She's a *girl*," I said in the same mocking tone he'd used before. "What does she care as long as her car is clean?"

Instead of uttering a response, he tucked his rag into his shorts' pocket and stomped over to the front of the car. Standing directly behind me, he placed one hand over mine to move my rag in small, circular motions. My heart thumped loudly when his hand gripped mine firmly, manipulating it in his intended direction across the car's surface. When he stretched to reach the middle of the hood, his bare chest pressed against my back, and I could think of nothing beyond his skin in contact with mine. "See? No streaks," he said as his cheek casually brushed mine while he worked.

I blinked. *Was that intentional?* His closeness caused my pulse to quicken.

Suddenly, I couldn't focus on his words as the thought of having him this near me weighed foremost in my mind. I let my hand effortlessly revolve in small circles under his, surprised by my changing perception of him. His strong grip covering my hand as his fingers laced between mine.

"Yeah. No streaks," I agreed belatedly, secretly hoping my agreement wouldn't encourage him to release his grip just yet.

As our hands swooshed across the hood of the car as one, my skin tingled from his touch. "There, that's better," he finally said, satisfied.

He released his grip on my hand, congratulating me with a pat on the shoulder. *A buddy type of pat*, I reminded myself, surprisingly disappointed. "Now you've got it." When he stepped away, his fingers softly grazed the length of my back. Was it my imagination, or did they linger near my waist for a deliberate second before he walked away?

I continued working in silence, my hand spinning in circles. My mind sorted through these confusing signs, pondering the root of his actions.

Was he trying to make me like him? Because if so, he was off to a pretty decent start. All my initial impressions of him began to fade when I let myself see his true personality. I caught myself sneaking furtive glances in his direction while he worked, eager for another reason to have our hands meet again soon.

"Looking good," he encouraged me with an infectious smile before he directed his attention to the doors and trunk.

Subconsciously, my free hand floated to my back. I imagined I still felt his fingertips linger near my spine.

It's not a rebound thing, I decided. *It's something more.* But how much more would I allow my heart to give before the other Elementals threatened to take him from me?

CHAPTER TWENTY

The sun broke through my window early the next morning. Thrilled for good weather on the ride to the volcano, I dressed quickly. I entered the kitchen and spotted a row of canned plum jellies lining the counter. *Yes! She finished!* I thought excitedly, grabbing a box of cereal from the cabinet. But the kitchen seemed oddly silent. I poured my milk and sat at the table, alone. Eager to visit Pele right away, I scooped huge spoonfuls into my mouth and cleaned the dishes in record time, before leaving the kitchen to search for Lulu. I couldn't find her anywhere—not in the house or out in the yard. Even her freshly washed Firebird sat patiently in the driveway, as if she had mysteriously disappeared.

Maybe she went over to a neighbor's house and would come home soon, I guessed, knowing Lulu never ventured far from home without her car. Only I couldn't figure out why she had left right then? Didn't she remember she promised to take me to Pele after she'd finished her canning?

I decided to wait by the car, impatiently drumming my fingers along its shiny orange paint, watching for her return.

Long minutes passed with no sign of Lulu. The warm sun beat upon my face and shoulders while I waited. And waited. When my legs tired from holding the same position for so long, I sat on the step of her front porch and let my head drop into my hands.

186

Had I unintentionally done something to upset Auntie Lulu? Why else would she break her promise and vanish without a word?

I heard a car engine coast up the driveway and roll to a stop behind the Firebird. I glanced up, expecting to see Lulu. Only it was Liam's blue Tiburon. I let my head plop back into my palms. Discouragement overwhelmed the recent change in my feelings toward him.

"Hey, Jordan. You busy today?" he asked. He shut off the engine and climbed from the car.

"Lulu was supposed to take me somewhere, but I can't figure out where she went. You didn't happen to see her, did you?" I muttered without lifting my head.

"Actually, that's why I'm here," he admitted.

I raised my head, my brow pinching together. "You are?"

Liam nodded. "Marvin had to go to the hospital late last night, so Gerard swung by first thing this morning to pick up Lulu to visit him."

My fingers covered my surprised mouth. "Is Marvin okay?"

"Yeah. He'll be fine. The doctors said he had appendicitis, but they caught it before it burst."

"That's a relief," I replied. Though I didn't know what would actually happen to him if his appendix burst, it sounded unpleasant.

"Anyway, since the store's closed," Liam continued, "and Lulu expects she'll be at the hospital for most of the day, she asked me to stop by here and tell you."

"Oh," I said, not bothering to hide my disappointment. I knew I shouldn't be upset. Lulu didn't plan for Marvin to get sick. Still I had thought today would bring me one step closer to completing my training.

"So, I was wondering," Liam added, sitting next to me on the stoop, "if you'd like to get away for a bit. I'm planning on hanging out at the beach for the day, and you're welcome to join me."

"Are you sure?" I was surprised he wouldn't want to hang out with one of his other friends on his day off.

"Absolutely."

"O-kay," I said, somewhat unconvinced. "But I'll need to grab a few things. Can you give me a couple of minutes?"

When Liam nodded, I leapt from my spot and darted into the house, quickly throwing on my black string bikini and shorts and grabbing a towel. If I hurried now, Lulu might be home by the time I returned and take me to the volcano later that afternoon. "All set," I announced. I bounded down the steps and slipped into the passenger's side.

As Liam backed out the driveway, I figured I'd make the best of my predicament and prepare for my next visit to Pele. While he drove about two miles down the road from Lulu's, I gazed out the open car window, the wind streaming through my hair while I rehearsed my conversation with the goddess in my head.

"Your arms are looking better," Liam noticed, his voice breaking the silence.

I gazed at the collection of long red cuts, newly covered in thin scabs. Honestly, I thought they looked worse than yesterday, but maybe he was only trying to be nice. "Yeah…and so is your nose."

"It's still pretty sore, but it's getting there." He laughed. "We make quite the pair, huh?"

I blinked, unable to utter a response, my mind fixating on the word "pair." Did he enjoy spending time with me or did he intend "pair" to refer to a couple of injured klutzes that drew attention away from the other?

Regardless, I had little time to ponder his meaning before we pulled up to a quiet beach shaded by tall, sweeping palms. Unlike the coarse black sand of the beach across the street from

Lulu's house, this one reminded me of the contrasting colors of salt and pepper, only in grains the size of pebbles. The entire length of beach consisted of small porous lava rocks interspersed with chunks of coral, rolled and tumbled smooth. Although the two types appeared separate and distinct—one made from a superheated rock spit from inside the earth and slowly cooled, the other formed by living creatures in the sea—here they harmoniously joined to form this solitary stretch of beach. I knew from experience that fire and water didn't belong together, yet in a surprising way, this beach seemed to make it work.

Liam tossed his towel and shirt on a large rock and sprinted across the black and white beach toward the sea. "You coming in?" he asked and splashed into the shallow water. The sunlight glinted off his bronze skin and accentuated the highlights in his hair.

I shook my head. "I'm good." Though my feelings toward Hydros had changed since I'd discovered more about her past life as the Irish girl, Shannon, I still hesitated in entering her watery realm. What if Gaia and Skye had already discovered a new Water Elemental? Wouldn't my contact with the ocean lead her directly to my spot? Would it even matter if they found me, now that my own powers had increased? Unsure of the answers, I made a mental note to ask Pele when I saw her tomorrow.

In the meantime, I decided to sit in a safe location of flattened lava rock with my feet tucked beneath me, careful not to let them get wet, just as a precaution. From my perch, I watched the activity of schools of tiny fish stranded in the tide pools, warily darting in one direction then another. Crabs traced the water's edge, scampering over lava rocks in a sideways motion. Corrugated shells shaped like conical hats clung tightly to the rocks to prevent the waves from carrying them out to sea.

I wiped a trickle of sweat from my brow, my skin growing warm from soaking up the sunshine. I looked out at Liam swimming happily back and forth, wishing I could cool off, too. If only I wasn't scared of the water.

Soon Liam paused to shake the water from his hair. A wide smile plastered across his face as he called, "Seriously, Jordan, you should come in. The water's great."

I stood, my entire body thirsting for a refreshing chance at the water. But logic and reason prevailed. "I can't swim," I admitted shyly, hoping my reason sounded convincing.

"You don't have to. See?" When he stood up, the water reached just above his waist.

"I dunno," I said, forcing my feet to stand their ground while sweat pooled across my forehead.

"Oh, come on. It's nice. Really." And to prove to me that he was right, he waded out of the water and up the beach. He stood before me, water dripping from his hair and shorts, and extended one hand.

I gazed at his hand, remembering how only yesterday I had longed for another chance to hold it. Despite my concern of entering the water, I reluctantly accepted.

Liam gave a pleased smile. He gripped my shaking hand securely and led me into the shallows.

I had to admit my first few steps seemed calm and relaxed. But as I waded in past my waist, I grew jittery, my heart racing with fear. He led me out past his original spot where the water soon touched my shoulders. A small wave washed over me and panic gripped my throat, remembering Shannon's tsunami that drowned Atlantis. Water rushed into my mouth. I struggled for a breath, coughing and sputtering on the salty sea.

"You doing okay?" Liam asked.

"Sorry, just a few too many close calls in the ocean," I said, recalling my near drowning in Atlantis. I mopped the stringy hair from my face, certain the new Water Elemental had already found me, if she even existed.

"Relax, I've got you," he said and slipped a comforting arm around my waist. When my breathing slowed and my rapid pulse subsided, Liam released his grip and cupped both hands near his mouth. "Try this," he suggested and blew into the water to create a huge bubble contained within his palms.

"How are you doing that?" I sputtered, my eyes wide with surprise that the bubble held its form underwater.

Liam shrugged. "It's no big deal. Can't everyone?"

I opened my mouth to declare, *No, I don't think so*, but paused instead. Fearful of Hydros's power detecting my presence, I had spent so little time in the ocean that I actually didn't know the answer to his question. Perhaps Liam was right and this bubble wasn't as difficult to accomplish as I had thought.

"Well, go ahead. Look inside," he suggested.

I shot him a skeptical glance.

"I mean it. I've got you." And just to ease my nerves, he balanced the bubble between his hand and one of mine, sliding his free arm around my waist once more. Surprisingly, it felt much easier to relax with him near, holding me close. I pressed my face against the bubble, providing a viewing window into the underwater world of the reef.

Looking through the bubble, I saw a latticed pattern of refracted sunlight dance across the rippled surface of the wave-swept sandy floor. A wide array of colorful fish darted through the clear water...some masked like bandits, others striped like convicts. Flashes of bright orange, yellow, and turquoise scooted past, belonging to a pair of fish painted in harlequin colors. An unusual grayish-blue fish possessed a horn that protruded from the middle of its skull like a mythical unicorn.

I pointed from one creature to another, unable to believe all I saw. "Unbelievable," I breathed, lifting my head from beneath the water.

Liam shook the water from his hair. "So...still wish you

stayed on shore?"

I surprised even myself when I exclaimed, "No!"

An amused smile crossed his face before I dipped my face into his suspended bubble again, amazed by the beauty of the underwater world. A world I'd never have experienced if it wasn't for his patience to help me overcome my seemingly irrational fear.

When we finally waded back toward shore, I cupped my hands, trying to blow a viewing bubble like Liam's. But all I managed to create was a flurry of small bubbles that quickly dissipated rather than fusing into a single entity like his.

"Y'know, Liam," I mentioned, abandoning my efforts. "Not everyone can do what you did."

He dismissed my comment with a casual shrug. "It just takes practice."

Yeah, I thought, *or I must be doing something wrong*. But before I could test a different technique, I heard a sharp bark. A few feet away, I spotted a white dog crouched on the beach, her eyes and ears trained on me.

"Kea," I exclaimed, leaving the water to greet my friend. "What are *you* doing here?"

She jumped up from her spot and trotted toward us, her tail wagging excitedly.

"Hi, girl," Liam said and patted the top of her head. Her mouth flopped open in what appeared a content grin.

Satisfied with her daily dose of affection, Kea leapt ahead, charging into the sea to frolic in the waves and chomping her jaws at the spray that kicked up in her path. She straggled from the surf and shook herself off, sending droplets in every direction. She bounded across the sand, knocking her wet body into my leg when she passed, tipping me off balance. "Kea!" I scolded, bumping into Liam. On instinct, he slid his arms around my waist to catch me from falling.

The blush rose high into my cheeks. "Sorry about that," I apologized and righted my feet beneath me once more. "She's normally not so playful."

"I don't mind," he said. The way his radiantly blue eyes looked at me in a deep, intent gaze made my breath catch inside my throat. All of a sudden, I realized he hadn't removed his arms from my waist. Stranger yet, I really didn't want him to. I thought of his closeness when we washed Lulu's car. His chest pressed against my back as he manipulated my sponge across the surface of the car. I searched for something to say, something to guarantee he wouldn't release me. Not yet, at least.

"You know," I whispered... The words stirred up strong feelings of emotion and longing while plans of a possible visit to Pele that afternoon fled my mind. "I'm actually glad Lulu was busy today. And that you swung by to get me," I added, hoping he'd realize my intent.

"Me, too," Liam said in a low voice, like he didn't trust himself to say anything more.

Overcome by the moment, I leaned forward, rising onto my tiptoes and tilting my head backward, ready to dare a kiss. A very small part of me warned against my action since Liam didn't have a clue about my true identity—but with a little amount of luck, I could keep things that way. And as far as I could tell, he liked me, too. Why else would he have gone out of his way to help me?

I gazed into his eyes with an unexpected stirring inside, realizing how much things had changed. Time slowed as I closed the distance between us, everything in my body telling me that this felt right.

Suddenly, Liam's expression froze. He studied me with confusion. And in that particular moment, he appeared torn, his face wrought with conflict.

I hesitated, baffled and somewhat hurt at the same time.

Wasn't he the one who'd shown initial interest in me? Hadn't he instigated our entire friendship?

Then it hit me. Maybe he only wanted friendship, nothing more. I felt stupid for misreading his expression, assuming the times he'd leaned close to me across the counter at Lipoa's were only to speak to me on the same level. And the time he'd held my hand and pressed himself close to my back was only to prevent me from leaving streaks on Lulu's car. Nothing more.

Disappointed by these realizations, I slowly sunk onto my heels. "I should probably get going," I muttered, wondering if I remembered the way home to spare Liam from having to give me a ride.

I turned to leave when Liam grabbed my hand and spun me toward him. But before I could analyze his intentions further, he pulled me into a fast embrace and his lips met mine.

CHAPTER TWENTY-ONE

Funny how one unexpected incident could really throw a total curve in your life.

Dreary skies masked yesterday's bright sun from the beach. I didn't consider the change in weather an omen, rather a common facet of life on this side of the island. The soaked scenery blurred as we sped past, the wipers swooshing back and forth.

Even though I should have spent my time rehearsing questions to ask Pele, I stared blankly out the passenger window of the Firebird where rivulets of rain streamed across the glass, thinking of nothing beyond Liam's kiss. It had held the magic of a first kiss unlike any other I'd ever experienced before, like the mere action of our entwined lips sparked feelings inside me I hadn't known existed. I couldn't say how long we'd stood together, our arms wound around each other, our mouths refusing to part. Even today, I could still taste Liam's kiss upon my lips.

But when we neared Kilauea, a pit of dread formed in the bottom of my gut—small at first, but gradually growing wider and wider. I realized once again I had unintentionally placed someone I liked in harm's way. It didn't concern me that I hadn't revealed my identity as an Elemental to Liam. If I had a choice, I would relinquish my powers in a heartbeat in exchange for a normal existence and a chance to be with him. Still, the threat of Gaia and Skye's return loomed in the back of my mind. So far, there had been no sign of their approach, but that didn't mean they weren't near.

After arranging to meet Lulu an hour before the park closed, I waved good-bye and headed out across the lava field that stood empty, a result of the light rain. I knew I no longer needed to search for the goddess directly; she would find me when she felt ready. I had only hiked halfway across the lava field when I felt a rush of hot air behind me. Turning into the heat, I saw the goddess standing before me, a red blossom tucked behind her ear. The molten ends of her hair steamed with each cool drop that fell from the sky.

"Follow me," she directed and led me out into the middle of an open basin, away from the designated trails. From her hurried pace, I could tell she seemed eager to start, so I decided to hold my questions and complaints for a moment and let my mind dwell on thoughts of Liam instead. What did it matter if my magic had failed and I didn't end up where I had intended if I'd managed to find happiness in my current location?

"Today," Pele announced, "we step your powers up a notch. Have you ever made a lava lake before?"

I scrunched my nose. "Considering I don't even know what a lava lake is, I'll say no."

Pele rolled her eyes, my sheltered lifestyle amusing her. "You'll start small to begin with, so you can get the idea." She placed her hands side by side, with thumbs overlapping, and focused her energy upon a chunk of lava rock, about the size of a bowling ball. An intense beam of heat poured from her hands, concentrating on that single spot until the solid rock gradually changed shape, its edges rounding and softening until it melted into a liquid state of matter. When her thumbs unlocked, the beam dispersed, leaving a puddle of molten material in the place where the rock had previously rested.

"That's pretty cool," I said, marveling at her work. I

196

considered the possibilities of this new skill in defending Liam and myself from the threat of the other Elementals. I mimicked her hand position and closed my eyes, forcing every ounce of my strength into a single, focused beam of heat that burst forth from my palms. Sweat beaded across my brow from the exertion and the magnitude of the heat aimed at the ground. Daring a glance at my progress, I watched proudly. The rock's solid form slowly softened into a red-hot mass.

Pele nodded, pleased. "Now bigger," she directed and traced a finger around the area she wished me to cover.

I wanted to protest that her designated boundaries seemed far too large, but held my tongue. *This is it. Finish your training*, I coached myself, searching deeper within my soul to call forth more heat. Keeping my thumbs interlocked, I aimed my palms at a spot in the middle. Surprisingly, the heat I produced helped melt the adjacent areas as well, allowing the puddle to fan outward and swell in size. Despite the coolness of the light rain, sweat poured from my brow and stained the sleeves of my shirt. When I finally reached Pele's set limits, I let my weary arms fall to my sides. I panted from the side of the lava pool, watching with pride as the lava bubbled furiously, like a pot of red-hot liquid boiling on a stovetop. I chanced a glance at Pele, gauging her mood before I asked the question that burned foremost in my mind. She appeared satisfied, which meant now was as good a time as any.

"So, do you think I'm ready?" I dared to wonder.

She tilted her head sideways. "Ready for what?"

"To take on the other Elementals and finish this thing once and for all," I explained between ragged breaths. My life would be mine to do with as I chose. *Finally*.

Pele blinked in surprise.

"Okay, I know what you're thinking," I continued. "I can never have my old life back and can never bring back those I've lost. But I'm strong enough to take them on and finish them like I finished off Hydros, right?"

Pele looked down at me, shaking her head sadly as she whispered, "An Elemental's body may perish, but not the Essence."

"Essence?" My eyebrows pinched together in confusion. "What's that?"

Pele sighed. "A long time ago, the four Elements of Earth, Air, Water, and Fire fused together with living beings to create the Elementals. As you have learned through experience, Elementals are capable of surviving extended exposure to their element in a way that would kill other humans, thus making them seemingly immortal through time. However, as individuals, you are still subject to mortal wounds, like you saw when Hydros perished in your last battle. Because of her Elemental powers, she did not die like other mortals. Instead, her Essence lives on in a spirit-like form."

"So Hydros isn't really gone?" I gasped. My body felt conflicted, a part of it relieved that I had not truly destroyed the innocent girl Shannon, the other part concerned she might return.

Pele nodded. "She will never be truly gone."

"But does she still have powers?" I wondered aloud, my hands trembling with every word.

"Yes, but they differ from the ones she had possessed before."

Different in a good way or different in a bad way, I didn't dare to ask. I gulped, suddenly frightful of her return. Perhaps I could pacify her temper, if I had a chance to explain my actions.

Wiping the sweat from my brow, I asked, "So can I speak to Hydros's Essence and apologize?"

"Not yet, child. She is still bitter."

Because of me. I didn't need Pele to finish her sentence to know who Hydros blamed for never seeing her parents or twin again. Gaia might have destroyed her home and chased her through time, forcing Shannon to accept her identity as Hydros and her role in Gaia's quest for power. But in the end, Hydros blamed *me*…and me alone.

"So what happens to the Water Element now that Hydros is no longer an active Elemental?"

"Why, the Element must choose a new life form to embody," the goddess explained.

"Meaning…a new Elemental has already been chosen?" My mouth went dry as my world crashed upon me. All this time I'd presumed I was safe with her destroyed. Instead, I only worsened my situation, infuriating Hydros's Essence and creating a new Water Elemental.

Oh. My. God.

A part of me finally understood why Pele had waited to share this truth with me. She was right—I wasn't ready for this news before. And to be honest, I wasn't even sure I was ready for it now.

"Do you know who the new Water Elemental is?"

Pele gazed into my eyes, but didn't reply. For a split second, I thought I saw a trace of pity in her expression. I hoped she would budge, but she didn't.

"Well, can I at least speak to the old Fire Essence?" I tried, desperate for an ally against so many foes.

Pele smiled softly. "In that regard, Hina may be able to help."

"Hina? The healer?"

"Hina is my friend, the Hawaiian moon goddess and the goddess of healing."

I blinked, remembering Cam's story about the two angels who visited his hospital room. "The one who saved Cam."

"And you." Pele nodded. "I have arranged for her to introduce you to the Fire Essence."

I opened my mouth to blurt a slew of questions, "When, where, and how?" when Pele placed a gentle hand upon my arm.

199

"Don't worry, child," she reassured me. "Hina already knows you. When the moon is full, you will see her."

"When the moon is full?" I repeated, baffled. "What do you mean?"

"You have so many questions," Pele said amusedly. "Trust me. On the next full moon, call for her. You will see."

I allowed a small grin to seep across my face. After everything I'd been through, I was finally getting somewhere. And I had a sneaking suspicion that Hina would tell me exactly what I needed to know. Still, Pele's explanations seemed limited, like she purposefully withheld other vital information about the history of the Elementals.

"So that's all I have to do to finish my training?" I questioned her. "Meet Hina and the Fire Essence?"

"You give up too easily," she said with reproach. "There is more you must learn." The Fire Essence will be accompanying you on the final journey of your training."

I sighed. "I thought you said I was done with my missions."

Pele shook her head. "There is still more you need to master. Your last journey is unlike the others. Inherently it is more dangerous, yet absolutely necessary."

"Well, that sounds fabulous," I said, my sarcasm spilling over the top. "I think I'll pass."

"It's too late for that," she cautioned. "I called you here for a reason, you know, and you *will* finish your training."

"But what if I don't? What if I can't do this?" I challenged.

Disturbed by my insubordinate behavior, Pele's eyes glowed red. "Don't tell me you're ready to give everything up? For what? A boy?"

"No," I exclaimed, my jaw dropping in mock surprise. The blush rose in my cheeks to belie my emotions.

Pele crossed her arms over her chest. "You think I haven't been in love many times before? I can see that look in your eyes."

"Look?" I asked, trying to make my voice sound innocent. "What look?" Especially since I hadn't realized I had actually fallen for him.

"Now is not the time to lose focus, Jordan." Pele stared at me with reproach. "Remember, call for her at the full moon."

"But where is the Fire Essence taking me? And why is it necessary?"

"I'm afraid I cannot tell you more at the moment," Pele said sternly.

I knew I shouldn't press her, but my curiosity got the best of me. "Can you at least tell me who the new Water Elemental is?"

She thrust one hand behind her, making the ground cleave and a molten jet of fiery lava spurt into the sky. "That is all for today." Dismissing any further conversation on the topic, she turned on her heels. The molten ends of her black tresses trailed behind her, melting everything they touched.

This time, I didn't bother to follow. Like I'd learned countless times before, Pele wouldn't volunteer any information beyond what she wanted me to know.

Dejected that things hadn't worked out, I sulked back along the trail as the drizzle worsened, grateful Lulu would return soon. Pele's remaining tasks repeated in my mind, even though I didn't fully understand what she expected me to do when I met Hina and the Fire Essence. Worse, what if the weather didn't clear and the clouds obscured the full moon? How would I call for Hina so I could complete the last portion of my training?

By the time I reached Volcano House, my clothes were drenched and my mind more muddled than before. My obligation to Pele and my desire to be with Liam warring inside my head, I wiped a brimming tear from my eye. From her hostile reaction, I knew she would never allow me to quit, not after all the effort she had devoted to my training so far. Somehow, I must learn to balance both sides of my life. I must find a way to complete the last of her tasks, so I could be with Liam and keep him safe.

I still had a few minutes to spare before Lulu pulled up in her Firebird. Rather than waiting by the parking lot, I stood amongst the tourists on the viewing deck and stared out across the expanse of black lava punctuated by a few straggly trees bearing red blossoms like the one Pele had tucked behind her ear. In the distance, the smoldering remains of her anger rose into the late afternoon sky. Visitors in cheap plastic ponchos found it exciting, snapping photos on their cameras and phones or dropping coins into the slots to peer through public binoculars mounted to the wall. But I knew the truth behind the active display—I had angered Pele yet again for letting my heart distract me from the tasks she set forth. I felt bad, not just because I disappointed the goddess—a feat I seemed quite adept at accomplishing—but because I doubted I could ever rise to her high expectations. Especially since every challenge she set before me only ended in frustration and failure.

CHAPTER TWENTY-TWO

Grayness descended upon the treetops the next morning, slowly soaking the earth with its steady drizzle. Despite the weather, I headed into town early, eager to meet up with Liam at Lipoa's, regardless of Pele's reservations about prioritizing him over my training. I can't return to Pele until after I meet Hina and the Fire Essence, so why not enjoy my freedom in the meantime? I shoved the threat of Hydros's Essence and the new Water Elemental to the back of my mind.

Only when I reached Lipoa's, Gerard told me Liam had asked for the day off because he said he had some things to take care of. *That's odd*, I thought, certain he would've swung by Lulu's house to see me if he wasn't at work. By late afternoon the drizzle had ceased, though my mind had grown muddled with conflicting thoughts. I decided to walk across the street to the beach, just for a break from the monotony of the house. Surprisingly, I found Liam sitting alone on top of one of the vacant wooden picnic tables.

Was he purposefully avoiding me? Had I done something wrong? I walked up to the table, unable to voice either of those thoughts. Instead, I simply said, "Hey, Liam. Mind if I join you?"

Liam shrugged. His gaze never left the sea.

"Is everything okay?" I gauged him with caution and scooted up the picnic table, careful to leave a fair distance between us.

203

I suddenly felt the need to apologize. "About the other day," I began. My throat went dry. I struggled to find the right words, but sufficed with a simple, "For what it's worth, I'm sorry."

Instead of responding, he buried his face in his hands, making me feel worse than ever.

I sat there, waiting for him to say something to contradict me and explain how I misunderstood his intentions. After all, *he* had volunteered to spend time with me working on Lulu's endless list of chores. *He* had invited me to the beach. Didn't that count for something?

Instead, he said in a low voice, "It's not you, Jordan. I mean it is, but it isn't."

My eyes stung. I blinked away the tears. Somehow, that obscure explanation was supposed to make me feel better? I pulled my shirt tightly around my waist, the chill seeping in. But he made no gesture to explain his behavior. In fact, he did nothing at all but stare into the distance.

Overhead, the clouds began to open, coating the ground with another sprinkle. For several long minutes, I sat in silence next to him, more confused than ever. Finally, I muttered a last, "Sorry," and slid off the table, my head slumping forward. I plodded across the beach toward Lulu's house. Soon, a thin layer of fine black sand caked my wet feet. I made it about halfway down the beach when I heard Liam call my name. I looked up expectantly, hoping he'd say something to clarify the confusion I felt. Instead, he remained seated, only offering a vague reply, "Jordan, this wasn't what I expected. I…I just need some time to figure things out."

My gaze left his face, grateful the rain masked my conflicted emotions. Disheartened, my shoulders slumped forward. I hurried for home through the intensifying rain.

Things were so much less complicated with Sully who spoke his mind, but I couldn't turn back the clock and make him like me again. Especially not when my time with Sully had lacked the magic I felt when I was with Liam…a magic I'd thought we shared. Somehow, I managed to ruin even that. Worse, I had no idea what I did to mess things up. Confused and hurt by Liam's reaction, I bolted up Lulu's slippery steps two at a time and slammed her front door with more force than necessary.

"Is everything all right?" she asked, intercepting me on the way to my room, drying her hands on a dish towel, leaving her work unfinished in the kitchen.

"Never better," I said, bitingly sarcastic. My wet clothes clung to my skin and my damp hair stuck to my cheeks.

Lulu's deep brown eyes narrowed with concern. "Is there anything I can do? Anything you'd like to talk about?"

I sadly shook my head, not trusting my voice to words.

"Jordan…" Lulu began and placed a gentle hand upon my forearm.

I glanced up, my moistening eyes belying my true emotions, and slipped from her grasp. I flew down the hall to my room, slammed its door behind me, and flopped on the bed in my clammy clothes, unable to contain the tears any longer.

Wasn't he the one who'd led me on? After all, I hadn't liked him one bit when I'd first met him, but he persisted, conveniently placing himself in different parts of my life until I could no longer resist his real personality. I'd given him an out the other day on the beach, hadn't I? I had started to walk away, but *he* pulled me into that kiss. And judging by its duration, I could tell he had enjoyed it. So why the sudden change? What had I done to make him so mad that he wouldn't even speak to me?

Lucky for me, Lulu let me cry myself dry without interruption, pondering those questions in hopes of reaching a justifiable conclusion. But not as lucky, soon after my tears had reduced to soft sobs, I heard a knock on the door. I peeked out my window and spotted a drenched Liam waiting on the front stoop. I made sure to duck out of sight before he noticed.

When no one answered, he knocked again, more urgently this time. As far as I was concerned, he could stand out there all night, but Lulu took pity on him and opened the door.

I expected the exchange to be brief, telling him to try another time after my heart had a chance to heal. Instead, they spoke in rapid, hushed tones for a considerable length of time. Puzzled, I craned my head to peer out the bottom of my window without notice, straining to hear their conversation. Eventually, their pitches rose, as if escalating into an argument. Still I couldn't distinguish a coherent word.

I knitted my brow and sunk to the floor, more bewildered than ever. I knew Liam had described Lulu as an old family friend, but I'd never seen him question her authority or stand his ground in front of her before. In fact, all the times I'd seen them together their conversations had been short and pleasant. Deep inside, I felt guilty for instigating this conflict between them, all because I hadn't bothered to answer the door myself.

Finally, Lulu heaved an exasperated sigh. "I hope you know what you're doing," she said, just loud enough for me to hear.

I inched closer to the window, desperate to catch a piece of Liam's response.

"I've got this," Liam replied in a confident and controlled voice. "I can handle it."

Lulu sighed again. "If you say so." But judging from her tone, she didn't seem convinced.

I blinked, wondering what he meant when I heard Lulu's footsteps coming down the hall. I quickly scrambled onto my bed, pretending I'd been there the entire time and hadn't overheard a single word.

She knocked softly upon my closed door, her hand bearing a despondent air.

"Come in," I conceded, curious to unravel the subject of their conversation.

The door handle spun slowly. "Liam's here," Lulu said, like I hadn't noticed.

"I don't want to see him," I declared, hoping my obstinate behavior might result in her divulging important details.

Lulu crossed her arms over her chest. Her eyes appeared weighted with sorrow. Or frustration. Or perhaps both. "I thought you might say that, so I asked him to give you a few minutes."

"You can give him a few hours, if you want. I'm not going out there."

"Stubborn child," Lulu muttered as she closed her eyes and pressed her fingers to her temples, like playing the role of mediator had given her a migraine. "Wait in here if you wish. I'll simply invite him inside instead."

"Fine," I grumbled in a tone that sounded anything but fine. I pried myself from the bed and lumbered down the hall with irritation that I hadn't uncovered a thing.

Under Lulu's watchful gaze, I opened the front door and snapped at Liam, "Yeah?"

"About earlier," he began, undeterred by the hostility in my tone.

I leaned against the doorframe, crossing my arms over my chest and waited, impatient.

His shoulders slumped slightly as his face softened. "I...I'm sorry," he said in a low voice. His damp hair plastered against his head, concurring with his regretful mood.

From the corner of my eye, I saw Lulu's mouth relax into a sympathetic smile. She returned to her work in the kitchen. I turned my attention back to Liam, waiting for him to explain.

He took a deep breath. "I'm sorry...for everything. I just needed some time to figure things out."

"Like what?" I asked, curiosity getting the best of me.

He shrugged. "It's complicated."

A faint smile traced across my lips. "Hey, that's my line," I said, remembering I had used those exact words when I couldn't actually explain why I bothered with Lulu's chores and why I needed her help.

My gaze left his as questions packed my mind. Did I really want to be with someone who withheld secrets from me? Or with someone whose moods could swing that dramatically? Could our relationship ever progress to another level if he couldn't trust me with the truth?

Then again, I hadn't shared my most dangerous of secrets with him. Not even a single word about my actual identity or my frequent visits to the volcano. How could I tell him that I was an Elemental and Lulu provided my link to Pele, the sole reason I came to Hilo in the first place? How could I expect Liam to reveal everything to me if I wouldn't share the same courtesy with him?

I looked back at Liam, trying to decipher his intentions.

He flashed me a knowing grin, watching me ponder those thoughts, like he'd carefully chosen those precise words to guarantee I'd accept his apology.

"But it's okay now," Liam reassured me. "Everything's okay."

"And how am I supposed to know that?" I asked. I held his stare, wishing his words were true—though skepticism still reigned over my heart.

"Here's how." Without another word, he cupped my cheeks in his palms and pressed his lips delicately upon mine.

Surprised, I stood there in the doorway, not caring if Lulu or anyone else saw. Softly, he continued to kiss me until my anger dissolved and my defiant arms dropped limply to my sides.

CHAPTER TWENTY-THREE

That night, I thrashed in bed while Hydros flooded the ancient city of Atlantis. Clinging to the Dragon Tree, I stretched out my hand toward the slave girl, Monifa, the rising waters swirling around her. Desperate for help, her fingers reached mine, clasping my hand tightly within her grip. I yanked Monifa toward me, carefully keeping her head above the water as the weight of the shackles bound to her ankles threatened to pull her under. Just before she reached the safety of the tree branches, the waters rushed back out to sea, dragging everything with their incredible current. Her fingers slipped through mine as I helplessly watched her sink below the dark water. The echo of her fading scream of panic rang inside my ears.

Suddenly, I was back in California, at the base of the mangled Bay Bridge. Fierce winds whipped my hair and pierced my clothes. I fought off Skye's tornado, infusing it with a jet of fire and aimed it at Hydros. Suddenly, I reconsidered and tried to alter the course of the fire tornado. But it was too late. Hydros had already fallen. Gaia rushed to her side, cradling her limp form. Gaia's gaze shifted toward the Bay where another wave grew in the distance.

She will never be truly gone, Pele had said. Hydros's soul lived on, but in a different form now. Meaning I hadn't destroyed the threat, only transferred it into another being.

209

I watched the incoming wave swell to enormous proportions. "Three on one," I thought grimly. "Just like old times." I raised my hands upward, prepared to defend myself.

In the distance, the next chosen Water Elemental rode atop the incoming crest, like the big wave surfers Sully and I had watched from our perch on the cliff. I craned my neck, desperate for a glimpse of my new threat when a bright light pierced through the clouds and straight into my window to illuminate my sleeping face.

The full moon.

I leapt out of bed, my brain startlingly alert. Dozens of questions swam through my mind, but they would have to wait. Pele said I needed to meet Hina and the Fire Essence at the next full moon. Hopefully, they might provide some answers to the uncertainty that filled my life. Desperate not to miss this opportunity, I threw on a shirt and shorts and tiptoed from my room, careful not to wake Lulu.

I crept down the hallway and out the front door. I stole down the patio steps slowly, praying they wouldn't creak under my weight. The moon snuck behind the clouds once more, but I didn't hesitate. The bright beam through my bedroom window was a beacon, reminding me of the significance of this night.

Barefoot, I jogged across the road toward the coarse black sand on the other side. When I reached the breezy beach, I wrapped my arms nervously around my waist and announced, "Hina, I'm here!" But the beach appeared empty, except for a few pale creatures that scuttled across the sand. Slowly I sat, watching their movements and waiting for Hina to arrive.

A series of hatched trails marked up the sand, each ending by the mouth of a deep protective hole that lay just beyond the water line. A pale ghost crab popped out of the hole, busily scooping sand to form a mound and dig out its home. The trails spread in different directions, but whenever they met, the marks intensified, as if a brief clash occurred in the open arena before the two crabs parted and went their separate ways. I couldn't help but think of how their nightly rituals paralleled my own life. Regardless of the time or place, I followed my own course until I encountered the other Elementals in another skirmish.

These small crabs, like pale ghosts on the beach, endured an endless battle against the sea similar to the one I must face. It didn't matter that I had destroyed Hydros if another person took her place. I hoped Pele was right about the importance of this final journey — that it would provide the answers I sought.

I glanced around, wondering where to find Hina when I noticed a shadowy lump curled like a ball under a tall palm tree. Its long fluffy tail lay neatly tucked over its nose as if keeping its moist skin warm in the cool night breeze. I recognized the lump immediately. *Kea.*

I left my spot on the sand and walked toward her, my footsteps rousing the dog. She lifted her head from under her tail with recognition. She stretched and yawned before rising from her spot. Shaking the sand from her white fur, she trotted over to join me. I patted her head, grateful for her companionship. "How can you stand sleeping there, girl?" I asked her. "Aren't you afraid a coconut might fall on your head?"

She tilted her head sideways, wearing an amused grin like she meant to say I worried too much. I scratched her belly, making her tongue dangle out one side as she panted contentedly. Suddenly, she paused. Her ears cocked as her nose twitched to sniff the air in an inquisitive way. She closed her mouth and looked upward, detecting the source of the interesting scent.

I followed her gaze toward the mountain that shared her name. Above its summit, thick clouds were backlit in a ghostly glow. Soon the clouds parted, revealing the light of the full moon. I blinked into the brightness, marveling at how the light and dark patches of the moon strongly resembled a human face, warm and caring.

"Is that Hina?" I asked Kea, though I didn't expect her to understand a word.

Kea's ears perked forward and she gave a sharp bark, confirming my question, before running off into the shadows.

In that moment, a bright moonbeam stretched toward the ground, right before my feet, as a path that led the goddess Hina to my very spot. Her figure appeared outlined in a silvery glow. Her soft, gray eyes—like the dark fields on the surface of the moon—alighted on me. A smile traced its way across her full lips, pushing her cheeks upward on her rounded face.

"It's a pleasure to meet you," I said in my most polite voice and gave a deep, reverent bow to the old goddess. "I cannot thank you enough for healing my friend, Cam, and myself."

Hina spoke in a soft, measured voice. "It's the least I could do. He has too much life to live and you are still needed. Besides, Pele does not ask many favors of me. And I couldn't refuse one of such importance."

My hands sought each other and I anxiously wrung them together. I thought Pele said Hina would answer my questions. Instead, she only seemed to raise more. Why was I needed? Why was it so important for Pele to train me? But Hina volunteered no further details and I feared to press the subject before I completed my final journey…and the rest of my training.

Taking a deep breath to restore my patience, I began, "Pele told me that you can communicate with the departed souls of the past Elementals."

Hina nodded her round face. "I can."

"She also said that you could introduce me to the old Fire Elemental."

"As you wish. The Fire Essence will be here soon," she said kindly.

"Is there any chance I can speak to Hydros's Essence, too?"

Hina shook her head. "Give her some time. She is not ready yet."

With a flash of boldness, I dared to ask, "Well, how about any of the other Essences? Like the Earth Essence?" Perhaps they could provide some background for me to help me better understand my greatest foe.

"There is no Earth Essence," Hina stated simply.

"No Earth Essence?" My brows pinched together. "What do you mean?"

Before Hina could respond, a washed-out, ghostlike mist swirled by her side. Tinted in a faint shade of orange, the mist quickly took on form, like an apparition of a human. What I imagined had once been a flaming red head of flyaway hair framed a steep nose, square jaw, and intense eyes. I gaped in astonishment and awe when the Fire Essence said in a clear voice, "Gaia is the original Earth Elemental. She is the first and only embodiment of the Earth Element. No others existed before her."

The Essence leaned toward me and whispered, "That's why she can be a little on the bossy side at times."

My mouth fell open. Partially from the shock of the honest revelation of Gaia's personality and partially because...

"You're a boy!" I exclaimed.

Mirroring my behavior, he let his jaw drop. "And you're a *girl!*" he squeaked in a mocking high-pitched tone.

"But...but..." I stammered, trying to think of a polite way to phrase my surprise. "I thought...well, with me and the other Elementals..."

"That only girls could possess such power? Ha!" He cackled to himself. "As if."

Hina slowly rolled her wide gray eyes. "Well, you two seem to have hit it off right away," she said with a surprise dose of sarcasm. "In case you hadn't already guessed, Jordan, I'd like you to meet the Fire Essence, Brandr."

"Brandr," I repeated, letting his name hang on my lips, the word representing a new hope in the form of an alliance against the other Elementals. With his brash attitude and sassy remarks, I couldn't help but like him from the start.

"It's Norwegian for 'fire,'" he explained. "But enough about me. I heard we have some work to do tonight." He stretched out his arms and legs like he pretended to run a long-distance race. "I hope you're ready."

"Pele said it would be dangerous," I offered, hoping to entice him to elaborate on our destination.

"You have no idea," he replied, his voice taking a surprisingly serious tone as his intense eyes held mine.

A shiver of fear traveled up my spine. I looked away from his gaze. Suddenly, I missed Liam's calm, comforting, playful demeanor, so unlike the ghostly form of the one who had previously shared my role. I looked out across the water, remembering the day I spent with Liam at the beach, hoping to draw comfort from that memory before I embarked on this journey into the unknown. The silhouettes of black lava rocks jutted into the indigo water. Moonlight shimmered like quicksilver off each rising wave, spilling over into white churning sea foam that tumbled toward shore. Meanwhile, the tiny crabs—pale like the soul of the past Elemental who stood before me—reappeared on the beach to begin the excavation of their holes once more. The sight before me now seemed so foreign and cold, completely unlike the bright day with Liam. I shivered once more, more frightened than ever about what lay ahead.

"Well, I am sure there is much the two of you need to discuss in preparation for your journey," Hina said politely, noticing my fear. Before she departed, her gray eyes flashed toward Brandr, as if warning him not to disclose too much.

He nodded in understanding.

I watched the moonbeam dissolve, returning the silvery form

of Hina to her place in the sky.

"So where are we going?" I whispered.

"That's for me to know and you to find out," he replied, like an irksome sibling.

I placed my hands on my hips and shifted my weight to one side. "Well, that's really mature."

"What can I say?" he said, puffing out his chest. "I guess you know me too well."

I sighed. "Can you at least tell me how dangerous this journey will be?"

He studied me intently for a moment, his lips drawn into a thin line. His mouth busted into a wide grin, unable to contain his laughter any longer. "*Re-lax*. Everything will be fine. Besides, by the time we're through tonight, you'll scoff at your old powers," he said, his eyes lit with a mischievous twinkle. As an aside, he added, "You can thank me later."

My face loosened into a soft smile, hoping what he said held true. Then I would gain the powers I needed to stop the other Elementals so I could continue my quest for a peaceful, ordinary life.

Chapter Twenty-Four

Before we departed, the Fire Essence turned to me. "You know, Jordan. I have to admit that the fire tornado you made back in California was pretty sweet. Way to think outside the box!" he exclaimed and raised his fist to knock his knuckles against mine in congratulations. Even though I saw our knuckles connect, I felt nothing but air, almost touching a ghost. I looked at him sadly, glimpsing the future that awaited me.

"So what exactly do you do?" I asked him. "Follow me around like an invisible babysitter?"

Brandr scoffed. "No! I've got plenty to keep me busy besides trekking around after you and your lovesick heart."

My jaw dropped. *Lovesick heart?* "Were you spying on me?" I gasped.

"As if. Like I told you before, I've got plenty to do. I only knew about the fire tornado because the other Essences and I try to catch the battles when we can. It helps us know what you're all capable of."

"You talk to the other Essences? Then you can tell Hydros that I'm sorry. Pele said she's bitter and that's why I can't see her yet. But you have to believe me, I didn't know. I didn't realize what she was like before." I paused for a moment, remembering how much the Irish girl Shannon reminded me of my own blind fear. "If I had, maybe things would've been different that day by

216

the bridge. Will you tell her that for me?"

"I don't think she'll listen. It's not like that's the only reason she's bitter," the Fire Essence said offhandedly. His pale face froze, as if he'd said too much.

My eyes grew wide. "There's more? Like what?" I prodded.

The Fire Essence shook his head. "We don't have time for this now. Your issues with Hydros will have to wait. Pele made me promise I'd take you on this journey tonight. And I think you know her well enough by now to understand why I do *not* want to disappoint the goddess."

I gave a dejected nod, frustrated that once again my questions waited on hold. "Can I at least ask you one thing?" I blurted before he began.

He heaved a deep sigh. "Go ahead."

"Did it ever bother you?"

"That I'm dead? Yeah, it still bothers me," he admitted, in a tone that sounded like I had rubbed salt on an open wound.

"No," I replied with a dramatic roll of my eyes. "Not that. I mean, did it ever bother you that you weren't as powerful as the other Elementals?"

"Not as powerful?" He chortled. "What gave you that idea? Aside from the fact that I died, of course."

I sighed deeply before beginning. "It's just that everywhere I look, I see the Earth beneath my feet or water extending as far as I can see with the sky stretching from one horizon to the other. Fire plays but a small part on the planet. So why is it we got stuck with the least powerful of the four elements?"

Brandr laughed deeply. "Way to time the questions, Jordan. That is precisely the reason Pele asked me to visit you tonight."

He pointed upward. "The sky does appear to extend into the vast reaches of space, yet it's but a thin layer over the entire planet. Skye's weather couldn't exist without water or the heat from the sun.

217

"And look out into space," he continued as he waved an arm across the pinpricks of light that dotted the black of night. "What do you think these stars are made of?"

I shrugged. "Burning masses of superheated gases," I replied, as if reciting a phrase from a textbook.

He excitedly ran his fingers through his flyaway hair. "Don't you see? Your power—*our* power—reaches beyond this planet alone. Earth, water, and sky do not exist everywhere in the cosmos, but *fire* does. You have powers that stretch beyond this world."

"So you're saying, if it wasn't for fire, there would be no planets or stars...nothing but empty space?"

"Exactly." Brandr's face lit into a cunning smile. He twisted his fingers together to crack his knuckles, but without the sound. "And I've got just the way to prove it to you. Okay, so the first thing you'll need to do is turn your core white hot, like when you make the flash blast Pele taught you."

I swallowed hard. "But I never learned how to master that skill," I admitted, suddenly guilty I hadn't tried harder during Pele's session, letting my emotions trump my drive to succeed.

He groaned. "You know, this would be so much easier if you'd simply come to accept and believe in your Elemental name, Pyr."

"But I'm not," I protested. "I'm Jordan. And if I had it my way, I'd give all this up in a flash just for the chance to be normal like everyone else."

"Not after tonight, you won't. Wait until I show you your true, full powers and we'll see how ready you'll be to give it all up."

I scrunched my nose. "My full powers? But I thought Pele had already taught me everything I needed to know."

"Not even close. I've got some news for you. This next experience will be anything but normal...or pleasant. But if you're going to be difficult and not believe you really are Pyr, then I guess we'll have to do things my way."

"Your way?"

"Hang on, sweetheart," he said in a mocking tone. "I'm sorry to have to do this to you, but we're about to get to know each other a whole lot better." And without another word, the Fire Essence stepped sideways and merged his body with my own.

"Ew," I squealed as a dank, stale smell flooded my nostrils. "You stink!"

"Careful I don't take over your mouth as well," he cautioned. "Besides, it's not like you're any better," he added in a disgusted voice. "You smell so perfumey sweet it makes me sick. And don't even get me started on the erratic beating of your heart!"

Angered by his comments and action, I tried to thrash my arms and legs to escape. But my body felt heavy and immobile, like my limbs would move only under his control. "What are you doing to me?" I shrieked.

"I told you this would be easier if you just accepted your Elemental name and believed it with your heart and soul. But noooo, your heart's too busy fixating on a boy," he said in a faux-girly tone. His voice turned hard and serious. "So now we do things my way. This is what it feels like when an Essence and an Elemental fuse as one. Once fused, our powers can work in unison—amplified and concentrated to achieve feats neither one of us could accomplish alone. So if you'll relax for a minute, I can turn up the heat and get this party started."

"But I don't get it. If you're the Fire *Essence*, weren't you around way before me? So how do you know how to talk like that?"

"Just because I died, doesn't mean I can't keep up with the times. Now I mean it. Relax."

As difficult as it seemed, I stopped resisting him. Deep inside, I felt his soul settle alongside mine, confident and strong as he revved up my core into a searing burn that coursed through my body with amazing speed. Sweat beaded across my brow, but instantly vaporized into steam. I glanced down at my hands, surprised to find my normal skin tones dissolve into a bright white that went from glowing to radiating a blinding light within seconds. The blistering heat caused the rock I stood upon to melt in an instant. I recalled Pele's words about how an Elemental was immortal within the realm of the Element. Only this act took her statement to a new extreme.

"How hot did you make my body that I can melt rock with my feet?" I asked, astonished as the ground liquefied beneath me.

His voice remained calm. "Oh, I dunno. Sixteen hundred degrees, give or take a bit."

"*Sixteen hundred!*" I choked on the stale air, desperate for a decent breath. "What are you trying to do? Turn me into a miniature sun?"

I heard Brandr chuckle. "Something like that," he said. "Now hang on."

Before I could blink with surprise, I sank knee-deep into the hole he melted in the ground. But we didn't stop there. Faster and faster we sank beneath the surface. Soon, our speed increased to an amazing rate. Our magical abilities combined, allowing us to travel deep within the Earth itself. The ground above me congealed, sealing up the hole and preventing our escape. "But the exit route..." I began, my voice rising two octaves in a panic.

"No worries. It'll reopen when we need it."

"God, I hope you're right," I said, trembling as I looked around, enclosed by molten rock on every side. Though I told myself to trust the Essence, I couldn't shake the feeling I had unwittingly sealed myself inside a fiery tomb. Besides, what did *he* have to lose? He was already dead. Me, on the other hand...

I forced my thoughts to Liam. And in that moment, I forgave

him for everything. I only wished to see him again. Whatever it took, I vowed I would make it out of here alive.

"I have to test something else. Tell me, Jordan," the Essence continued. His voice sounded like an unsettling echo inside my head. "Can you hear me now?"

I laughed. "You sound like a cell phone commercial."

"But you actually *heard* me?"

"Yeah. I mean, it was kind of weird because it sounded like the voice came from inside my mind."

"That's because it did," Brandr said in an exuberant tone. "Don't you see? This allows us to communicate with each other without spoken words!"

"And that's exciting because why…?" I asked dryly.

"Think of the possibilities," he exclaimed. "We can talk to each other without others knowing! This gives us a huge advantage in the future."

"I'd rather not. As far as I'm concerned, this is the one and only time I ever plan to let you fuse with me again. Did I mention I still can't get the smell out of my nose?"

"You'll live," he said sourly, a hint of jealousy lingering inside each spoken word. His voice prattled on inside my head about the massive power of fire that lay beneath the Earth's crust and how it was my responsibility to understand my full potential in harnessing this power when needed.

"So we're down inside the core of the planet now?" I guessed.

"Not even close. This is still the crust. It's only a thin section of our overall planet, but beneath the crust is a whole different story. That's where things heat up…literally."

"Are you planning to take me all the way to the center of the Earth?" I wondered aloud, expecting we'd pop out somewhere on the other side.

"No. The inner core is solid, plus the pressure is intense, almost three million times greater than at sea level. Even with our magic combined, we couldn't stave off pressure of that intensity. If we tried to go all the way to the core, we could be crushed to the size of a marble."

"That doesn't sound good."

"Not good at all," he agreed as we melted our way down into the next layer of the Earth where extremely hot rock flowed like a very thick, very slow moving liquid.

"Where are we?" I dared.

"This is what I wanted to show you. This is the mantle... the section beneath the crust. This is also the unseen source of your power. You asked why your powers seem less than those of the others, but I am here to prove you wrong. This is where rising currents form new ocean floors and sinking currents make plates collide as their crustal materials are recycled back into the mantle. You know, Gaia will never admit it, but I think she feels threatened by you."

"Me? But why? She's beaten me every time."

"Only because you didn't understand your vast untapped potential at the time. That's where I come in. In case you hadn't realized it, our element creates the underlying force behind Gaia's power."

"Meaning...?"

Brandr sighed. "Meaning you alone can govern her ability to lift mountains or generate earthquakes, all from the heat within the mantle, rising and falling like currents that drive the plates of the crust."

His information might have surprised me more if we had been someplace else. Yet as he explained, I noticed the rock around us had begun to lighten in color from its original deep orange into a faint yellow and gradually into a bright white. "Is that normal?" I asked the Essence, gesturing to the changing colors.

"Oh my God," Brandr gasped. "Pele will kill me if I don't get you out of here alive."

"Why are you worried?" I teased. "You're already dead."

"Oh, shut up. You know what I mean," he snapped, his playful attitude fading in an instant. "I need you to focus! This is bad...really bad. I think our fused heat may have accidentally created a new mantle plume."

"Mantle plume? What the heck is that?"

"Think of it as a hot spot within the mantle, like a huge embedded pillar of tremendously hot molten rock that acts like a blowtorch on the ocean's crust to create a chain of massive underwater volcanoes. And when the volcano swells large enough, it breaks through the water, forming an island like Hawaii. To make a long story short, I think that our extended presence in this area may have created a new hot spot in the mantle as the surrounding rock absorbed our temperature..." His voice trailed off, as if he pondered the monumental consequences.

I braved a question. "What are you saying? I thought you told me everything would be fine!"

"Don't you see? We have to get out of here now before our superheated mass triggers an unexpected eruption on the island that could threaten the lives and homes of tens of thousands of innocent people."

"You're right." I swallowed hard. "That does sound bad."

"*Really* bad."

"So can't you just turn down the heat a little?" I suggested.

"Negative. Unless you don't plan on escaping...ever."

For a moment, I saw Liam's face flash before my eyes as his deep blue eyes gauged me with concern. A face I'd never see again, unless we left right now. "I'm afraid that's not an option. Do whatever it is that you need to do to get us outta here."

"I thought you might say that." And in that second, the Fire Essence's soul seized total control of my body. My mind felt helplessly trapped inside an alien body as he turned up the heat by my feet, like thrusters to rocket us from that spot. Faster and faster we spiraled up toward the surface, the hot thick rock parting just before my head sliced through its space. I prayed the rock beneath us cooled quickly in the absence of our radiating heat and silenced the unintended mantle plume forever. During those long minutes, we traveled upward at a rate that made my head spin, until we finally reached the cool, dense rock of the oceanic crust.

"Aaahhhh!" I screamed as he pushed us harder still, desperate to reach the surface. I couldn't fathom how much further we had to go, but just when I thought I'd never see Liam or Lulu or Kea again, we shot out through the rock into the cool evening air, and landed with a thump on solid ground. The impact ejected the Essence from my body. And once our fusion had broken, I cooled dramatically, my white-hot skin quickly assuming its normal color. I lay beside the ghostlike apparition of the Essence, unable to move from my spot, my clothes miraculously intact, but drenched with sweat. I wasn't sure how he felt, but my heart thudded like a giant brass drum inside my chest from our narrow escape.

"Don't. Ever. Do. That. Again," I managed between panting breaths.

Brandr gasped for air before retorting. "Believe me, sister. Repeating that experience is *not* high on my priority list. But I think we did it. I think we made it out in time."

"I hope you're right," I whispered, afraid of what might happen if he wasn't.

As we lay under the dark skies, I half expected a spire of lava to jettison from underneath my spot. The ground remained solid, leading me to believe him after all, that we escaped before creating a new mantle plume.

Still, something weighed on my mind. "Can I ask you a personal question, Brandr?"

For a long time, he silently gazed up at the night sky, as if contemplating how to respond. Finally, he replied with a joyless, "Go for it."

"I was just wondering, if you are so strong within the realm of our element and know so much about your powers, how did you die?"

Brandr slowly rolled his head to face me, a profound sadness filling his weary eyes. "It's a long story. Ask me again some other time," he said softly and slowly dragged himself off the ground. "Some time when I'm not so tired."

I nodded, dissatisfied, even though I fully understood his response. After enduring so many tragedies in my time on this planet, I couldn't imagine the emotional toll I'd feel if I had to describe my own loss of life.

"So I guess I'll be seeing you around?" I wagered.

Brandr gave a small nod. "Perhaps sooner than you think," he murmured as he staggered away. His Essence spun into a wisp of orange-tinted haze and floated into the distance just as the hint of dawn began to touch the sky.

Chapter Twenty-Five

I stumbled back to Lulu's house, more drained from that journey and the Fire Essence's fusion with my body than I'd ever been before in my whole life. After stripping off my sweat-stained clothes and taking a much-needed shower, I slipped into a clean pair of pajamas and crawled into bed, shutting the shades against the bright light of the morning. Even lying still, I could feel the trickle of perspiration against the back of my neck, as if my shower didn't really take. So I kicked off the sheets and stretched out beneath the overhead fan, letting the gentle breeze cool my skin and seep into my core.

My heavy arms and legs sunk into the mattress, my muscles clumsy and inoperable from overuse. I lay, incapable of movement until sleep quickly found me. And I dreamed refreshing thoughts in an attempt to soothe the burn.

In my dream world, waves quietly lapped the shore as the sea breeze lifted my hair and brushed my skin. No longer in fear of the water, I waded into the shallows, eager to revisit the beauty of the coral reef. As I drifted through schools of striped and spotted fish, Liam suddenly appeared by my side. A gasp of surprise escaped my lips, trapped underwater in a bubble that swelled between my hands. My eyes grew wide, marveling at my achievement. Liam smiled proudly and slipped his fingers into mine. With a gentle tug, he lifted me toward the surface and said,

"See? I told you it just took some practice." He congratulated me in a way that spoke louder than words and swept me into an amazing long, deep kiss, bordering on magical. I felt the blush rise high in my cheeks, warming my skin, my heart, my soul.

I crawled out of bed, the image of Liam kissing me in the shallow water replaying in my mind. I staggered into the kitchen to replenish my depleted reserves, wondering if reality would match the expectation of my dream.

I grabbed some food from the fridge and noticed the answering machine light blinked red. I glanced around the empty house, wondering where Lulu had gone. Puzzled, I pressed the button to play the message, excited at hearing Liam's voice. "Hi, Jordan," he started, before slipping into a long pause. My initial enthusiasm quickly faded when I detected a note of worry in his tone. "I stopped by earlier to see you, but Lulu said you were still sleeping. Are you feeling all right? Anyway, I need to talk to you. It's really important. I'll pick you up at six, okay? See you then." A loud, obnoxious beep concluded the message before a computerized voice declared, "Saturday, four-fifteen p.m." Another annoying beep followed.

Suddenly, I forgot all about my meal. *Four-fifteen in the afternoon?* How long had I been sleeping? I peeked at the kitchen clock, startled to discover that not only had I slept the entire day, but forty-five minutes had already passed since his call. Though my body seemed lethargic and sore from exertion, my mind whirred at an incredible rate, infusing new energy into my weary limbs.

I replayed Liam's message, trying to remember his every word. The second time through, his voice seemed to carry a different tone. Perhaps it wasn't worry after all, I decided. Maybe he sounded a little nervous about asking me out over the phone, especially when Lulu could hear. *And maybe he's simply anxious to see me again,* I concluded, my heart fluttering with anticipation at the thought.

I flitted around the room in a daze, unable to believe how much my life had changed in such a short time. Sure, I had an irritating first encounter with Liam when I broke his nose. But now Pele had confided some valuable secrets about the history of the Elementals, the Fire Essence had taken me inside the Earth, and Liam had officially asked me out. Overwhelmed with my good fortune, I wanted to tell Lulu I'd be gone for the evening.

Strangely, she wasn't anywhere in the house, so I ventured into the backyard, barefoot. I soon spotted Lulu perched quietly on a lava rock by the side of the koi pond, tossing handfuls of pellets across the surface. She wore her long gray hair loose, letting it fall around her shoulders, like the weight of the bun upon her head was more than she could bear.

"Lulu?" I called, but she didn't look up. Instead, she peered at the water with a vacant stare.

A part of me felt a sense of personal accomplishment as I gazed upon the yard. Where weeds and leaf litter had previously stood, a thick carpet of grass now lay. The faded pink exterior shone in its fresh coat of that ridiculously named paint, Luscious Lilac. Piles of porous red and black lava rocks lined the wall of her koi pond. And neat corners trimmed the hibiscus hedge, covered with full blossoms.

Despite all the work I'd completed, the other part of me felt like I'd disappointed her in some way. Was she sad that I'd spent so much time with Pele and Liam? Or was it something more?

I neared the pond, gazing across its surface, wondering what worries preoccupied Lulu's mind. Leafy water plants—like floating heads of lettuce—bobbed on the surface of the pond, agitated by the hungry fish. Piebald orange and black heads broke the surface as their large gaping mouths gulped down the pellets of food with vigor. Their scales gleaming in bright splashes of ivory, black and gold, the koi skimmed the surface, anxious for

Auntie Lulu to scatter another handful of food across the water.

"Lulu? Are you okay?" I asked and crouched beside her.

She paused in a contemplative way while the fish clustered right below the surface, eagerly awaiting another handful of food. Yet she didn't answer.

Maybe she just wants to be alone, I thought and decided to leave her in peace. But I only made it a few steps before I heard her faint, withered voice. "I had a dream that one of my friends was in danger."

I turned around, my voice reassuring. "But I heard Marvin was feeling better from his surgery. Gerard even said he expected his brother to be back at the store by the end of next week."

Lulu slowly titled her head to face me. Her grave brown eyes gazed into mine. "A different type of danger," she whispered grimly. "I'm afraid my friend might get hurt...or worse...die."

I blinked, surprised by the severity of her words. I recalled how many nightmarish dreams I'd experienced, none of which ever occurred as I'd foreseen. Gruesome scenes of mass destruction and unnecessary death, all figments of my imagination. "Oh, Auntie," I said with a lighthearted sigh, "it was only a dream."

By the wilt in her shoulders, I could tell she didn't believe me.

"Come on, let's get you inside." I said, coaxing her from her spot. "I'll make you some tea. It'll help you feel better, I'm sure." Still, a sorrowful look filled her eyes when I took the bag of pellets from her hand and led her into the house.

As I fixed Lulu a cup of tea, I glanced up at the clock, noting its hands read just before six. Despite Lulu's unease, a small smile crept across my lips. Liam would be picking me up soon and I had to admit, I could hardly wait. I ran back to my room to get ready, certain that nothing—not even Lulu's worry—would spoil my cheerful mood.

Chapter Twenty-Six

Reaching into the back of my closet, I pulled the sundress I'd borrowed from Vanessa Sullivan off its hanger and held it against my body. Normally, I wasn't a fan of pink, but something about the dress made it work. With pale blue flowers surrounded in green leaves, it fit in well with the style of clothing here in the islands. Plus, this particular shade of rosy pink seemed to perfectly accentuate my black hair and ebony eyes. I had brought this dress along for a special occasion, but hadn't had the opportunity to wear it since I'd arrived. Tonight seemed as good a reason as any. After all, Liam asked to see me, so that sort of counted as a date, didn't it?

I slipped into the dress, zippering the tight fitted top up my back and adjusting the straps—as thin as spaghetti noodles—over my shoulders. I spun back and forth in the mirror, secretly hoping he'd notice my changed appearance, when an urgent rapping came at the front door. My heart leaping at the sound, I slid into a pair of sandals and dashed to the door, eager to greet him.

After fanning my hands down the dress to straighten out the remaining wrinkles, I swung open the door. My face instantly brightened. "Hi," I told Liam, my smile growing uncontrollably wide.

"Hi," he replied in a surprisingly nervous tone and dropped

the car keys into his pocket. For a second, his eyes searched mine with urgency. Before I could worry about Liam's reservations, his gaze shifted to trace my body from head to toe. "You look really nice," he admitted. His cheeks turned a fast shade of crimson.

I figured he wouldn't have blushed that much if he didn't actually like me. "Thanks," I replied bashfully. But inside my head, I congratulated myself. *He noticed the dress!*

The color quickly drained from his cheeks. "Jordan, I have to tell you something," he blurted.

"Not here," I said and grabbed his hand, pulling him down the front stoop before I swiftly closed the door behind me.

With a short glance for traffic in both directions, I dashed across the street with Liam in tow. When we reached the edge of the sandy beach, Liam spun me to face him. "Jordan, I—"

"Hang on. It's not far," I said, having a more private spot in mind.

He sighed before reluctantly acquiescing. I kicked off my sandals, grabbing them with my free hand, and picked up the pace. Hand in hand, we climbed over a stretch of rocks and ducked under a few branches from the small grove of trees. Soon we reached the edge of a secluded stretch of fine black sand, lit by the bronze glow of the setting sun. "This is it," I announced and dropped my sandals on the ground. I gazed deeply into his eyes that reflected the muted purple of the rugged peak of Mauna Kea—almost like the color sample of Pandora's Box from Lipoa's. It reminded me of the first day we met, causing an amused smile to form on my lips, thinking of that first awkward moment when I'd accidentally smashed his nose upon entering the store.

My smile grew wider. "Okay. I'm ready."

Liam blinked. As desperate as he had been to speak to me before, he now seemed surprisingly silent.

His fingers caressed my cheek as he looked at me intently. I detected a slight trace of worry on his face.

I looked at him in the fading light of day. "Go on," I prompted, my voice a mere whisper carried on the wind.

He released a heavy sigh. His eyes searched mine. "This past week has been…well…"

"I know," I finished his sentence for him. "Not what you expected. I didn't think it was possible, either."

"What wasn't possible?" he asked.

My smile widened. "You. And me." I squeezed his hand, hoping he'd understand my intent.

Only Liam shook his head. "It's not just that. I'm not exactly who you think."

"I know that now," I said with a nod. "I probably shouldn't tell you this, but when I first met you, I thought you were a bit too…" I paused, hoping my admission didn't hurt his feelings.

"Helpful?" he suggested.

"Bingo. I mean, it wasn't a bad thing," I explained. "It was just a little over the top."

"Yeah, well, that wasn't exactly me."

"But I know that now. You are so much more than the guy I first met who seemed overly helpful in a slightly irritating way." As soon as those words left my lips, I regretted every one, certain I'd upset him.

One of his eyebrows perched high on his forehead. "You thought I was *irritating*?" he asked.

I gave him a sideways look. Did I detect amusement in his tone? I studied Liam's face as he strained to keep his lips flat and allowed myself a huge sigh of relief. *He's not mad. He may try to look it, but deep down he's about to bust laughing.*

"'Slightly irritating," I replied, unable to contain my widening grin.

"Oh, is that it?" he asked. He squinted his eyes to appear angered by my reaction, but his mouth belied his true emotions. As one corner perked up in a knowing smirk, he leaned toward me this time to kiss the smile from my lips.

Phew.

When our mouths parted, I rested my forehead against his, drawing comfort from his warm touch in the cooling night. "But none of that matters anymore, now that I know what you're really like."

His face paled as he swallowed hard. "That's the problem, Jordan. You *don't* know."

"Of course I do," I told him. Regardless of whatever concerns he had about himself, I carried a far more dangerous secret. Only that secret no longer frightened me. With my knowledge and powers, I could protect Liam from any future threats.

"Jordan, there's more I have to tell you," he admitted with a puzzling hint of sadness.

I pinched my brows together. "Like wha—?" Fright robbed my voice from completing that sentence. From the corner of my eye, I caught a flicker of movement in the shadows. I watched in horror as two figures I recognized far too well emerged from the grove, their silhouettes clearly visible against a backdrop of darkening skies. Together, they stood upon the black sand on the edge of our secluded beach—one with a head of untamed curls, the other with pale flowing hair that gleamed in the moonlight.

"Oh, God, no," I murmured, my body trembling with fear. Instinct prevailed over logic and reason. Still, one thought triumphed above all others: I must protect Liam.

I released Liam's hands and stepped in front of him, ready to aim my full destructive forces upon Gaia and Skye to guarantee his safety. "You have to run," I told him. "I can handle it from here."

Only he didn't move as the other Elementals steadily approached.

"I'm serious, Liam, they're dangerous. I promise I'll protect you, but you've gotta get out of here. *Now.*"

Instead of heeding my warning, he planted his feet firmly in the sand.

His reaction surprised me. I glanced backward for a split second, noticing moisture clouded his bold, bright eyes. With a small frown, he mouthed, "I'm sorry," then stepped in front of me, unafraid.

Gaia strode up to his side and slipped her arm around his waist. The Earth Elemental flashed me a cunning, satisfied smile, like she'd just played her trump card. But instead of speaking to me, she turned to face Liam. "You've done well, Lir," Gaia congratulated. She moved to kiss his lips, but at the last second he turned and she caught his cheek instead.

CHAPTER TWENTY-SEVEN

I felt the blood drain from my face as my jaw hit the ground with a resounding thud, unable to fathom what I'd just witnessed. Gaia had kissed Liam?

Gaia had kissed Liam!

Sure, his expression had stiffened and his head flinched slightly at the caress of her lips against his skin, but he'd made no attempt to stop her. Meaning their presence tonight came as little surprise to him. I had no idea how or why he knew her, but at that moment I didn't care. Not when that awareness rocked my entire perception of reality, knowing the guy I thought I liked had allowed my enemy to get close to him. Too close, in my opinion.

My eyes turned steely cold, fueled by the pain of his betrayal. A high-pitched stream of questions flowed from my mouth at once, without permitting him the time to respond. "How did this happen? Do you even know who she is? And why did she call you *Lir*? Doesn't she know your real name?"

Apology filled Liam's face. "I thought you'd've made the connection by now."

"Connection? What connection?" I stammered and crept backward, viewing him as a complete stranger.

He shook his head with disappointment. "That Lir is the name of the Irish god of the sea."

I stared at him blankly. "What are you talking about? How is *that* something I should've known? You never gave me a single clue!"

"Really," he replied with a heavy dose of sarcasm. "Not one?"

I was about to utter some witty retort when the answer dawned on me. I thought back to the first time he had introduced himself as Liam Innis Reilly. At the time, I'd considered him a dork for actually stating his middle name. But why else would he have bothered, unless he wanted me to know his initials spelled *LIR*?

I recalled how the color of his eyes seemed to change with the mood of the ocean, from bright and bold on sunny days to steely blue when rain speckled the sea. And perhaps the biggest clue would've been completely obvious to me if I'd ever spent any time underwater in the past. Regardless of Liam's claims, there was no way he could have produced a viewing bubble underwater.

Unless he was the new Water Elemental.

I couldn't believe I hadn't seen it before, that I let my infatuation with him impair my perception of reality.

"Oh. My. God," I gasped, stepping backward. A newfound fear twisted my gut into a tight knot. How did I miss this before? He was long and lean, just like her. His eyes even matched hers in color. Liam's voice echoed in my head, *Lir is the name of the Irish god of the sea.* "So you're actually...?"

"Yep," Liam said as his lips drew taut. "You guessed it."

"...Hydros's twin *brother*," I breathed. And all this time I had assumed Shannon's twin was identical, safe and secure back in their ancient hut in Ireland. Not a boy. Not here. And definitely not Liam, someone I'd thought I knew, someone I'd trusted... someone I thought I was falling for.

I took another step backward, shaking my head in disbelief. "It can't be. You're lying."

Liam's face steamed. "You think this was easy for me? You

killed my sister!" he seethed. "Then Gaia found me. Told me to get close to you. To gain your trust. But that was all."

I drew in a huge breath, incredulous. "How could you do this to me? I can't believe that everything we had—*everything*—was built upon a lie. Our whole relationship was a complete farce, wasn't it? And you know what's worse? I actually fell for it." My chest heaved upon finishing my rant.

Liam took a step toward me. "Jordan, you have to listen. There's more you need to know. More you must understand."

"No. *No.* You've had so many chances to tell me before and you didn't. Why would you possibly think I'm going to listen to you now?"

He stretched out his hand, placing his fingers tenderly upon my arm. "I couldn't. I wanted to tell you, but I couldn't."

I slapped his hand away, despising his touch upon my skin. "Right. And I'm supposed to believe you? After all of this? Well, forget it. I want nothing to do with you. Did you hear me? *Nothing.* And I swear that is the God-honest truth."

Skye's eyes flashed like quicksilver as she took a step forward to aid Liam. But Gaia held up one hand to restrain her, advising, "Give him a minute, Skye. He needs to handle this on his own."

The Air Elemental pouted. She flitted her stormy eyes toward Gaia, seemingly disappointed to miss the opportunity to defeat me. Crossing her arms over her chest like a petulant child, she shifted her weight to one hip, waiting for the moment to strike.

But I was too infuriated with Liam to concern myself with Skye's desires, at the moment. I glared at him, my nostrils flaring at his treachery.

"Jordan, don't you see?" Liam asked, reaching for my hand once more. "None of this was supposed to happen."

"What are you saying?" I bristled, the truth behind his confession wounding the depths of my heart. His feelings for me had all been a sham.

237

"I thought you were some heartless, evil person," Liam explained as his fingers clasped mine. "Who else would take Shannon from me forever? But you weren't at all what I expected. I only tried to act super helpful so you'd be a fool to turn down my offer. But why did you have to make things so difficult for me? Why did you have to like me back?"

"It was more than *like*, Liam," I spat as bitter tears of betrayal built in the corners of my eyes. "I can't believe I was so blind. You're right; I was a fool. None of this should've ever happened."

Ripping my hand from his grasp once more, I turned on my heels and ran, my irritating dress trailing behind me. What was I thinking, wearing a ridiculous outfit like this tonight? Or perhaps a better question might have been, what was I thinking, falling for another *Elemental*? Now I had nowhere to go. No one left to trust.

I had only made it a few paces before I heard Gaia command, "Stop her! We need her, Lir, before we run out of time." I increased my pace, taking long strides across the cool black sand, eager to be rid of them all forever. My heart pounded inside my chest and my pulse thundered through my veins from Liam's treachery.

Near the end of the beach, I darted to the right and ducked beneath low branches. I sprinted down the narrow path and bolted to the left, hoping he would lose my trail.

Suddenly, Kea emerged from the darkness and loped by my side. Spinning her head to face mine, her intelligent brown eyes twinkled while she playfully kept my pace. Only for her it looked effortless, like we engaged in a friendly game of tag rather than a race toward freedom. Her panting tongue dangled from her mouth in what appeared an amused grin, as if my unfortunate change of fate somehow humored her.

"You knew. You knew all along, didn't you?" I accused her in an acidic tone.

My words didn't faze her. For a trace of a second, I thought

I saw her wink at me before a reddish-orange tinge flickered through her eyes. Yet I couldn't be sure if I'd imagined the change since the color vanished almost as soon as it had appeared. Loping by my side, her mouth widened into a knowing smile.

"Why didn't you tell me?" I screamed, wheeling on the stray. "You liked him, so I thought it was okay for me to like him, too. And now look what happened. I can't believe I actually listened to a *dog!*"

Kea's mouth closed. She cocked her head to one side, appearing both puzzled and hurt by the anger in my tone. I kicked myself for treating Kea that way. I had no right to yell at her. She was only looking for a little bit of food and attention.

I didn't have a chance to apologize to my poor, homeless friend because in that very instant, the dog's body dissolved into a misty trail of vapor that streamed over the black grains of sand and danced on the light sea breeze. In shock, I tripped over my feet and stumbled to the ground. My elbows and knees skidded across the coarse beach as my eyes gaped wide. Utterly stunned at Kea's mysterious disappearance, I lay on the beach, breathless, staring at the dancing trail. Then, in slow motion, I watched the dog's vaporous mist inexplicably coalesce into the aged form of Auntie Lulu.

CHAPTER TWENTY-EIGHT

I gasped from the shock of what I had just witnessed and from the exertion of racing across uneven terrain. In an instant, I completely forgot about my desire to distance myself far from the other Elementals as I gawked at Auntie Lulu.

"What the…! But how'd you…?" I sputtered, unable to form a coherent thought as this new information bombarded my senses. I waved my hands from the spot where the dog had been to where Lulu now stood, as solid and permanent as myself.

"Haven't you heard the legends?" Auntie Lulu asked simply.

I opened my mouth to speak and then shut it again without uttering a word.

She shook her head, disappointed I hadn't made the connection between her and the white stray who'd followed me essentially everywhere I went since my arrival on the island.

I blinked again, things suddenly clearing within my mind. Never once did the stray appear at the same time as the withered old woman. How could they have coexisted when they were one and the same? I finally understood how Kea had made it to the volcano shortly after Lulu dropped me off. The dog hadn't hitched a ride in a pickup like I'd thought, but still, I didn't understand why she cared. I decided there must be something else she intentionally hid from me.

"Legends? What legends?" I asked, forgetting about Liam for

a moment while I demanded an explanation.

But instead of a response, Auntie Lulu reverted into her misty vapor trail and encircled me twice before transforming into a concrete being. I expected the dog to reappear when the mist coalesced once more.

I easily recognized the vapor's new form, though it definitely wasn't Kea. Instead, a beautiful young maiden with long flowing tresses stood before me. Her eyes flashed like molten lava. I gaped at the form of the powerful goddess, Pele.

"I don't believe it," I breathed. "All this time, it's been you!" In all the days I'd spent in Hawaii, Pele had never let me wander far on my own, had she? Instead, she'd watched and guided my every move, as the stray Kea, the old Auntie Lulu, or the striking young goddess herself.

"One of the benefits of being a goddess. My Essence can take on many forms, just as the Hawaiian legends describe."

"So why didn't you tell me before? I can't believe it was *you* who stole my sleeping bag and made me sleep on the hard lava. You who followed me everywhere. Why, you even licked my face!" My chest heaved, infuriated with her deception. "I don't get it? Why all the secrets? Why didn't you trust me?"

"You had to learn the truth when you were ready," Pele replied in a calm, clear voice.

"Oh, so I could find out this way instead? In a twisted web of lies! All those chores, those trips to Lipoa's Hardware Store, having him check up on me when you were visiting Marvin in the hospital...they were just a way to get me close to Liam, weren't they? Why bother? So he could break my heart? Thanks a bunch. Thanks a whole heap."

My face boiled with anger. I continued to shout, "This whole summer, all my training—everything—was a complete waste of time. I couldn't even get one stupid bit of magic to work. Take me where I'm needed," I muttered. "Like *that* actually happened."

241

"But it did. Don't you see, child? He needs you. They need you. I merely wanted you to trust Liam so you would willingly join the Elementals. The fact that you fell for him was an unexpected bonus."

"Fell for him?" I chortled madly. "Oh, please. You set me up. You knew," I yelled at her, tears stinging my eyes as I realized that everyone I knew and trusted here had officially turned against me. "You knew about all of this in advance. And you intentionally set me up to get hurt."

"No, I wanted to train you to prepare you for whatever situation you might encounter. I originally told Gaia to do whatever was necessary to gain your alliance, but I never expected you to be so headstrong or disagreeable that it would result in the loss of life. You must believe me, I never intended for her to kill your family and friends. But do not let their lives pass in vain. Your action against Hydros—as tragic as it was—proved the break we needed to reform the team and gain your support… using alternate means."

"Alternate means?" I fumed. "You lied to me. You toyed with my heart."

"Only because you have the power to complete this team and tackle the rising threat," Pele replied in an even tone. "That was the main reason I had you complete all those missions."

"What a fabulous idea," My tone dripped with sarcasm. "How can you possibly call that 'training' by deliberately sending me to the most dangerous situations imaginable?"

Pele explained, "It was extremely necessary that you gain sympathy for Hydros—and indirectly Gaia as well—by having you understand more about her past life as the girl, Shannon. And it was critical that you meet the Fire Essence to better understand the full extent of your fused powers. Yet, I admit, I had an ulterior motive in sending you on so many missions into the past."

My brow crinkled. "You did?"

"I needed to detain you at the volcano. That way, it gave me the opportunity to work a little of my own magic."

"Magic?" I asked, dumbfounded. "What are you talking about?"

"At a certain bonfire on the beach." She gave me a pointed look.

My jaw dropped open. "Are you saying that while I was off nearly getting myself killed, you were playing Cupid with my ex-boyfriend?"

"It worked far easier that I imagined," Pele said in a proud voice. "I suspected if I kept you away from Sully, he would soon lose interest in you. All I needed to add was a little magic in my firelight and the next thing I knew, Bethany kissed him."

"Like that was a big accomplishment. She practically threw herself at him when she visited me in the hospital." I glanced away, ridding the thought from my mind. Unfortunately, it didn't work—I could see nothing beyond the two of them sitting side by side on a driftwood log in front of the bonfire, their lips locked.

Blood boiled inside my veins. "How dare you! Shouldn't *I* be the one to choose who I like?"

"Of course, dear child. I merely helped you in reaching that conclusion." Her lips twisted up into a knowing smile, confident in the success of her methods.

I opened my mouth for a rebuttal, but silently shut it again. She was right. Kea and Auntie Lulu had both told me in their own ways that they approved of Liam. And I *had* liked him until he revealed the truth about his identity.

"Jordan, please, you must trust me. You needed this to happen," Pele reminded me. "It is of utmost importance that you join forces with the other Elementals. It is the only way."

"The only way for what? For them to rule the planet?"

"No. Not at all," Pele admitted, shaking her head. "It's so

you can protect everyone from a future threat."

"Future threat? What are you talking about? *They* always posed the threat to my life."

Pele gave me a sympathetic look and turned away. That same sympathetic look I'd seen in Lulu's eyes earlier by the koi pond.

"So I suppose this means that again I have to wait until I'm ready to understand?"

"I am afraid I cannot tell you more," the goddess said softly. "That information is something that Liam himself promised to disclose to you when the time was right."

"But I don't want to talk to Liam. I don't want to have anything to do with him again."

"Sometimes, child, you must look beyond your own wants and see what is needed for the greater good."

And before the goddess revealed another word, she returned to her vaporous form of wispy trails skittering across the ground. I watched them weave across the path, dip suddenly toward the earth, and erupt into an electrifyingly red spire that shot high into the air, piercing the dark skies in a blinding flash of light. It quickly reached its pinnacle before dropping to the ground in fiery globs of superheated molten rock.

Because, like always, Pele did what Pele wanted to do, leaving me with more unanswered questions.

Goddess, old woman, white dog, molten lava—all these forms contained the Essence of Pele. Why hadn't I seen it before?

I was naïve and trusting, that's why. Well, that time had ended. Now I could trust no one beside myself.

No one.

Never before had the world felt so cold and isolated. I blinked into the distance, unable to spot any trace of Pele. Not like I really wanted to see her again after she used me, lied to me, manipulated me. Only I wished she had finally trusted me enough to tell me the whole truth, instead of leaving me miserable, confused, and alone once more. I closed my eyes, letting fresh tears trickle down my cheeks.

I heard a rustle in the bushes lining the beach. I turned, realizing Pele's eruption had a different intent. She hadn't opened the earth in anger, but used her sign as a beacon to direct Liam to my precise location — making me realize I had no allies in this battle. Clenching my fists in fury, I purged the innumerable confounding thoughts from my mind so I could focus on the approaching threat.

CHAPTER TWENTY-NINE

"Listen, just listen," Liam said in a strained voice.

I spun on my heels and took off down the sand, not caring to hear a word he intended to say.

"Jordan, it's me. I haven't changed," he declared and tried to catch me. "I just need you to listen for a minute so I can explain."

"You had all the time in the world to explain before, and you didn't!" I shouted over my shoulder and sprinted toward the rocky hillside on the distant end of the beach. "Why should I listen to you now? All this time, you were using me. You never even liked me for real, did you? Everything between us, it's all been a lie."

"That's not true. Not everything," he yelled, trying to close the gap between us.

"I hate you," I spat. Blood boiled within my veins. I stopped suddenly in my tracks, spinning to face him. My palm glowed red-hot and I aimed it at Liam, launching a ball of fire at his feet.

But rather than jumping out of its way, he summoned a wave to douse it before it contacted the ground. "Jordan," he pleaded, "you don't understand."

"What's to understand?" I yelled. Fury mounted inside me as I tossed another fireball in his direction, shouting at him, "I mean it. I *hate* you!"

"Just listen to me, will you?" he screamed. Another ocean

wave broke against the shore, instantly drenching the fireball.

My face steamed. With a fierce look of determination, I extended both palms in his direction. *I will never listen to him again*, I decided and split the ground to summon help from the molten layer beneath our feet. Four fissures opened, one on each side of Liam, as lava burst forth from the cracks like a blazing prison that surrounded him on all sides. "You're a liar," I said with finality, surveying my work. "I can't believe I ever trusted you."

"Jordan...please," he pleaded from inside his molten cell.

"Leave me alone!"

He flinched, whether surprised by the intensity of my anger or uncomfortable from the heat of his cell, I couldn't decide. He looked around, as if contemplating his options. He spiraled, shooting water at the inside of the lava to create a solid wall of rock that boxed him within its four sides.

Ha, ha, I laughed to myself. He thinks he won this time? His efforts only made my lava prison stronger.

A forceful stream of water blasted a hole in the base of the rock, large enough for the ocean to enter. He called upon the sea so when the next wave neared shore, it channeled all of its power through that hole until it rocketed Liam into the air. He rode the fountain upward out of his rocky cell, his arms extended for balance like he surfed a cresting wave. "But I'm still the same person," he protested. He landed on the ground in front of me, a smile of satisfaction stretching across his smug face. "Nothing has changed."

"How can you say that when you know this changes everything?" I screamed. My voice choked on fresh tears. "You manipulated me. You lied to me. And stupid me fell for it." My head spun and suddenly I felt very weak. Everything I knew about him was founded upon a series of lies—his name, his charm, even his feelings toward me. Worse, I was naïve enough to buy into it and grow attached to *him*, thereby giving Gaia the checkmate.

Bursts of fire shot from my hands, creating a superheated wall between us. "I don't know anything about you. It's like I don't even know who you are."

Worse, I realized as I stared at him through the roaring wall of flames, *I don't even know who I am.* So many details remained shrouded in mystery. I frowned, realizing Pele's explanations of the history of the Elementals only left me with more questions than answers. More confused than ever, my wall of flames unintentionally dwindled.

Liam took a step closer, pointing one hand toward the sea as an enormous wave reached the shore. It fell with a loud crash upon the earth, extinguishing the firewall and drenching my entire body. I mopped the hair from my eyes, choking on salt water as I glared at him, certain he deliberately magnified that rogue wave.

"Look around, Jordan. Can't you see the power of the water surrounding you? You'll never win. Not here, not now," he taunted, his voice taking a surprisingly arrogant tone. "Earth itself is covered mostly with water. The human body can't survive without it. What happens if we don't have fire? It's not like we need it for warmth or cooking anymore. You don't stand a chance on your own. So why not give up right now and admit the truth?"

"The truth?" I narrowed my blazing eyes. "*What* truth?"

"That water can beat fire every time. I possess the power to extinguish anything you throw at me, so why bother even trying? Seriously. Jordan. It's time to give up and give in to Gaia."

"We'll see about that," I muttered and thrust my palm behind me, slicing the ground to reveal the boiling lava deep beneath. Gritting my teeth to focus, I willed the lava to rise into a tall molten plume. It branched high over Liam's head, forming spherical lava bombs that rained to the ground. Liam responded with a douse of water from the sea that enveloped the bombs, instantly cooling each into an orb of glossy black obsidian that dropped from the sky and shattered into jagged shards of volcanic glass about his feet.

It's not enough, I scolded myself and closed my eyes, collecting my energy within my core. Too infuriated to feel the pain, I quickly grew hot. The power radiated from deep within, fueled by the ache of betrayal. The rock around my feet melted into puddles under the intensity of the heat generated inside me. I glanced down at my hands, amazed to find my skin glowing white-hot like the midday sun, just like Pele had claimed possible. *Now watch this*, I thought and balled my fists. I concentrated the light into a pulse that shot from my palms, directly at Liam's face. Inside, I congratulated myself for finally accomplishing this challenging feat, without having to fuse powers with the Fire Essence, Brandr. Yet the power of the flash blast was greater than I imagined, making Liam howl in pain. He crumpled to his knees.

"God, Jordan! What are you thinking?" he screamed, his hands smothering his eyes. Momentarily blinded by the flash blast, he shielded his face. In desperation, he stretched his hand toward the ocean to unleash a towering wave of water that buckled above me, dropping its full force upon my very spot. The seawater rocked me off my feet, interrupting my concentration. It doused the molten puddles, making me sprawl across the slippery rocks, but wasn't enough to cool the intense heat of my sun-like core. Instead, the water vaporized into a steamy mist the second it contacted my skin.

"See?" I cackled as I slowly rose to my feet. "Water can't *always* beat fire. My powers might seem insignificant to you, but what about the vast untapped reserves of fire that lay beneath the surface? Or the widespread power of fire in the universe? Water barely even exists beyond our planet."

Using his forearm to block the intense brightness of my illuminated body from his eyes, Liam retorted, "That's what I've been trying to tell you. That's exactly why we need you. This is your future, your responsibility, your destiny. I've come to accept my Elemental name. Why won't you, Pyr?"

Hearing him call me by that name came as a shock. How much did he actually know about my past? I closed my eyes, instantly allowing the blinding heat to dissipate until my skin returned to its normal color. "Don't call me that," I seethed, rejecting his notion. Though my core had cooled, my palms still burned hot. I aimed them at Liam once more.

He laughed at my expense. "I'm not worried. You may be a threat elsewhere, but as long as you're on the surface of our planet, I still have the upper hand."

My eyes steamed, frustrated with his conceited pride. "Not if I make a solar flare and engulf the Earth. All I need to do is penetrate the protective magnetic field and destroy the atmosphere. Then the waters would disappear, leaving only rock and fire. Air and water would be gone forever, leaving me with only Gaia to defeat."

Though I wasn't positive I could actually make the sun produce a flare of that magnitude, it sounded like a good comeback to his cocky remark.

"You're bluffing," Liam said. "Even if you *can* make something that large, you'd never really do it. You don't have it in your heart to be evil. Why, you probably couldn't even kill a fly, much less destroy our whole planet."

"And what if I told you I had meant to take out your sister?" I goaded, my eyes cold and cruel.

His face fell, like I'd struck the perfect chord.

"Just try me. I dare you." I shot Liam a threatening glare and raised my arms toward the sky. He was right, even after everything I'd been through, I couldn't hurt so many innocent people. But I would never admit that to him, not after his deceit. Before I could summon the power within my core to transform my body white-hot once more, Liam sprinted toward me. Throwing his arms around me, he tackled me to the ground, unwilling to take the risk.

CHAPTER THIRTY

"Let me go!" I screeched, kicking at his legs. I thrashed my body in a desperate struggle to break free. It only made him hold me tighter.

"Jordan, I'm serious. I need you to listen," he began, pinning me beneath the weight of his body. He pressed his lips to my ear. "At first, you were right. Gaia wanted me to get close to you. It was my job to get you to like me so I could gain your trust."

My eyes narrowed into thin slits. I writhed violently, struggling to break free from his grasp. "Why would you ever listen to Gaia?" I seethed. "She's evil and manipulative, cruel and calculating."

"She's *desperate*," Liam corrected. "Don't you see? As the oldest of the Elementals, the original embodiment selected by the Earth Element itself, and the only one who lacks a former Essence, she feels personally responsible for leading our team. But when Gaia's plan didn't work out like she had hoped, Pele decided we should try something different to win your support."

My nostrils flared, outraged by his revelation. "So is that what you've all been doing? Scheming behind my back?"

"No. Well, not exactly." He squeezed me harder and continued, "I'll admit it was hard, very hard, especially once they told me what you had done to my sister. That I'd never see her in the flesh again...ever...because of *you*."

I paused my struggle for a moment as his words stabbed my heart. Hydros wasn't as evil as I'd initially thought. True, she did order William's death in Old Salem Village, but only after she had lost the guy she loved onboard the *Titanic* and wanted to protect Liam—Lir, whatever his name was—from Gaia.

And I never would've known the truth about her if I hadn't gone back through time to track her former self, the frightened girl named Shannon. Without learning about her past, I never would've understood that Hydros wasn't much different from me. Over the course of those missions, I watched Gaia break Shannon's soul into submission, leaving her with a single choice to protect those she loved. Shannon had accepted her Elemental identity as her way out, hoping she could quickly end the fear and return home to ancient Ireland. Was that too much to ask? For a return to normality? I sniffled, realizing that I had unintentionally prevented Hydros from realizing her dream, a dream that we had shared.

"Then that day you came into the store," Liam continued, interrupting my thoughts. "I could see the fear and frustration in your eyes. Lulu said she had assigned you all of those chores because she wanted to teach you patience, discipline, and the perseverance to finish a task—all skills you would need for the future.

"But you looked so drained and exhausted, I couldn't help but feel sorry for you. At that moment, I realized you were just trying to protect yourself. You never intended to hurt her, just like you never meant to break my nose...and that's why I guessed you were bluffing about the solar flare right now. I'd thought by offering to help you finish your tasks I could easily win your trust. Only Lulu told me you found my help annoying, so I had to change my tactics."

"What a good plan," I said, my words bitingly sarcastic. I attempted to wiggle free of his hold once more. "Too bad you hadn't stayed your original annoying self so I never would've wanted to like you."

I tried to twist around, but he continued to pin me down, his chest pressed close to mine so our faces hovered only inches apart. Under different circumstances, I would have longed to be this close to him and gaze into his bright eyes. With anger boiling inside my veins, I only wished to escape.

"You don't understand," he said, shaking his head. "You ended up being so different than I had expected, so different from the stories Gaia had told me about you. I tried staying away and tried to stop thinking about you. But it only made me want to be with you even more. Fire and water shouldn't be together; you said so yourself. And now I've jeopardized our whole team by letting my feelings for you get in the way.

"This wasn't supposed to happen. I was only supposed to make you like me enough to gain your trust, nothing more. For God's sake, Jordan, you killed my sister!"

I flinched at the finality of that word.

"So I suppose this is the 'favor' you were talking about?" I said glumly. "The one I owed you for all the chores you helped me with?"

He heaved a deep sigh. "I wanted to tell you before. Honest, I did. But I wasn't allowed to reveal my identity—that was part of the plan. So I thought if I left you some clues, you might figure it out for yourself."

I held still for a minute, gazing straight into his face and contemplated the sincerity of his words. Even though he had lied to me so many times before, this time I could tell he was speaking the truth. *Not lied*, I reminded myself. *More like he withheld important information.* Information that would have entirely changed the way I viewed him and prevented my heart from growing too attached.

Besides the obvious link between his name and that of the

Irish Sea god, I recognized some other clues he had left for me. "Like the day we had the hose fight while washing Lulu's car," I mused. "There wasn't really a kink in that hose, was there?"

"No," he admitted. The smallest of smiles snuck across his lips, remembering my humorous look of surprise when the hose shot me directly in the face.

The more I thought about it, the clues were everywhere. His surf shorts resembled ocean waves. The fish seemed to cluster around him when we swam underwater. Even the color and name of his car held a clue, if only I'd taken the time to notice. "Doesn't *Tiburon* mean...?"

"Yep, you nailed it. It's Spanish for *shark*." He paused, letting my mind chew on his subtle hints. "But then, everything changed. All of a sudden, it felt right to be with you. Not because I had to — but because I wanted to."

I stopped resisting, finding myself hanging on his every word. Liam loosened his grip slightly as he explained, "I don't know what it was, but maybe I realized that you weren't the person I expected you to be. You only killed my sister to protect yourself and thousands, perhaps millions, of people you didn't even know."

He was right; I killed her. Now Liam would never see his twin in person again...all because of me. Suddenly, the reason for my action no longer mattered. I stared at my hands in horror, knowing moments before I had used those same powers against him. Defeated, I made no attempt to flee as he loosened his grip from a restraint. He lifted himself off me and sat beside me on the sand, wrapping his arms around me as he had before.

He was right. I had no intention of fighting him now. But I didn't want to stay there, either. Not after he had hollowed out my heart. Rising to my feet, I slipped from his embrace and marched down the beach, too emotionally drained to run. Liam leapt after me, "Jordan. Please, just hear me out," he said and grabbed my hand.

But I pulled away, wheeling on him as renewed anger surged through my veins. "What do you want from me anyway, Lir? You have accepted your Elemental name, haven't you? At least Gaia thinks you have."

He recoiled, stunned by my harsh tone. "Forget about Gaia. This is just between you and me."

"How can I forget about her? You helped her. Plain and simple. You were on her side and you used me, made me think I meant something to you. Still, she kissed you. How can you expect me to ignore that?"

But as I spoke, my voice cracked, knowing those words did little to erase the pain in my heart. Despite everything that had happened, deep down I knew a part of me still liked him. Worse, I could never admit my feelings to him, not now that Gaia used him to get to me. I didn't know what was real and what was pretend. I dropped to my knees on the sand, burying my face in my hands as my body heaved with sobs.

Liam knelt beside me. "Jordan," he said, placing a soft hand upon my shoulder. I brushed it away as if a pesky wasp buzzed around my ear.

"Jordan, please," he repeated and cradled my weeping body in his arms. Only this time his voice sounded tired. So very tired. In that instant, I realized the conflict that warred inside him, not just between right and wrong—but between attraction and obligation. Gaia had never expected him to complete his job this well. That much was obvious from the look of displeasure upon her face when he flinched away from her kiss.

So when he leaned closer to give me a gentle kiss of apology, I turned my head, letting his lips graze the side of my head.

"You have to believe me, Jordan," he whispered in my ear, "I'm still the same person. Really, I am."

But my whole body felt numb, my heart devoid of emotion.

256

I killed his sister, I repeated in my mind, purposefully having avoided that choice of words until now. It sounded so final to hear him speak about her. And even if I went back to that day when we had fled San Francisco and I'd battled The Three, I still couldn't change the outcome. There was nothing—absolutely nothing—I could do to bring her back.

"I'm sorry. I didn't know what she was really like," I murmured sadly, knowing those words offer little consolation for the void in his life. "She only wanted to protect you."

"What's that?"

"Shannon. She only did all those things to prevent Gaia from getting to you. Gaia manipulated her—made her believe she had to do all of this to keep you safe."

"You're not making this any easier for me, you know," he said with a sniffle.

"It's true. I saw her."

He didn't bother with a response as I imagined his mind swam with this new piece of information. For a long time we sat in silence, Liam's arms wound loosely around me. Finally, he spoke. "You know, Jordan, I didn't think this was possible." He hugged me tighter, pulling me toward him until my head rested upon his shoulder. He held my drenched body for a long moment. Placid waves rolled up the beach and the moon rose higher in the sky. Yet a part of me seemed surprised that Gaia had not yet returned. Perhaps she trusted him more than I'd imagined.

"What was possible?" I muttered. "That you'd actually catch me?"

"No," he said with a light chuckle. He unwound his arms from my back, pulling away so he could look directly at me. His fingers brushed my cheek, sweeping a wet strand of hair from my face. "I didn't think I could grow to like someone this fast. Especially not you." His deep blue eyes searched mine and I saw sincerity and compassion in his expression.

Still, I couldn't help but feel betrayed, unable to ignore the anger that festered deep inside. *I don't need him. I don't need any of them.* The stubborn, resilient part of my soul clung fiercely to a burning need for independence.

"I know. I thought things were different this time," I said, wistful. *But they weren't. I learned I can't trust anyone but myself.*

"They were. And they still can be." His voice carried a hopeful tone.

I pulled away from him, wary. "But what if I won't join your team? A long time ago, back in Pompeii, Gaia told me she could find someone to replace me."

"Maybe then she could've, but not anymore. There's not enough time. It has to be you."

"You keep saying that again and again. That there's 'not enough time.' Time until what?"

His face paled. A grim look clouded his eyes, making his normal bright blue color fade into the bleak grayness of the sky above, dismal and foreboding. "Promise you'll trust me," he said softly. "Promise you'll listen." He pressed his hands to my cheeks, willing me to hold his saddened gaze.

I looked at him in silence for a long while, weighing my options. From what he said, I now held the upper hand. Curiosity getting the best of my mind, I agreed to his request. "I promise."

"There's more you need to know." His voice sounded wearied, yet sincere. And suddenly, I wanted to listen. I wanted to believe. I wanted to trust him.

Even though I wasn't sure I should.

END OF BOOK TWO OF *THE ELEMENTALS* TRILOGY

Before You Go...

HELP AN AUTHOR

write a review

THANK YOU!

Share your voice and help guide other readers to these wonderful books. Even if it's only a line or two your reviews help readers discover the author's books so they can continue creating stories that you'll love. Login to your favorite retailer and leave a review. Thank you.

ABOUT THE AUTHOR

After graduating from Cornell University with degrees in Biology and Education, Debbie Kump taught middle and high school science in Maui, Seattle, and the Twin Cities and worked as a marine naturalist aboard a whale watch and snorkel cruise. Debbie lives in Minnesota with her husband, two sons, and three Siberian huskies. She especially enjoys writing early each morning; teaching; coaching youth soccer, hockey, lacrosse, and baseball; and dogsledding her kids to school.

For more information, please visit her website: http://sites.google. com/site/debbiekumpbooks/